SHOTGUN HONEY
PRESENTS

Locked
AND
Loaded
BOTH BARRELS v3

edited by
Irvin • Conley • Arneson • Phillips

Shotgun Honey Presents: Locked and Loaded
Both Barrels Volume 3
Copyright © 2015 One Eye Press LLC

ISBN-13: 978-0692434307
ISBN-10: 0692434305

www.OneEyePress.com
www.ShotgunHoney.net

TABLE OF CONTENTS

TABLE OF CONTENTS

for A.J. "Bill" Hayes

FOREWORD
Ron Earl Phillips

A couple weeks ago the Shotgun Honey flashzine turned four. I am not sure whether that is called a birthday or an anniversary? In social media circles, the site was wished a happy birthday, though it seems the latter would be the proper term. Either way, four years is a sizable amount of time, not to mention an accomplishment that would not be had without the dedicated writers, readers and editors.

The *community*.

It is a community that goes beyond Shotgun Honey, and goes well beyond my first inclinations to accept its warm embrace in 2010 when I wrote my first bit of flash fiction for a challenge. It featured a nameless hero who learns the hard way that "No Good Deed" goes unpunished. And at a mere 550 words would have fit right into the Shotgun Honey criteria. If you do a search on my website you'll find that little gem. It didn't win any awards, but it did garner a few kind words.

That was my hook into the crime writing community—the immediate feeling that I belonged, and while I might dabble in horror, sci-fi, or the paltry attempt at lit, crime fiction was where I belonged.

It took a mere 18 months, but after I had been invited to participate in challenges, anthologies, and other venues,

I felt like I wanted to give back. I wanted to interact with other writers, give them a venue to share and grow their words. I didn't know how, but I wanted to do what Steve Weddle, David Cranmer, Neil Smith, Christopher Grant, and numerous others had done—they gave their time to promote new writers and to build the community.

Then Kent Gowran happened. Shotgun Honey happened. Things kind of stuck, morphed, and marched on as time has a tendency to do. And through Shotgun Honey I got to work with many of the writers/editors that I admired. Weddle, Smith, Grant. I got to share their words.

Over the past four years, through a circulating gauntlet of editors, Shotgun Honey has published more than 500 stories and marching towards half as many writers, with thousands of comments from avid readers of the genre getting their 2-3 blasts of fiction weekly.

Bam! That's community.

Shotgun Honey Presents: Locked and Loaded is our third foray into the short story marketplace. Created as an extension of the flashzine to allow our contributors a little elbow room and as an enticement for writers we have wanted to work with, but who had no desire to write in the limited form of flash fiction. With perseverance, and a little hen pecking, I managed to get the original Shotgun Honey ringleader to contribute, not to mention a story from Mister Noir Bar himself. Kent Gowran and Jedidiah Ayres. Both giants in my book, partially because they stand well above my 5' 10 ½" stature, but mostly because they are damn fine writers.

I've gone into each volume with a wish list—or should I say hit list—of writers I'd like to include. And it doesn't always pan out with the desired result. Understandably, most cases it's a conflict of events. After all, you ask writers in the middle of edits, you are likely to be the lower priority. Other times, well, you just run out of time.

From the very first days of Shotgun Honey, one of the biggest contributors to the flashzine wasn't a writer—though that's not entirely true, because he was a damn fine writer—rather, it was a commenter named A. J. Hayes, Bill to his friends. As clockwork like our weekly three-story cycle most of the first two years, A. J. would comment on stories as only A. J. could: genuine, knowing, with a beat of poetry. When he gave you his praise, you took it as words off the mountain. He made you want to reach in that well again and again. There was passion in his love of crime fiction, and it was infectious.

We were privileged to publish two of his stories: "All You Got" and "Small Separations."

In March of 2014, around the time I was making my wish list for *Locked and Loaded*, A. J. Hayes let go of this world after a courageous battle with lung cancer. It was a great loss to the community.

It is inevitable to lose those who inspire us to be better writers, but it is a tragedy to lose those who inspire us to be better people.

I'd like to believe that Bill considered us all friends—a community of friends sharing words and a passion for words.

I think A. J. would have enjoyed all 25 stories included in this anthology, and would have had a unique riff on each and every one. It's a good collection with eclectic stories from authors around the world. Best sellers and newcomers. A bit of something for everyone.

Welcome to the community.

A KID LIKE BILLY
Patricia Abbott

Everyone knows a kid like Billy. You've seen him at the grocery store bagging food or stocking shelves, or in a pet store feeding the animals and cleaning cages. Or maybe at a nursery dragging a Christmas tree to someone's car. That's the sort of place you regularly find a boy like mine.

His mother was killed by a careening car when Billy was three. When I surfaced from the bottomless well of grief, I counted myself lucky Billy was off in pre-school that morning and not in Ellie's arms.

The years passed slowly for us. Billy repeated fourth grade and then ninth. On the night I watched him walk across the squeaking stage to take his diploma, I knew in my heart he still didn't understand what a fraction was or where to find Michigan on a map. But in a town like West Lebanon, anyone who puts his butt in his seat eventually gets a certificate. And I made sure he stuck it out.

People advise you to get a boy like Billy into plumbing or carpentry—jobs where you use your hands more than your heads. Billy hands weren't his strongest suit either, but I called in a favor and got a friend in construction to hire him.

"What're you doing home?" I said, finding him in front of the TV one day when I came home unexpectedly to retrieve a file. He should've been down at a work site on State Street, sweeping up nails or toting 2 x 4s.

"I wanted a tuna sandwich today. Came home to make one."

He looked around the rumpus room, seeming surprised himself that he was watching *The Ellen DeGeneres Show*, his shoes kicked off, and the half-eaten sandwich drying up on a plate. His feet smelled bad, and I wondered when he'd last changed his socks.

"I packed you tuna," I said. "Did you even unwrap it to look?"

"You usually pack ham on Wednesdays."

"Today's Tuesday," I said, grabbing the dirty plate.

Al Ferguson gave him a job at the IGA the next month. About the only things Billy had to do was stock shelves, sweep the sidewalk, and help customers tote bags to the car. But Billy took it into his head to begin organizing the cans by colors—markers he could relate to more easily than the brand names.

"Oh, no you don't," I said, coming in one day to pick up some Hamburger Helper. He was on his knees, sorting the cans. I began replacing the cans, getting angrier with each one. "Look, just do what Mr. Ferguson tells you. Bear down."

But he couldn't keep that job either. Don't get me wrong. There was no meanness in my boy, no cunning or ill-will. He wasn't lazy or dishonest. But neither was there an ounce of common sense. I lay awake nights wondering what would happen to him, wondering if a town like West Lebanon was the best place for a boy like mine.

West Lebanon's in the northern part of the Lower Peninsula in Michigan. In summer the population swells to

5000, but for nine months a police force of six keeps order for the 1200 permanent residents. In my years as Chief, we've never had a murder or even a suspicious death. Drug problems, more than enough DWIs, a few marital disputes, one or two suspicious fires, some B & E's, especially in the summer, a bully or two raising hell over at the high school, lots of traffic accidents. But spread that over 365 days and it's a peaceful spot.

In the tenth year of my tenure as Police Chief, I hired Billy. I took some heat for it—both with my men and with two members of the City Council.

Patty Harmon, the Council President that year, put it bluntly, "I guess you're the one who'll take the blame if he screws up. Right?"

Gradually my men came around. Billy turned out to be a pretty good crossing guard at the elementary school. He also saw the squad cars were washed and serviced, answered the phone, and ran errands. These were the chores my men disliked most and after a few months nobody was complaining about his doing them. I never sent Billy out on a dangerous or complicated job. He didn't carry a gun or even a nightstick. He didn't do patrols. If he answered a call asking for serious help, he passed it on.

"A good kid," Sam Hunter, my second in command, told me. "A high IQ isn't everything, Chief." He laughed a little. "As I can testify."

The winters up north are filled with slow days when a crossword puzzle or crime novel often occupied us. Rummy and solitaire were popular. So was *The Price is Right*.

It was a lousy February, like most of 'em up here, one of those months where it never seemed to be fully light. Cold, snowy. In the second week, four of us came down with a terrible stomach virus. The headache that came with it was crippling. Billy didn't catch it though. He'd never been sick a day in his life.

So it was just Billy and Ed Stuyvesant at the station that day. Around noon, the bug hit Ed like a bullet to the gut. He high-tailed it into the bathroom.

"All right out there, Son?" he called to Billy between bouts. Ed wasn't worried. Half the town was down with the bug too so things were even more quiet than usual.

The call was clocked at 12:45, coming from a house out on Badger Creek Road. Helen Clayton's. She told me later she'd expected Billy to pass the phone on to someone senior.

But after hearing her first sentence or two Billy told her he'd see to it and hung up.

Ed said he'd heard Billy talking through the john door, but since he hadn't heard the phone ring, he thought it was Billy just babbling to Ed about something. Maybe asking if he was all right. Ed mumbled something back and returned to the business at hand, never dreaming Billy took off to answer a call.

Billy drove out to Badger Creek Road on his motor scooter at 12:55. The roads were recently plowed from a storm the day before. Mrs. Clayton had reported the disturbance as coming from the Ryans' summer home. We'd checked the house for a disturbance the week before and came up empty. But Helen was no hysteric and breaking into summer homes is an ongoing problem where houses are deserted for months. Mostly it's teenagers looking for a place to have sex and drink. But not always.

As a year-round resident, Helen didn't want a long driveway to plow so she was smack-dab alongside the road. She couldn't see much, if anything, because the Ryans' house was set further back. She described the noise as a radio playing at full volume, laughter, swearing, shouting, a car pulling in and out too noisily. She thought it was teenagers—out of school for President's Day. Skiers maybe. It was odd for a party at noon though.

The racket finally died down, and she assumed one of us had come out to quiet things, and went back to whatever she was doing. It wasn't until an hour or two later that someone stumbled into the station saying he'd seen something—probably a body—holding the door open at the Ryans' place.

"No, I didn't go any closer," the fellow told Ed. "Didn't know what I might be walking in on." Embarrassed, he muttered, "Looked like he was past any help from what I could see."

Ed'd been wondering what'd happened to Billy by then. But since wandering was one of Billy's most aggravating traits, he hadn't been too worried. He took the guy's statement, asking him how he happened to be tramping around out near Ryan's. The guy whisked his hunting license out, told Ed where he was staying, and left, pretty shaken up. Of course, the hunting season for anything other than crow, squirrel and rabbit had been over for months, but Ed had other things on his mind.

After checking the phone log and talking to Helen, Ed called me, trepidation in his voice. We drove out there, seeing Billy's figure sprawled in the doorway. It was almost certain someone had hit my boy with the iron shovel lying next to his body. There was blood everywhere: blood and parts of Billy's skull and brains. My stomach, which had been churning all day from the damned virus, went suddenly calm. Ed's reaction was different: he ran right inside, making it to the john in time but defiling the crime scene. Me and my men weren't used to such things—either the body or the proper procedure.

Within fifteen minutes, the area swarmed with my little army and men from the neighboring town. I put in a call to Traverse City, a bigger place, and they sent over their forensics team and a detective more experienced in handling crime scenes and homicides.

"Do you realize these bloody footprints probably belong to your own man?" the detective asked me.

I nodded. "We've never investigated a murder."

"You get the same training we do."

"It's his kid, you know," Ed told him, going quickly from ashamed to angry. "The body you just carted away."

"Sorry for your loss," the detective said quietly.

Those were the words we'd been taught to say, and for the first time, I realized how hollow they sound. How perfunctory.

I hung back from the start of the investigation, letting others take the lead, allowing others to turn my son's body over, letting other men carry him away. I never set foot in the house. It wasn't up to me to find my son's killer. Anything I did was likely to screw up a subsequent trial because of my inexperience in homicides and my relationship to the victim.

At least a dozen times in the weeks ahead, Billy's actions were questioned, and I repeatedly admitted Billy shouldn't have been there, shouldn't have been employed by a police department, shouldn't have been allowed to think himself capable of answering such a call.

If I'd grieved over Ellie's death twenty years earlier, Billy's death damn near sent me 'round the bend. Why had Billy gone out there? Certainly because the rest of us were down sick but why hadn't he called me. I hadn't given enough thought to a situation like this one arising, and Billy paid the price. The only thing keeping me sane was the conviction the murderer would be caught and brought to justice— that I would see him put behind bars for the rest of his days.

But it didn't look like there was going to be a trial anytime soon because the one and only piece of potential evidence was a Spider-man wristwatch, the kind you can buy in any department store. It wasn't even certain that the watch—found about ten yards from the door—hadn't been lost by some summer guest months earlier or a more recent passerby.

It'd only been spotted because the glint of the glass caught someone's eye when the sun made a brief showing.

"What do you think, Chief," Ed asked. "Has it been lying out here since last summer?"

We both looked at the watch. It was in pretty good shape for a watch supposedly lost six months earlier. The band was surprisingly long for a kid.

"Do adults wear these things?" Ed asked.

"A girl might think it was cute or something."

Billy would have loved a watch like that I thought to myself.

I looked at it again. "It may not belong to whoever was in that house, but it hasn't been here for long. It would've been a foot deeper in the snow and a lot dirtier. Nobody would've found it in that case and I don't think it'd still be running."

We both consulted our own watches and found Spidey kept pretty good time.

"Plus," I said, "if it'd been here since last summer, the

time would be an hour off."

Ed looked impressed that I'd thought of that; this was the depth of investigation our force could undertake: remembering daylight savings time.

There were other signs people had been there: cigarette butts, beer cans, a few empty bags for snack foods. These items were eventually run for fingerprints but none matched any prints on file.

I buried my boy five days later, putting him next to Ellie, the spot where I was meant to be. There was nothing to hold up a funeral when a shovel to the head was all there was for evidence.

"One quick jab," the coroner decided. "Guy must have been an ox."

The whole town turned out and the folks in most of the neighboring ones. That's the way people are up here. But I'd be damned if Billy's murder was going to end like this, so the investigation continued. But finally the new leads, the people to question, the timetables to work out faded away. There was no way to keep it going.

I am a patient man. Billy taught me that. I knew that whoever killed my son had found another crib—if that's the current term—but they hadn't disappeared entirely.

Small-time drug dealers, and that's who I thought it was, don't disappear. They're peasants like me. And peasants don't travel well. They like their own john if nothing else.

They'd never return to the Ryans' house, but the area had hundreds of similar setups. I just needed to wait it out. And I waited through spring and summer with nary a report of noise or unusual traffic.

Summer fills the houses in northern Michigan, but by

October, the houses are being boarded up for winter. It was then that reports of unusual activity began to surface, lighting up our phone lines or coming across the Internet. Local kids partying a bit too hardy, odd movement at night, a few DUIs that didn't seem like the usual beer-induced euphoria. I spent most nights driving or walking the streets of our town and the ones nearby.

"You're not sleeping much are you?" Ed Stuyvesant asked as we stood in front of the coffee machine in November. "Saw your car out on Huron Street last night, Chief."

"Just making sure our taxpayers are safe." We watched silently as the machine dripped its God-awful coffee into the scarred pot. "And what were you doing out there, Ed? A little far from your regular beat, too."

"Marge's sister, Brenda, lives out that way. Her dog had some pups in the middle of the night. Ever since I delivered that girl's baby in the squad car, those women think I'm an ob-gyn." He held his hands up. "Do these look like the mitts of a skilled vet?"

I smiled. "She hear anything? Brenda, I mean."

"Sometimes, Chet, if you're looking too hard..." Ed said, calling me by name for once. He sampled the brew and made the requisite face. "But if you come across anything, give me a call—no matter what time of night, Chief. Don't take it on alone. I never did care about eight hours sleep."

"I'll give you a call, Ed. I'm not aiming to screw it up now."

"Still hoping to convict someone?"

I nodded. "I'm gonna see someone brought to justice. If I don't, I'll never get beyond it"

"Odds are against it by now. Those cowboys are probably long gone."

"And where would they go? Detroit? Chicago? Bet they can't even read a map."

It wasn't until the week after New Year's that I picked up two reports of activity in Duck Hollow. Duck Hollow's fifteen miles down the road. It's less of a town than West Lebanon, mostly attracting folks who just want to fish or hunt.

Loners. There's a general store with a gas pump outside and not much else.

Most of the houses sit deep in the woods. They're really just bare bones cabins—not meant for families. Duck Hollow uses the schools, police, and services of the neighboring town to get by. Off-season population is 166 and mostly men over fifty, holed up in tiny cabins they knocked together with a few drunken buddies over a couple of weekends thirty years ago. Nobody tells them how to live their lives in Duck Hollow; taxes are among the lowest in Michigan.

The first suspicious report came from one of the few married couples. They reported New Year's Eve had been celebrated eight hours straight at a cabin nearby. The man said

it sounded like a machine gun was being fired. It may have been a pump BB gun, but the officer who took the information thought it was probably a semi-automatic shotgun.

Two more reports came in: the sound of windows being broken, cracking branches at night, possibly more gunshots.

When I looked at a map, the locations called in as suspicious were in a straight line if you traveled through the woods. Maybe someone without a car, who was tramping through the woods from house to house, looking for food or stuff to steal. Ed and I went up there, scouting every cabin we could find and succeeding only in drawing attention from two men with shotguns.

"Police," Ed yelled. Both times, the gun was silently withdrawn through a crack in the door. No idle chatter in Duck Hollow.

But the third time, we found their lair. Although the boards facing the dirt road were still up when we cautiously circled the house, the ones over the back door and window had been pulled aside just enough to allow entry and a bit of light. Smoke curled out of the chimney and two pairs of dripping boots sat at the back door. Nice they'd removed their boots before entering the cabin. Someone had taught these guys manners.

"Think we need to call for more help," Ed whispered as we eased closer to the house.

"Looks like it's just two of them," I whispered, gesturing toward the boots.

Ed kicked in the flimsy door and I peered in cautiously. Inside was a barely furnished room with a kitchen at our end. Two guys sat at one of those fifties kitchen tables watching a tiny TV. It must have run on batteries since the electricity was turned off. They both looked up, blinking at the sudden light and at the poised Glocks in our hands.

Before they could move, I yelled, "Freeze," which they immediately did.

The older one, a beefy, red-faced guy, was around forty-five; the other, a kid who was even larger, was maybe eighteen or twenty.

"Put your hands where I can see them," I added. I'd hate to tell you how rarely I've said words like that. They took it as the genuine thing though and the kid's enormous arms shot right up—probably something he'd seen in movies too.

"Like this?" he called out in a surprisingly pip-squeaky voice. I could see his wrists clearly, and it nearly took my breath away. He was wearing a Spider-man watch. Red band this time. The one we found was blue.

"Where d'you get that watch?" I asked, grabbing his wrist.

The kid screamed, nearly falling off his chair. I yanked him back onto it and he sat there, his mouth hanging open, not saying a word.

I repeated the question, "Where did you…"

"Look, he ain't right," the beefy guy broke in. "And all you're doing is scaring him half to death." His voice softened considerably. "His dad bought that watch for him when he lost his old one. Right, Johnny." The kid nodded. The older man looked at me. "What's with the watch anyway?"

"Could you be the guys killed a boy out in West Lebanon last year?" I asked. "Left him dead in a doorway."

The beefy guy shook his head. "No way. I was down inside Jackson 'bout then. Didn't get out till June." He looked at me, answering my next question. "Stole a car."

"What about him? He do it?"

"He ain't right," the beefy guy repeated. "He don't remember what he did yesterday. His dad lets him hang around." He looked around as if that father might be listening, then added, "He don't know what else to do since Johnny's mom took off. He's got some place gonna take him after the holidays. Up near Marquette."

"Ever hit a guy with a shovel? A guy wearing a shirt like mine?" I asked Johnny, knowing I shouldn't be asking questions like that. Knowing I should call the cops in Traverse

City and let them handle it. Knowing I was screwing things up. But I had to know. I could feel Ed flinching with this knowledge beside me.

The kid shrugged.

"I toll you. He probably don't remember," the beefy guy said. "And if he did do it, which I ain't saying he did, it didn't mean nothin'. A kid like Johnny, well you know how it is. Everyone knows a kid like Johnny. Right?"

"Either of you have guns?" I asked, ignoring his last comment. I nodded to Ed and he started to search them.

"Nah, I'm just a minder, you might say," the guy told me. "John here gets minded since those events. I'd just as soon stay out of Jackson so it's okay with me, Money's less but it's something. Not that I'm saying anything happened over there, mind you. Who knows how scared a kid like John might be to see a uniform come through a door. Who knows what he's liable to do."

"You're not saying that, huh?"

"It's just daycare," the guy continued, in case we still didn't get it.

I looked at the table where the boy sat, head down. A tear slid down his cheek, his hands still up in the air.

"Why don't the two of you get out of here?" I said, avoiding Ed's shocked face.

"What 'bout the other stuff going on?" Ed asked me. "The break-ins. You know."

"These fellows won't give us any more trouble. Right?"

"Right. Right! You mean we can go?"

The guy was rising already, looking for his coat "Get your coat on, John."

Johnny lowered his arms slowly. "I don't need a coat, Shep." He looked longingly at the TV where Oprah Winfrey was interviewing a female guest. One of those skinny blondes you saw everywhere nowadays. "You ain't gonna leave the TV behind, are you?"

Shep shook his head. "You do too need a coat, Johnny. It's not ten degrees out there."

"Get out of this county now," I said from the doorstep. "As far away as possible. 'Cause next time it'll be different."

I stood at the doorway, watching them head toward the forest.

"I may not remember what it's like for a kid like him." I was shouting the last words and Johnny had to cover his ears.

BORDER CROSSING
Michael McGlade

Onwards we continued, stacking time on the blacktop. Our thirty-six-hour drive thus far had taken us from DC, through Knoxville, Nashville, Fort Worth and Tucson.

"Wait till you hear this, Daddy."

Missy pointed to a listing in the Arizona Penal Code directory on her lap.

"Says here it's unlawful to smile if you have teeth missing. Donkeys are not permitted to sleep in bathtubs. And cutting down a cactus is punishable with up to twenty-five years in prison."

That's my wife, Missy. Equal-stakes partners since the moment I met her two years back and we've been skating asphalt together ever since. She calls me Daddy on account of the age difference—she being twenty-five, me thirty-four. My real name's Jackson: not many living people know it.

Midnight Rider jangled on the radio and I cranked it up. We were heading for the border crossing into Mexico with a priority pigeon-express delivery for Eduardo Guzman. Let me explain. I used to run my own export business out of Mexico City, which means I'm a seasoned transfer specialist. Back then I learned subtle techniques guaranteed to navigate the myriad nightmare bureaucratic red-tape complexities of border crossings such as smuggler tunnels, improvised cannons, trebuchets. Even used nuns with dodgy habits.

I'm ex-military. Blackjack brigade. Army training is a good grounding for border jumps but I'd be nothing without Missy. She's in charge of logistics. It's her plan.

"We can't risk going through a border checkpoint," she said. "So we'll drive straight over the top of the fence."

She had prepared a makeshift ramp to scale the fourteen feet high US-Mexico border fence in Yuma, Arizona. What's not to love about that? I had to go, just to see if it even worked.

Not that this type of border crossing was strictly necessary considering the cargo. Eduardo Guzman had family papers and deeds he'd been keeping from the IRS which are presently contained in a steel lockbox which could easily be hidden in my Jeep and we'd pass through any checkpoint with a high degree of certainty. Even though I'd guaranteed Eduardo's delivery, I wasn't worried about being stopped by the border guards at somewhere like El Paso because if those border guards discovered the lockbox, me and Missy would just use my homemade grenades to blast our way out. It's why we were being paid two hundred thousand dollars, half up front.

But I wasn't doing it for the money. Like I said, I wanted to drive my Jeep Wrangler right over that fourteen feet high fence.

Near noon we tooled along Interstate 8. Yucca trees, sagebrush, cactus, sand dunes. Every now and then, and I don't know why, there were these little piles of pebbles like some bored child had taken it upon himself to tidy up the whole desert. Didn't see sandcastles though.

The roadside sign said five miles to Yuma, which was where we'd jump the border into Mexicali and find Eduardo waiting for his delivery.

"Ever wonder where the phrase *son of a gun* came from?"

Travel doesn't often broaden the mind, just lengthens the conversation.

"During the Civil War a Minié ball pieced a young rebel's genitals, passed right though and struck a woman's belly. She conceived a child because of it."

Missy chuckled.

"Now that's an immaculate conception."

Earrings of Spanish moss dangled from a roadside oak.

A single pickup approached from a mile off.

I checked the rearview and noticed that two vehicles in the distance drifted over the hazy ridge like wind-bullied tumbleweeds and both of these vehicles then slowed to a stop on the lee of the hill with a clear, uninterrupted line of sight. There was no reason for them to stop there except…

A golf ball-sized hole fractured the left upper corner of the windshield. Glass powdered like ocean spray. Another hole. Closer to the center. Missy clutched her face.

Our Jeep caught the gravel apron. Tractionless tires. Lurched into the ditch and struck an outcrop of rock and everything went upside down.

Pressure, like a lead weight, squeezed the air from my lungs.

Everything stopped.

Sound and time no longer existed.

I don't know how long I lay there but burning electrical

wires and gas fumes brought me back. The vehicle rested on its side. I leveled a boot at the windshield and struck at it till it shattered.

I retrieved my Beretta M9 pistol from the glove compartment. There had been no more shots fired which meant our attackers were probably winding their way toward us. Missy's seatbelt was caught and I cut it off . Her face glittered with glass fragments but she seemed uninjured. We scrambled out the vehicle and took shelter. The Mossberg 500 twelve-gauge was in the trunk, along with Eduardo's steel lockbox, and to get them we'd be exposed.

I peered out. The two cars were coming, still a mile off.

My head thrummed. Took a hard hit during the crash.

There were no clean surfaces on the Jeep and it had rolled almost into a ball. Coarse smoke billowed from the engine.

"Who'd you upset enough to shoot at us, Daddy?"

"Didn't annoy nobody," I said. "Nobody knows we're here. Except Eduardo."

"Then who did Eduardo irritate?"

The shooters' cars approached from the wavering horizon and between me and Missy and them was a stretch of blacktop caught in the flux of the endless desert sands.

Reek of gasoline intensified.

"Get us out of here, Daddy."

Missy's voice as crisp as the clack of a cocked gun.

I certainly didn't revel a shootout.

A pickup approached from Yuma direction and I limped onto the pavement and waved it to a halt. Missy got the Mossberg and Eduardo's steel lockbox and we piled in the back of the pickup.

"What happened?" the woman said. "You run your car

off the road?"

"Just drive," I said.

"But you're cut. You're bleeding."

I hadn't noticed the gash on my head.

"Get us out of here," I said. "I got money."

"I don't want money. Are you OK?"

"Drive. Just drive."

I pointed toward Yuma and the woman turned the pickup in that direction.

Sharpness drilled into me. I heard the rifle bullet hiss and then I collapsed. Pain flared. A gunshot wound is terrifying and invigorating. Adrenaline kicked in and it felt like a series of doors slamming shut inside my chest. I stood but it was worse than I expected and I went down, down, down into darkness.

A dark green corrugated steel fence fourteen feet high in a solid contour receded into the heat shimmer for miles unbroken. Beyond were some low bald hills pocked with shrubs, then Mexicali. We had dropped the woman off near town and proceeded to the border crossing point. We weren't followed, not after I lobbed a grenade at our pursuers, but that didn't mean we couldn't be found.

Not long ago, out of this dead-grass landscape and sand and the stone plateaus smelling of burned bricks and heat lines that imposed a soft focus effect which caused the horizon to seem like some unreachable destination, we had willingly come toward the blue hills of Mexico, vegetation diluting from green until only dead yellow remained.

This woman's pickup, which I'd bought for ten thousand, was aimed at the makeshift ramp which spanned the US-Mexico border fence.

"Don't know if the pickup will make it," Missy said. "I designed the ramp with the Jeep in mind. Gradient might be too steep."

She removed her sunglasses, blew a watermelon-scented bubble and popped it back into her mouth. She took the pickup onto the ramp and up the incline and at the change-over from incline to horizontal, the chassis caught and sparked on the ramp edge. Tires slipped. A little gas and the pickup made it onto the level. We were crossing the border. The way down was like a teeter-totter and she had to go easy and let gravity take us from horizontal to decline at the fulcrum, otherwise we'd stick.

We crossed into Mexico, the nearest town and our end destination Mexicali five miles off. Here was a featureless area, easy to get lost in. Withered shrubs. Fat cactuses. Stony roads that led nowhere.

Missy's hired hands set about dismantling the ramp.

She took the steel lockbox onto her lap and picked the lock. Inside were five of the largest emeralds I'd ever seen. They must've been worth ten million dollars.

"He tricked us, Daddy. Eduardo played us."

I'd lost a lot of blood and had a tourniquet on my leg. The bullet had gone through the meat of my thigh and somehow missed the femoral artery.

"I'm bleeding," I said. "Thanks for your concern."

"He lied to us. You know I can't stand liars."

"I can't *stand* either. Literally. Still bleeding here."

"There's a veterinarian I know nearby."

"While you're at it gonna get me neutered too?"

⊙ ⊙ ⊙

Pale yellow walls. In a room now. Hot, too hot. I kicked the bed sheets off. Body flamed.

I cremate.

Incinerate.

I am napalm.

Missy dabbed a damp cloth against my forehead and the drapes ghosted in the blowtorch breeze. This hotel room stank of sourness and sick. Missy sat next to me on the bed.

"You've got a fever, Daddy. It's the infection. You're fighting it. Get some rest."

My voice croaked like a bullfrog. Missy gave me water and I wanted to douse myself in it or I'd catch alight. She gifted me a few sips and took the glass away.

My leg wound crawled like fire ants. It had been stitched and smelt like spoilt milk.

⊙ ⊙ ⊙

Almost six o'clock. I'd been in bed a day and a half, and decided I'd been static too long—that's how you get caught, get dead.

The sky stormed and crashed like timpani. Rain daggered down and muscled through the vacancies in the rotten wooden window frame. This hotel room carried a distinct Bates Motel vibe.

If we had to, we could make a stand here, and at least I'd be able to stretch out on a bed in the meanwhile. I sure hoped Missy had slept because she looked worn and stretched and pinched thin. More than anything I wanted to curl up next to her and forget all this was happening. All I could think of was a shower. I needed icy water to crave it all away, freeze the blacktop from my skin. Instead I stared at the ceiling where a jagged crack ran its length cleaving it in two, a bit like the Mississippi.

Missy changed my dressing because the bullet wound had been oozing. She sprayed it with iodine which stung to high heaven but I couldn't let her see it hurt.

I am rock.

Solid granite.

Unflinching.

She squirted more iodine. I laughed. She took it as a challenge.

"Daddy, you don't yelp some, I'll have to put it in your eye."

"Won't matter. They trained me not to feel."

"Is that so?"

"Indeed it is."

"You don't feel nothing?"

She leaned across, bosom in my face, and scenting of wild daisies. I embraced her, took her closer but she shrugged me off.

"Hope you enjoy being a rock."

The phone rang and she lifted the receiver. I took it.

"We know you're mad at us," the man said. "But you gave us no choice, Jackson. We want the emeralds. They're ours by rights."

He sounded almost apologetic. The grenades I had lobbed at him during the escape must've changed his tune, and I guess my reputation held some sway. Although, I'd speculate this coward much preferred to finish me off from distance.

"Come on in this room," I said, "see what happens."

"Just want what's ours back. Give me the stones and I guarantee your safety. Eight o'clock, leave them outside your room or we're coming in with the heavy artillery."

◉ ◉ ◉

A scripture quotation that hung in a frame on the wall said, 'I have engraved you on the palms of my hands.' The accompanying illustration showed a pair of praying hands clutching a candle.

Missy stopped reading her cell phone screen and set it on the hotel bed. It was seven o'clock.

"News report says them stones were heisted in DC a month back."

I said, "Eduardo showed me the lockbox contents in his study. I saw only papers inside. Must've swapped the box out when I turned my back."

"He tricked us into moving stolen objects," she said. "And them's his crew been shooting at us. Eduardo paid us over the odds because he figured his disgruntled crew, the ones he double-crossed, would be taking potshots at us."

I noticed the wild glint in her powder-blue eyes.

"No, not a way, Missy. Don't be thinking that."

"I want an apology from Eduardo."

"An apology?"

"He lied. I hate liars. I deserve an apology."

"I'm the one been shot. Don't I get a say?"

"What do you want to say?"

"We've a whole heap of gemstones here. What's to stop us keeping them?"

"I despair, Daddy, sometimes I do. You've got brains, yes you have. But they don't always work. We can't keep them gems. It ain't right."

"I'll refer you back to the bullet hole in my leg."

"We didn't earn them. And we're not stealing them. We're not thieves. We had a deal with Eduardo to deliver his lockbox and that's what we're going to do."

"Did I just have a stroke? Deliver them? After him lying to us, playing us for a fool?"

"You want me to give you a matching hole in that other leg?"

"Nope."

"Then we're committed to this assignment," she said. "Eduardo will get his steel lockbox, as promised."

⊙ ⊙ ⊙

We parked opposite a squat white adobe building where a double rainbow had formed in the slow drizzle illuminated by the setting sun.

Missy said, "Wonder what it means?"

We hadn't been followed to Eduardo's home. Out here, on the edge of Mexicali, the housing had sprung into existence recently with no aesthetic consideration, and was a jumble of huts and shacks stacked each on top of the other like something from some Asian slum. Almost medieval with its narrow streets.

The evening darkened by degrees into the hazy spectrum of gray and the sky drafted with ill-humor. It would soon crack again but for now there was a void of soundlessness that jangled my nerves like a steel guitar. It was half-seven. Something told me that if the gemstones weren't outside my room at eight, Eduardo's would be hit next.

Four armed guards manned the perimeter of this property. I entered alone while Missy kept the engine running.

It was disorientatingly dark inside. The surface of a wall looked like it had been smeared with effluent and I knew somebody had died here recently. A guard led the way into an unlit hallway, narrow and twisting to confound intruders.

Inside the room was Eduardo, a wedge-shaped man in his fifties with a greying mustache. He noticed the steel lockbox and extended his hand. He was unarmed. Big mistake. I had entered weaponless but the guard next to me had a nice submachine gun, so I struck him next to the ear at the jaw and had his gun before he collapsed to ground.

⊙ ⊙ ⊙

Missy drove into town and it was almost eight o'clock. Eduardo knew not to put up a fight and had elected to submit immediately. With a gun to his head I was able to get out without having to kill a soul. I don't like wet work.

"I will give you all the money you want," Eduardo said. "Double what I was going to pay you."

"It's too late for money," I said. " I'd never have taken this job had I known you were a bank robber and a thief. I'd have said no to the job. No matter how much money."

"But you were willing to transport my deeds, items I had concealed from the IRS."

"That's different," I said. "They're your deeds. You don't want to keep it in the country, fine. But I'm not a thief. I don't steal. And I don't appreciate being put in a jackpot."

"You crossed us, Eduardo, yes you did."

"Where are you taking me?" he said. "To the authorities?"

Not exactly.

◉ ◉ ◉

Missy and me were waiting in the pickup outside the El Rancho hotel when Nine Federal Police cars crisscrossed the street. Wind of a huge robbery bust had attracted half the on-duty officers. We had left Eduardo hog-tied in the room. His ex-crew arrived on time and shot off a few fireworks but the cops caught them all in one place. Five handcuffed men were being led into the street and an officer had secured the lockbox of gemstones.

"Eduardo looks a bit peaky."

"Sure does. He might just regret his trickery after an unsupervised night in the cells with his old friends."

"Missy, remind me never to cross you."

We were the only gringos in Mexicali which was something pressed that needed to be remedied.

"You any bright ideas how to get back into the US? Forgot to bring my fake passport."

"Daddy, you can fly an ultralight, right?"

LOOKING FOR THE DEATH TRICK

Bracken MacLeod

The cutoff denim skirt rode up over Honey's hips, exposing her ass as she bent over to get the attention of a driver slowly passing by. Although the men she signaled couldn't see from where they sat, Comfort and his top earning girl—his bottom bitch—Chai, insisted she show ass *every* time she leant into a car window. "For the customers still rollin' up," Comfort said. She did what she was told and didn't try to pull the fabric down, flashing her ass and pussy at the girls waiting behind her. It didn't bother Honey too much to show pink, but the other girls were always looking for a way to get ahead, get closer to top of the food chain. It wasn't like the movies; they weren't a sisterhood or a tribe. If she unconsciously displayed some modesty, word would move up the food chain and she'd pay for not marching in perfect step.

She didn't have much of a figure, but a lot of guys liked the girl next door look. That skinny, hasn't-quite-grown-out-of-being-a-tomboy-but-is-trying look worked for her surprisingly well. She had long, dishwater-blond hair and wore "natural" make-up. Her tight camisole tops left her shoulders bare so the johns could see her freckles—if they could tear their eyes away from her nipples. Many of the men who trawled the block were looking for something familiar they couldn't have at home. The neighbor's daughter. The babysitter. The day care teacher. All forbidden fruit, juicy and ripe and hanging low on the tree waiting to be plucked and fucked—if only it wouldn't wreck their lives. She looked the part. All except for her hands. They were bony with big blue veins and she chewed her cuticles, leaving most of her fingernails with blood crusted around them. She kept her hands out of sight as much as possible.

She filled a niche in her pimp's business model. The suburban tourist. Comfort tried to convince her she was doing a public service. Saving other girls from what had driven her out of the 'burbs into his embrace. She was a protector, Comfort said. "Keepin' those innocent at-home bitches from gettin' preyed upon. You a one girl rape prevention program, Honey."

He called her Honey because she was his "golden girl." "My ray of sunshine at night," he'd say, his words fat with hollow praise that filled the empty spaces in her heart.

Other girls on the stroll didn't have the luxury of looking like a type. Or rather, they looked like the type they were: drive-through convenience. A quick suck or fuck in the alley for someone with a hard-on in a hurry. Those girls wore tight lace outfits not much more concealing than lingerie. A few kept it even simpler, opting for a bra and thong under a big coat. Drive by and they opened their petals like moon flowers, blooming in the light of the streetlamps.

The car slowed and Honey got a glimpse of a face in shadow. White. Middle age. Athletic, going to seed. What she looked for was whether a john made eye contact. And how. If he looked her in the eyes, she could get him to stop. If he looked too hard, she might not be able to get him to stop when it mattered. It was the john angry with his wife or girlfriend who wanted to pin a working girl to prove some-thing to "those bitches" who was trouble. The men needing to express power and virility were the ones who liked to hear Honey gag, hear her gasp when they shoved it in dry. Those were the ones who all wanted to ride bareback. They paid extra for that privilege.

So did she. Usually with abrasions and tears.

The man beckoned her with a thick finger. She stood up, not pulling the skirt down, making sure he got a good look at her bald pussy as she walked toward his car. Honey leaned over again, resting her forearms on his windowsill. "Wanna date, Daddy?" she asked.

His face contorted briefly before his neutral expres-sion returned. The change had been so subtle, so brief, that Honey couldn't tell whether she'd imagined it or not. Either way, it made her regret approaching the vehicle. She was preparing to shove off the car and let him roll on down the road when he said, "How much?"

"It depends, lover. What do you want?" she asked, delivering her line, locked into the role that the Director expected her to perform. He had to tell her he wanted to fuck for money if they were going to continue the play.

"I want the blue discount," he said pulling back his sport coat to reveal the gold badge clipped to his belt.

"I seen fake badges before."

"This one's the real deal." When she didn't respond, he added, "I can take you off the stroll for the night, book you and let you go in the morning, or you can come with me for a few minutes and get paid the rest of the night. Either way you're getting in the car." His expression didn't change again—he kept his mask in place—but the last sentence held all the threat the fleeting shadow that had passed over his face promised a second earlier. Another man saying one thing and meaning something else. *Get in the car or I'll give your pimp a reason to tune you up for lightening his roll.* It was like they had their own silent language always running under what you could hear them saying.

She opened the door and slipped in.

"Good girl."

"Whatever," she said. "Pull around to that alley so Chai don't think I'm a rat."

"Chai?"

"You know Comfort, but not his bottom bitch? You ain't vice."

"Nope. Homicide." He put the car in gear and asked where she wanted him to park. She silently pointed toward the alley a half block away. He pulled into the gap between buildings and drove until she told him it was good enough. He backed the car into a berth next to a dumpster and killed the lights, but left the engine running. The smell of trash fermenting in the humid heat of the night floated into the car through the vent. She thought about pushing the recircle button on the air conditioning, but had learned long ago about messing with a john's controls. Instead, she hoped his cock smelled clean. Sometimes the odor of the garbage dumpster was preferable to that of the man in the driver's seat.

Honey knelt on the seat, leaned over, and ran a hand over his crotch, squeezing gently, trying to work him up so she could get back on the track under the relative safety of the streetlight. He grabbed her wrist and set her hand back in her own lap. "I said I want to talk."

"About what? You too cheap for therapy?"

"About this guy." He pulled a photograph from the

inside pocket of his jacket and handed it to her. She reached for the overhead light switch. He deflected her hand, pulling a small penlight from his pocket and shining it on the picture. "You seen him?" he asked.

"No. I don't know. All y'all look alike to me."

"Where are you from that 'all y'all' is something people say?"

"I'm from up that block," she said, pointing out the window.

The man sighed heavily and said, "Fair enough. Take another look at the guy. Study his face real hard. You recognize him or not?" He shone the light on the glossy paper, trying to get an angle that didn't obscure the image with glare. It was a grainy black and white, but taken from a close angle. The man in the picture had a goatee, odd shaped sport sunglasses, and wore a baseball cap. His mouth was open, but it wasn't to say anything. It just looked like he breathed with his lips parted.

The creep in the photo was as familiar as anyone else she'd ever seen—white guy with a chin beard and a Red Sox cap. Almost every single john who rolled down her block looked like him. She said so.

"This one is special," the cop said.

"Nobody's special."

"He is. Believe me. You see this guy, you call me." He handed her a business card. A gold shield like the one he'd flashed at her was embossed on the card next to the logo for the Boston Police Department. Beside the shield it read,

LIEUTENANT DETECTIVE
WILLIAM P. DIXON
HOMICIDE UNIT

The precinct address was listed on the bottom left opposite his office number, fax, and direct dial. "What's the P stand for?" she asked.

"Pepper." She laughed. He didn't even grin. "What's *your* name?"

"Honey."

"What's the name your parents gave you?"

She blinked a few times. He hadn't asked for her "real" name—"the one her parents gave her." Honey was as real as a name got for her any more. "I was... my name is Mindy."

"Well Mindy, you keep that picture. You see this prick, call the number on the back of my card." She turned the small white square over. He'd written a cell phone number on the reverse side in blue ink. "Give me a description of his car and the plate, but *do not get in*. You listening?"

"I hear you," she said, playing with a strand of her hair.

"Help yourself, Honey. I've got only so many eyes I can put on the stroll."

"You mean you don't want to spare none for the track."

"I'm out here, aren't I?"

She chewed on the end of her hair for a moment before asking, "Where am I supposed to keep all of this shit?" She indicated her outfit. No pockets; barely any fabric. She spread her legs slightly, giving him another look, wanting to see his expression change again. It didn't. He shook his head.

"Keep it out. Show the picture around. Let everyone know any working girl who gets in this freak's car is turning a death trick. You hear me?"

Her breath caught. He'd said he was homicide, but all she'd cared about when she got in was that he wasn't vice. He asked again if she was listening. She nodded and stared a little harder at the image. "He's killing working girls?" she said when she was able to find her breath.

"Sometimes."

"Sometimes he lets them go?"

"Sometimes he murders citizens too. But he mostly sticks to 'low profile targets.' Do you know what I mean when I say that?"

"No one cares if he does one of us."

The cop didn't say anything.

"Why me?"

"What do you mean?" he asked.

"Why did you pick me? You should be talking to Comfort's bottom girl. She's the one who runs the track. She can get the word out." Honey waited for him to tell her that he endangered her by jumping the chain of command because she looked smarter than the other girls. Friendlier and more likely to understand. She listened for the lines Comfort used when he explained why she was destined to out-earn all his other bitches except Chai.

He let out a long breath and said, "Because you look like the girls we find behind the dumpsters."

She sat staring at him for a long minute. He cracked his window and lit a cigarette, letting her have all the time she needed to picture herself lying lifeless behind a stinking trash bin, bled out and stiff. Dixon offered her a smoke. She shook her head, refusing.

"You're organic Honey, huh?" he said replacing the pack on his dash. "You keep that self-preservation instinct. Use it out there." He took one more deep drag. "You need me to drop you?"

"You don't know nothin' about The Game, do you? You gonna get me hurt worse than a bad date." His forehead wrinkled as if he didn't understand. 'A bad date,' she repeated, as if it was self-evident she meant a violent john. When he didn't seem to be getting it, she said, "Nobody ever drives me home. Especially not no cops. I ain't s'posed to talk to you."

"Then you better get going." He pushed the button on the door handle unlocking the car, but not moving to open her door. Electric chivalry.

She held out a hand. "Forty."

"A blow job on this block is twenty," he said.

"*Now* you think you know something, huh? You kept me longer than it'd take to blow."

"I have stamina."

"Not with me. No one has that much stamina."

He handed her sixty dollars and said, "Buy something to eat."

Honey snatched the money and let herself out of the car trotting for the end of the alley. She hesitated at sidewalk, glancing over her shoulder. The detective's car remained where he'd parked. She turned the corner and listened for a moment, waiting for the sound of him driving away. If he left, she couldn't hear.

She stared at the man in the picture, memorizing what she could see of his face. Dixon didn't know anything about how she worked and survived. Taking the picture around the block was more likely to get her marked as a snitch than it was to be taken seriously. Still, she figured he might know a thing or two about the kind of people who got off on killing girls like her. She decided to take his word for it that he was looking out for her. Comfort would understand that she was looking out for him by warning them.

She was his golden girl.

⦿ ⦿ ⦿

Comfort's fists left Honey with an ache in her guts that reached up her spine and down into her bowels. She lay on the sidewalk, crumpled up like the detective's photograph. Chai spit on the picture before kicking her in the crotch with the wedge toe of her platform shoe. Honey's back arched and her cry echoed against the monolithic brick factory wall opposite the park. Comfort gave her another punt in the guts with his Timberland, silencing her. "You a snitch? You a snitch?" his bottom bitch yelled as she tore up the detective's business card. She threw the pieces in Honey's face.

She wanted to tell them she wasn't. She wanted to say that she was looking out for Comfort's girls by showing them the picture, but she couldn't get enough air in her lungs to give volume to her words. She whispered "I'm sorry," in between shallow breaths.

"God damn right you sorry. Gonna be more sorry if you don't get correct. You don't talk to five-oh. You don't open that mouth except to suck a dick. You feel me?"

"Ye—" Chai kicked her in the stomach as she tried to agree. She nodded.

Comfort said, "You learnin'. You got an hour to get back on the block, or else I'm callin' up a party. Get some motherfuckers to jump on the train." He stomped off, leaving Chai to finish explaining what was expected of her.

She squatted in front of Honey and flicked the crumpled up picture at Honey's face with a dragonlady fingernail. "If you see this iceman, you come to me. I'll get Comfort and *he'll* take care of it. You don't go to the police for shit, you hear?"

Honey nodded. Chai stood up and brushed the hair out of her face, preening for her return to her man's side. He wouldn't tolerate her looking disheveled. She was not his most expensive piece of jewelry, but she was the prettiest. "You got forty-five minutes to get up and earn." She sashayed away, making sure that the other girls on the block saw she was queen.

Rolling over, Honey sobbed and held her stomach. It hurt so bad she worried she might be bleeding internally— that the two of them might have ruptured something. But she couldn't go to the hospital. She couldn't go anywhere except maybe around the corner to the "pharmacy." L'il Bentley would have something to get her through the night. She'd give him the twenty she'd stuffed in her shoe for an Oxy. It might not get her through the night, but it'd get her back on the track and in the game. She pushed up onto her hands and knees, waited until the cramping and nausea subsided enough to stand on her feet, and staggered off to find the dealer, leaving the picture where it lay. If Comfort or Chai found it on her, there would be no amount of Oxy that could dull what they'd do to her.

It was days before she could stand fully upright without cramping. Days during which it was a welcome moment to lean over and rest her elbows on the doorframe of a john's car and ask, "Wanna date?" Still she did it. Pushed through the pain until she'd skimmed enough to afford a pill or two.

She wasn't earning as well as she had been before the beating. But Comfort didn't say anything to her about the money or how she looked. While he was always reciting mystical-sounding shit to the people hanging around him, he didn't say anything to her at all anymore. One of his street soldiers asked why she was looking so used up and he thumped the book he always carried around, *The Art of War*, like some street corner preacher about to drop the word of Almighty God on an acolyte hungry to be fed the gospel of original pimping. "Once upon a time in China, the Emperor asked General Tso to make all his hos into an army," he said, holding court. "So the general, he lined all those bitches up and put the Emperor's favorite in charge. He tell them, 'turn left,' and when they didn't do shit like he said, he beheaded the bitch in charge. What do you think those hos did when he promoted the next one to bottom bitch and said 'turn left'? I tell you, they turned the fuck left." He laughed and nodded his head toward Honey. "She was an up-make-you-comer. Look at her now. That's what happens to snitches and bitches who don't do what they told." His golden girl was now his object lesson on how to keep the troops in line. And when she looked at him hungrily, she was left to starve.

Chai, in turn, was leaving Honey with less of her own money at the end of the night, claiming that it wasn't Comfort who was going to suffer if she wasn't working hard enough. Honey was doing the best she could, but as much as it hurt to stand up and even breathe, it hurt worse to fuck. And her increasingly despairing look was driving away the johns. If it wasn't the sleeplessness caused by the pain, it was surely the physical effects of the painkillers. The Oxy had left her looking pallid, with dark gray bags under her eyes. She tried to compensate with make-up, but she ended up looking... "trashy," her mother would have said. She was beginning to look like a junkie. Like a whore.

The man behind the wheel of the car looked her over as she asked him for a date, his face turning down with disappointment and contempt. Without a word he goosed the gas and the Mustang lurched off. The edge of the door banged Honey in the temple and she went sprawling to the ground, long skinny legs kicking out instinctively, shoving her out of the way of the car's rear wheels before they crushed her legs. Before another man left her alone to suffer.

She picked herself up and staggered to the street. She didn't bother to pull down the tight jersey skirt bunched up over her hips. Another girl on the block laughed as Honey held her stinging face and sobbed. A long purple bruise was going to make her even less attractive. She could already feel the side of her face growing hot, swelling. Although, she didn't see how that could make business worse.

Another car slid up the block and stopped a few yards away. The girl who'd laughed wiggled her ample hips as she tottered on too-high heels toward the open window. Honey watched as she curved her spine to the side so the john could see both her cleavage and the curve of her bare hip while she set up the deal. She stared, watching the woman twitch her hips, listening to the crack of her cackle as she amused herself with her wit. But she wasn't opening the door. In a moment, if the john didn't agree to the terms she offered, she'd shift from flirty to furious. Screaming "faggot" while kicking backward at his car with her heels like a donkey, trying to dent the door or at least scratch the paint so he'd have something to explain when he got home to the missus. Punish him for not helping her make her ends.

Honey glanced at the john. Her heart beat hard in her chest and she lost her breath. He looked like all the others.

Goatee, Oakley halfjackets, and baseball cap with a big white B shading his face. His mouth hung open, but not in a way that suggested idiocy. He looked hungry, like someone had just set out supper. He wanted to taste. He was a wolf who wanted gobble the girl up and take her inside himself where she would be his forever like in a fairytale.

Honey thought about her huntsman, Detective Dixon. He told her to call him and he'd come running. He'd barge into the cottage and slay the wolf and rescue the girl.

She thought about Comfort and Chai. The bottom bitch had said to call her and Comfort would descend on the wolf like angry villagers protecting their lambs.

The man nodded and moved his head, indicating the girl should get in. What was her name? Something like Crystal or Quartz... or Ruby! That was it. Ruby—pulled open the door to climb inside.

Honey shouted, "Wait!" Tottering toward the car in the heels that she used to be good at walking in, but had become uncertain as her back had been made weak and crooked, she called out for the man to stop. "How about a double date?" she shouted.

Ruby stuck her hand out the open window and stuck up her middle finger as they drove away. The car slipped off into the darkness, pulling around into the alley. She ran after it. Huffing and out of breath, she rounded the corner in time to see the silhouette of the man pull his hands away from Ruby's face and lay her limp form gently against the seatback. The red taillights of the car flashed as he stepped on the brake before putting it in gear and then they dimmed and he drove away.

"Wait!" she screamed, knowing he couldn't hear over the sound of the engine. Honey calling out after, "Not *her*!

Me! Take ME! I'm the one you want!"

She memorized the license plate and make and model of the car. She tried to file away everything in her mind, making sure every detail was there to be recalled, despite the fog of her dulled Oxy mind.

The next time he rolled up the stroll, she would know it was him before she even saw his face. She'd see the car and she would be at his window, smiling and showing him that she was everything he'd ever wanted: the girl next door, the babysitter, his daughter, anyone as long as he let her in the car and took her away. He could do anything he wanted to her, as long as he took her away for good.

Except, of course, she knew he wouldn't come again. He'd move on to another track in another part of the city. He'd hunted this ground. He'd go looking for a new girl who was fresh and everything he desired. Not her. Not anymore.

She fell to her knees. The concrete dug into her shins and scuffed her skin and added another set of blemishes that tarnished her looks and no one would ever want her again.

Not even a killer.

MAYBELLE'S LAST STAND
Travis Richardson

Maybelle **eases back and forth** on her rocking chair, slow, but steady, on the front porch of her single room abode. Keeping her cataract eyes on the dusty road ahead, she rubs her arthritic hands together underneath a quilt, trying to keep her fingers agile. A tall man approaches her shack with the setting sun behind his back, silhouetting him. She's not sure who it is, but he's white by his swagger and definitely the law because of the gun hanging off the belt on his hip. When he finally reaches the porch, propping his boot on the first step, she can tell it is the devil himself, Sheriff Reed.

Maybelle prays, hoping that her grandson is quiet now. No need to agitate a cowardly lawman. The sheriff takes his hat off, wiping away beads of sweat.

"Howdy, ma'am."

Maybelle nods, but doesn't smile. She doesn't smile for any white man, especially if he's on her land. Smilin' and yessirin' was something her parents did against their will when they were another man's property. This was hard land that she, her parents, her brothers and sisters, her husband, and her children toiled over to make a living.

"I'm looking for your grandson, Ernest Young." The lawman wouldn't meet her eyes.

"Ain't around here."

The lawman chuckles to himself as if he is dealing with a half-witted child. "That ain't gonna fly. You're gonna let me look around here. I don't need to be askin', I'm just tryin' to be polite."

"What is it that you want Ernest for?"

The sheriff turns and spits on the cracked earth. "We got another dead girl. A white girl. She was raped and then strangled to death."

Maybelle chuckled and shook her head. "That's a cryin' shame."

"Yes, it is. And I don't see nothin' funny about it."

"She'd be the fourth one now, right, Sheriff? And yet three good men have been hanged."

"They ain't good. None of 'em. They're rapists and murderers"

"Every one of them?" The lawman wouldn't meet her eyes. "I suspect it's a white man."

"Impossible," he says too quickly.

"You know, I think you've got a little strategy goin' on here, Sherriff."

"I don't care to hear any of your theories right now."

"Seems the land of three negroes, rightfully given to them by the United States is bein' taken. Amassed, you might say."

"Now you best watch your—"

"And sweet little girls seem to be dyin' every couple of months. So I'm wonderin' which is it you like more, Sheriff? The flesh of innocent young girls or land?"

The sheriff's nostrils flare, but fear widens his eyes. "You ain't to talk to me that way. I'm gonna teach you some manners, nigger bitch."

He yanks the pistol from his holster. Maybelle's quilt explodes from under her. Her body rocks back in the chair from the blast. The sheriff drops his gun, having brought it only halfway up. He looks at the burning hole and black powder marks around the quilt and then down to his stomach. His pot belly pulses out crimson goo.

Maybelle pushes the quilt onto the splintered porch and stomps out the flame. She takes the heavy, old Colt peacemaker and puts it in her left hand. Shaking her fingers, she feels like she might've fractured something.

"Kick like the dickens, don't ya," she mutters to the gun.

With both hands, she points the gun at the sheriff's head. Blood oozes between his fingers from the hole in his belly, dripping into a red pool next to his pistol on the porch steps. Maybelle thinks his face is almost as white as the sheets he and his kind put over their heads some nights when they get the spirit of the devil in them.

"Any last words, lawman? I hear you've never had the decency to've asked us coloreds that before you lynched 'em. But I suppose I'm better than you. A whole lot better."

The sheriff reaches for his gun, but it slips from his bloody fingers.

"They'll kill you, you and your grandson. Hang ya'll up by that tree in the front." He gasps, wincing in agony. He glares at her as mean as a dying man can. "You can't shoot a sheriff out here, not in these parts." If he had the strength, he would've spit on her porch.

"But it looks like I most certainly did shoot myself a sheriff. See, I've been havin' a dilemma for quite a while now. Either I kill a sheriff, that'd be you," Maybelle says, pointing the unsteady gun at the lawman. "Or let him live and keep killin' white babies. Truly it don't matter 'cause we get hung all the same."

She cocks the hammer back with her left hand. Much harder than it oughta be.

"They'll kill your boy, you know."

"No they won't. I can guarantee you that."

Holding the pistol with both hands, Maybelle pulls the trigger. Sheriff Reed's brains blast out the back of his head as he falls to the ground. She would've never suspected he'd had so much in that dull, perverted head of his. But maybe it's all putrid meat. Sure smelled that way.

More white men would be coming along shortly. And they'd be mad and outraged like a bunch of hornets knocked out of their nest. She supposes she has three bullets left, but isn't sure and doesn't even know how to open the noisy contraption to check. She'd been surprised when the gun fired the first time. It had been handed down from her father to her brother and then to her after Willie had been hanged. Must have been the Lord's doin' to make such an old device still work. She says a quick prayer of gratitude to God for being there in her time of need.

Yep, them white men will definitely kill me whenever they decide to show, she thinks. At least they'd never get grubby hands on Ernest. Standing on aching legs, she hobbles from the rocking chair to the door.

"Please, Lord, let me take a couple of 'em to hell with me."

She knows that's where's she's going. No doubt about it.

Opening the front door, she sees her grandson sitting at the table with his bowl of beans. Almost the same way she'd left him when she went out to the porch. Except the poor boy's face is planted in the bowl. Stone cold dead.

No, sir, Ernest isn't going to be hung, left swinging for

days in the sun under the bridge so white kids can disgrace his body. She's seen too much of that awfulness already. Running her calloused fingers through his unruly hair, she inhales a quick, shallow breath. Just fourteen years of age, the dear boy. The child was so sweet, so honest and sincere it broke her heart when she thought about him, even on the good days.

Ernest came running to her house an hour earlier, eyes full of tears and fright. He had the misfortune of seeing the sheriff pick up a little white girl in his car a few days before. When she turned up dead this morning, he told a few folks what he'd seen, only to find out the sheriff was looking for him. Maybelle knew what was in store for her grandson. And she swore to him, invoking the name of Jesus and the Father himself, that she'd keep those white men from harming him.

Sitting the boy upright, Maybelle takes a washcloth and hobbles over to a pail. Dipping the soiled rag into the water, she wrings it out, twisting it back and forth in her gnarled hands. She hates to turn around, to bear witness to the murder she has committed, but she must. Looking at her grandson, she sees the poisonous red beans sticking all over his face.

"Oh good Lord, Ernest. Can't you go anywhere without makin' a mess," she says in a tone she'd used on all of her grandbabies. "Let me wash you up. Just hold still now."

With the cloth she pulls off a bean one at a time, dropping them into the bowl. "Now I know you're up there in heaven, Ernest, looking down at me and wonderin' why on earth I'd do such an awful thing to you. The only blood I got left in this world." She exhales and starts washing up his face. "I want you to know it wasn't easy for me to mix the poison into the pot of beans I had boilin', but you see there just wasn't another way. With the sheriff comin' after you and nobody but a decrepit old ninny to defend you..."

Maybelle shakes her head, looking into the boy's wide opened, unblinking eyes. "This harsh, evil world wasn't designed for somebody like you. There are too many damnable jagged edges out there that'd rip a soft boy like you to shreds. I've lost too many loved ones to horrors, you see. My brother hanged on the word of a lying white man, your mama died in childbirth, your daddy sliced his arm on rusted plow and no white doctor'd see him until it was too late. No, sir, Ernest. You had nowhere to go. Not with an evil lawman like Sheriff Reed on your tail and the demons that'll follow him."

She hears an engine and the crunch of gravel in the distance. This is it. Armageddon on the homestead. Maybelle closes Ernest's eyes and steps back. He looks peaceful in the chair. She prays to God again, but doubts He's listening anymore considering the fact she killed her grandson. But didn't He sacrifice His own son for a greater cause? Maybe Jesus could intercede for her. She hears voices, white, shouting in horror and disbelief.

"Sheriff Reed's dead. That nigger boy done shot him."

She prays for strength and the ability to kill as many of them as there are bullets left in the old gun. Swinging the door wide open, she sees three men in tan deputy uniforms standing over the dead sheriff. They look up in shock. She raises the pistol and begins firing.

PREDATORS
Marie S. Crosswell

Los Angeles
2014

It's a little house tucked into the middle of Montecito Heights in the hills of East Los Angeles, nondescript enough that anyone would drive past it without noticing it there. She parks her black '69 Chevy Caprice up the street a ways and walks to the front door in her undercover costume: skinny jeans, a tight-fitting cropped tank top that shows off her muscular abs, A-cup bra with almost enough padding to stop a bullet, and a shoulder-length blonde wig made of human hair. She hopes to God that the men peg her for an early twenty-something or like her looks enough not to care about her age.

She knocks instead of ringing the doorbell, gentle as the part she's playing. She's got a gun in her oversized handbag—her Colt Government Model .45, not some bitch piece—but she's still nervous. She wants to turn around and look for Detective Blythe's unmarked sedan across the street somewhere, but she doesn't.

Somebody cracks the door open, peeking at her through the screen door mesh.

She tries to smile. "Hi," she says, raising the pitch of her voice. "Are you Dogfish?"

Black eyes gloss over her face. "Martina?" the man says, his voice rough and deep.

Gabriel nods, forcing a fake smile.

The man slides the chain lock and holds the door, standing inside the darkened house. The screen creaks when she goes in, her stomach jittery as he shuts and locks the front door behind her.

A white man sits on the ratty living room sofa with a lit cigarette in his fingers, looking at her as she stands in the foyer across from him. Even in the dimness of the house, Gabriel can see he has pasty skin and snake eyes: narrow and flat. He must be Gerald Lee Kitchen, convicted sex offender in the state of Louisiana and the brains behind this sex trafficking operation. His accomplice is Santos Escamilla, an ex-con with a record in Albuquerque and Vegas, the one in charge of finding johns for their prisoners.

Detective Blythe and his partner, Detective Quincy, work the LAPD's Human Trafficking Unit. They've been tracking Kitchen and Escamilla for almost a year, building a case against them. The two men have rotated through three different sets of slaves since the beginning of the investigation, holding them prisoner and pimping them out to men they've done business with before and strangers they solicit in the right bars and clubs. The detectives figure that Kitchen and Escamilla replace their slaves every few months to keep their client base stimulated and willing to pay a consistent rate. They dump the girls with nothing but the clothes they have on in random public places, usually gas stations or street corners. Not one of the ex-victims voluntarily filed a police report prior to Blythe and Quincy approaching them. Some still won't talk.

Gabriel isn't a cop, but she is a private investigator, bounty hunter, and a friend of Blythe's. Three weeks ago, she agreed to help him. She posed as a nineteen-year-old interested in a one-time hook up for cash, in a phony ad on Craigslist. Kitchen took the bait. They've been emailing and texting ever since, holding off on meeting in person until Blythe and Quincy got their strategy straight.

Kitchen grins and sucks on his cigarette, looking at Gabriel's face. She resists the instinct to run, feels her muscles tense and her stomach churn but faces her opponent with a cool exterior, something she's spent years practicing in the bareknuckle boxing scene.

"That's Dogfish," Escamilla tells her, looking at Kitchen along with her.

"I didn't know there was going to be two of you," she says, doing her best to sound juvenile.

"My friend José likes to watch," says Kitchen, his voice like skinned knees on gravel road slick with blood and whiskey. "Ain't you a tall thing. Come here, baby. I want a closer look at you."

Gabriel takes cautious steps into the living room, stopping at the wooden coffee table. Kitchen's eyes travel down and up her body. She can feel Escamilla appraising her backside.

"They make em good in California," Kitchen purrs.

"So, you got the money?" Gabriel says. "I'm ready to go as soon as you give it to me."

"There somewhere else you have to be?"

"No. Not for the next few hours. But this isn't a date, right?"

"It's sure not," Kitchen says, leaning forward to tap his cigarette into the ash tray on the coffee table. "But we don't have to rush things. You want something to drink?"

"Bottled water if you have any," says Gabriel, anxious to find her way to the bedrooms before either one of the men realizes she's a hell of a lot older than nineteen.

"Sorry, we don't. How 'bout a little something else, help you relax."

"Like what?"

Escamilla moves behind her, disappearing into the kitchen and coming back to sit in the recliner adjacent to the couch, on the other man's right. He's got a blunt in his lips and lights it up. The smell of marijuana fills the room when he exhales a long stream of smoke.

"You can have a drag on that," Kitchen tells her, nodding at Escamilla. He reaches into his shirt pocket and holds out his hand, two red pills in his palm. "Or you can have a taste of this. Make you feel real good."

Gabriel glances at Escamilla, then rests her eyes on the pills. Is that how these guys capture their victims? None of the girls Blythe and Quincy spoke to mentioned drugs, but it's possible they kept it a secret or never knew they'd been slipped any. Maybe these creeps keep their slaves dosed up the whole time they're in captivity, regardless of how expensive it must be.

"No, thanks," Gabriel says.

Kitchen sticks the pills back into his pocket. "Suit yourself."

A moment of silence passes, the two men staring at her as they smoke.

"Could I use your bathroom?" she asks.

"Down the hall on the left," says Kitchen, lifting his chin toward her.

Gabriel turns around to look at the dark corridor behind

her, across the foyer. She can see another door that must be a second bedroom. The girls might be in there.

Pearl Simon and Kayla Green, fourteen and seventeen-years-old, have been prisoners in this house for the last three months. They showed up on surveillance a week apart. It took six weeks for Blythe and Quincy to ID Pearl, another two for Kayla, both of them listed as missing persons. Pearl Simon disappeared in Park City, Utah, where she lived with her family. The detectives aren't sure how she ended up in Los Angeles. Kayla Green is a runaway from Bakersfield who likely came to LA on her own. She left home a couple months before turning up here in Montecito Heights.

Gabriel heads for the bathroom, feeling Kitchen's eyes on her bare back, passing the shut door of the second bedroom as if she doesn't notice it. She closes the bathroom door and finds the lock in the knob busted. She stands still and listens for noise on the other side of the wall but doesn't hear anything.

Gabriel takes her business phone out of her handbag and texts Detective Blythe: *Both targets present. No sighting on vics. Weapons status unknown.*

He replies in seconds: *Secure payment and proceed with plan. Standby ten minutes.*

She checks the cupboard under the sink and the bath tub but doesn't find evidence of violence. There's nothing that could be used as a weapon: not a knife, a nail file, a pair of scissors, or cleaning agent. She looks at herself in the mirror, at the make-up she never wears and the blonde wig, her face belonging to a feminine woman in her late twenties instead of the masculine thirty-five-year-old she is.

She jumps when someone knocks on the bathroom door.

"Ready when you are," Kitchen says on the other side.

Gabriel takes a deep breath, flips the light switch off, and opens up. "You have condoms, right?"

Kitchen licks his lips, looking at her. "Sure do. A girl shouldn't have to worry about that."

He steps aside to clear her path to the master bedroom, and she follows the cue.

"What about your friend?" she says, as he shuts the bedroom door behind them.

"He'll join in later," he tells her, pupils blown with animalistic lust.

Gabriel puts her handbag down on the bed and stands facing him, reactive fear beginning to seep into her brain like lake water finding the cracks in a car. "I'd like my money before we start."

"How much did we say?"

"A hundred."

He reaches into the back pocket of his jeans and pulls out a few wrinkled, folded bills. She half-expected him to blow her off and start pushing for the sex, but maybe he's smart enough not to give a girl reason to distrust him this early on. He offers her the money, and she counts it before sticking it in her purse, glimpsing the gun inside.

Kitchen unbuckles his belt and unbuttons his pants, as he steps up to Gabriel. He grins like a child's nightmare, stained teeth glinting. She resists the urge to lunge for her Colt and smiles back at him. She doesn't shiver when he rests his hands on her bare shoulders and dips his head to kiss her, his mouth landing on her neck when she turns her head away from him. She can taste bile in the back of her throat, but she starts lifting his shirt up as he inhales the scent of her skin, some girly perfume Gabriel would never wear as herself.

He pulls back to finish taking his shirt off and flings it away. His skin looks stretched over his rib cage, his chest hair thin and sparse, faded tattoos on both upper arms, his left pectoral, and covering his right shoulder. He has a scar about three inches long high on his left side; whoever did the stitch job wasn't concerned about how it would look healed.

"Your turn, dirty girl," he says, voice deeper now and rough.

Gabriel tries to make a flirty face. "Why don't you help me out?" she says and turns around, giving him access to the zipper in the back of her cropped tank. She eyes the handbag on the bed as he unzips the top, her muscles twitching with restrained fight moves. She slips the top off and drops it on the bed. Blythe has about two minutes before she breaks character and kicks this sicko's ass.

Kitchen presses his naked chest to her back, wraps his arms around her, and inhales. Her whole body clenches. She can feel him getting hard. He starts kissing her neck, swirling his tongue against the corner of her jaw, left hand groping at the padded cup of her bra as his right hand flicks the button of her skinny jeans open. "You wet for me?" he says.

He's going to stick his hand down her pants, and she's about to jab her elbow into his face.

There's a loud banging on the front door, Detective Quincy bellowing, "LAPD, open up!"

Kitchen pushes Gabriel away from him, and she falls forward onto the bed, bracing on her hands.

"Shit," he says, hissing. He zips up his jeans, buckles his belt, and dashes out of the bedroom shirtless.

She takes a deep breath, shoulders shaking, and composes herself. She rips off the blonde wig and the wig cap trapping her dark pixie cut, pulls the gun from her handbag, and slinks into the corridor. Quincy bangs on the front door again. She lingers behind the wall, out of sight, and eyes the door to the second bedroom. She waits to hear the detectives enter the house.

Blythe and Quincy come in. Gabriel darts to the bedroom door and tries the knob.

Locked. From the outside.

She goes back into the master bedroom for her snap gun in the handbag, brings it to the second bedroom and busts the lock open. She hears the men talking in the living room, the detectives just getting warmed up.

She slips into the bedroom and shuts the door behind her, sticking close to it like she's cornering a dangerous animal. One messy mattress and no sign of the girls. She eyes the closet and says, "This is Gabriel Kidd talking. I'm a bounty hunter, private eye. I'm here with the cops. I'm looking for Pearl and Kayla. If you're here, it's safe to come out. You're not in trouble. I just want to get you out of this place."

She pauses, waiting for a response.

One of the closet doors slides open enough for someone to poke their head out. A girl's face slowly emerges from the darkness inside, green eyes full of fear and surprise and hope. Her natural blonde hair's pulled back into a ponytail, smooth over the top of her head. She's iconic California beach babe pretty.

"Kayla?" Gabriel says, because the girl looks seventeen. She nods.

Gabriel holds her gun behind her, wanting to appear as nonthreatening as possible. "You got Pearl in there with you?"

Kayla hesitates, then nods again.

Gabriel nods back. "I want you to stay in here until the cops get you or until I do. Those creeps who hurt you are about to be arrested. You're going home. Just sit tight."

Most of the fear melts out of Kayla's face. She slides the closet door shut again.

Gabriel steps out of the bedroom in time for the men to look her way. She meets Detective Blythe's gaze and nods.

"Hey!" Kitchen yaps. "What the fuck are you doing in there?"

He glances at the two detectives, then back at Gabriel. She can see him taking in her real hair, the gun in her hand, realizing she played him.

"You bitch!" he shouts and sprints toward her.

Blythe throttles him from behind, the two of them hitting the floor. He pins Kitchen to the tile, wrenching the other man's right arm behind him and sandwiching it between their bodies. Kitchen writhes underneath him, glassy snake eyes rolled up to look at Gabriel's feet in the corridor ahead of him.

Detective Quincy orders Escamilla to lie face down on the living room carpet with his hands behind his back. Escamilla stands frozen with his hands raised in the air, an old pro at the arrest show. He stares at Quincy like a dumb cow clubbed over the head, about to take the cattle gun shot. Quincy tells him over and over to get on the floor, his back to Blythe and Kitchen.

Gabriel lingers in the bedroom corridor and watches, well-acquainted with her part as civilian support to cops. She's supposed to hang back and let them do their jobs, unless they need her help. She could take the girls outside to wait for their ambulance, but she wants to stay available to the detectives.

Blythe's muttering to Kitchen, still pressed into the man's back. Escamilla's not cooperating with Quincy's order, and Quincy reaches for his sidearm holstered on his waist. She wants Blythe to look up at her and give the signal to call in the back-up on standby in their parked cars on the street, stares hard at his head and hopes for it to come up with a nod, but she might as well not be here .

Quincy, now holding his gun at his side, asks Escamilla to turn around and put his hands behind his back. Escamilla begins to obey.

Blythe sits up, straddling Kitchen's waist and reaching for his cuffs with his free hand, holding Kitchen's right arm to his back. He ignores Gabriel, who's taken a few steps toward the men.

Escamilla stands in position to be cuffed, as Quincy steps closer to him and tries to pull his cuffs off his belt one-handed. He's pointing his gun at Escamilla's lower back. He opens one cuff and starts to hook it around Escamilla's left wrist.

Escamilla whips around and punches him in the nose. Quincy staggers back. Escamilla seizes him with both hands by his suit jacket and head butts him, throws him to the living room floor. Quincy's still holding his gun, but he's dazed. Escamilla kicks the weapon hard out of his hand, drops to one knee, pulls Quincy's upper body off the floor by the detective's shirt, and punches him again. Twice. Escamilla lets him go and starts choking him with both hands around Quincy's neck.

Blythe jumps up off of Kitchen to help his partner, brandishes his stun gun, and zaps Escamilla in the back with an electric sizzle. Escamilla collapses, unconscious, body rolling off of a passed out Quincy.

Gabriel starts to aim her gun at Kitchen.

He runs for the dining table, out of her sight.

Blythe turns around to look for him, still at Quincy's side.

Kitchen returns, wraps his arm around Blythe's neck, and plunges a knife into the left side of Blythe's belly.

Gabriel fires her gun twice, blowing a chunk of his skull clean off. The second round pierces his neck straight through. He slumps to the floor in front of Blythe, who stumbles a few steps to the wall next to the front door and slides down to sit.

She kneels at Blythe's side, eyes roaming over his body, heart rabbit beating in her chest. Blood's seeping out of his belly around the knife handle, shirt soaked brilliant red, and he's got his eyes closed as he wheezes. His muscles are rigid from head to toe. His face and neck gleam with cold sweat. His hands tremble on the floor.

She cards her fingers through his hair and says in her crisis-cool voice, "Blythe. Look at me. Look at me."

He opens his eyes. They're pink and glassy.

She keeps stroking his head. "I know it hurts like nothing you've ever felt, but you have to breathe. Okay? Breathe."

He nods several times, sucks in a breath, and yelps like a dog. Tears roll down his temples, and his face reddens. "Fuck," he says, the sound strangled. He raises his hand to the knife handle.

"I'm going to get you out of here in a minute," says Gabriel, hushing her voice and stopping him from pulling the blade. "You're going to be fine."

Blythe sucks in a breath and whimpers. She can feel him

almost vibrating with pain, and she's grateful that he isn't alone—the way she was two years ago.

She realizes she's still holding her gun, palm sweaty and warm on the hot metal.

Escamilla's groaning awake.

Blythe catches her arm as she stands up and gives her a pleading look. His bottom lip quivers, and he curls his fingers hard into her forearm. Gabriel looks at him with a grave sense of calm. She rests her hand on the side of Blythe's head, leans down to kiss his silvery hairline, and says, "You're in pain. You don't know what you're seeing."

She breaks out of his grasp, stands up, walks into the next room and shoots Escamilla in the head as he starts to push himself up off the floor. She lowers her gun to her side and looks at him, at the splatter of his blood and brain matter, with a stone cold face and not one iota of remorse.

Gabriel's worked alongside law enforcement long enough to know that the legal system never punishes men like Kitchen and Escamilla enough. Killing them isn't about justice. There is no justice when children have been violated, but one more sex offender dead is one less cockroach in the world.

Blythe gasps her name, and she turns around, breaking her dissociative trance. She goes into the kitchen, calls 911 on the landline phone attached to the wall, and picks an ice cube out of the freezer. She goes back to Blythe, sits on the floor cross-legged and lays his head in her lap. She starts to run the ice cube over his lips, pressing her other hand into his wound, his blood warm and slick.

A few minutes pass before she can hear the police and ambulance sirens in the distance.

The girls stay silent in the bedroom.

TWENTY TO LIFE
Frank Byrns

1.

Justine woke, Rodney's breath hot on her neck.

"Stop it," she said, rolling ever. But he wasn't there. He never was.

Not anymore.

2.

"No. I told you I don't want her seeing me like this."

"She's begging me, Rodney."

"I said no, Justine."

"You know she's telling her friends at the school that you're dead?"

"Well... Maybe it's better that way."

3.

"Good to see you, baby—it's been too long."

"I just wanted to tell you in person, Rodney, lest you heard it from somebody else."

"Go on, then."

"I'm pregnant."

"What? How—"

"It's Dickie's."

"Goddamn, Justine. Dickie?"

"It ain't like we was ever married."

"Yeah, I know... But Dickie?"

"I'm keeping the baby."

"*Dickie*. Really?"

4.

Dear Rodney -

Hope this card finds you well
Merry Christmas.

- Justine

5.

Hey Daddy -

Mama said it's all right to send you this picture of my softball team. I'm in the back row, third from the left, case you forgot what I look like.
Happy Father's Day.

- Mary Ellis

6.

"You look good."

"Thanks—I'm still working at the rest of that baby weight."

"I couldn't tell it."

"Asshole."

"I'm serious. You brought some papers for me?"

"The bank man came last week and took the trailer

—need you to sign this here title so we can sell off your car."

"How you gonna get to work?"

"I got the new baby—I can't really work right now anyhow. We moved out to Dickie's for the time being."

"*Dickie.*"

"He's a piece of shit, yeah, I know... but he's around, Rodney. You know?"

7.

"So does Mary Ellis still call him Uncle Dickie, or does she got to call him Daddy now?"

"Goddammit, Rodney, why you got to be such an ass-hole all the time?"

"Look around, Justine—what kind of place do you think this is?"

"You was always an asshole, Rodney—that's how you got here in the first place."

"So I guess you're Mrs. Booth now after all."

"I guess so. We just figured it was the right thing to do for Chase's sake."

"My mama come?"

"Naw. It was just a little quick thing at the courthouse. She was invited, but she didn't come. She's still mad at me about the whole thing, I guess. She loves both the kids, but she don't think much of me at this point."

"Me, neither, I don't reckon. I was never her favorite, anyhow, even in the best of times."

"Well, I guess we still got that in common, then."

8.

"Stop it, Justine."

"She just wants to see you, Rodney."

"I can't do it."

"She's been crying all the time—things haven't exactly been so great at home with Dickie—"

"That asshole lay a hand on her?"

"Naw, nothing like that—it's just hard, you know? She wants her daddy."

"Stop it. How many times do I gotta say it? I just can't."

"Then you tell her. I'm done with it."

9.

Mary Ellis -

Thank you so much for the little care package you sent by your mama. That candy bar was just about the best thing I ever eat. I hope your Uncle Dickie's taking good care of you and your mama. I love you so much . it would tear me up for you to see me like this. Please stop asking. I hope you understand.

- Your Loving Daddy

10.

Daddy -

I don't care what Mama says. Soon I'll be old enough to drive myself. I'll come see you then. See you soon.

- Mary Ellis

11.

"Dickie put you up to this?"

"He just don't like it, is all, me spending so much time

up here."

"So much time – what, three visits in two years is too much for him?"

"He just thinks it's inappropriate."

"Inapp—I'll tell you what's inappropriate. Marrying your niece's mother when your brother's in prison, that's what's goddamn *inappropriate*."

"Good bye, Rodney. I don't reckon I'll be stopping by again."

"The hell with you, Justine."

12.

Rodney -

I know it's been a long time. You must think I'm the worst mother in the world. I know this has been hard for you. But it's hard for me, too. I just wanted to say I forgive you for what you done. I'm working on trying to come and see you some day soon.

- Mama

PS   Your brother's taking real good care of Mary Ellis and her mama.

13.

Hi Daddy -

Uncle Dickie's an asshole (don't tell Mama I swore). Save me.

Mary Ellis

14.

Hi Dad -

Things are better this week. I met a boy. His name is Shane. He's real nice. I think you'd like him.

- Mary Ellis

15.

Dad -

I just wanted to let you know I'm gonna be staying with Grandma for a while. If you need me for anything. I just can't take it anymore.

- Mary Ellis

16.

"Christ, Justine, I don't hear from you for *years*, then you show up with something like this?"

"You gotta talk to her, Rodney—I don't know what else to do."

"Dickie can't help you?"

"Dickie's a piece of shit—you know that. If I had any other way, do you think I'd be here. This kid's trouble, Rodney. She's got enough of that in her life already—she don't need this boy Shane."

"What kind of trouble?"

" He reminds me of you."

"I don't know what you want me to do."

"Goddammit, I want you to talk to your daughter, Rodney. Please.

SO MUCH LOVE
Keith Rawson

he liberals and kids loved judge Marshall Knot. The
liberals loved him because his conviction rate of blacks
d Mexicans was the lowest of any judge who had sat the
nch in fifty years. The truth, he hated the fucking liber-
. Pantywaists. But they kept re-electing him because they
ɔught of him as progressive. Really he just thought most
vs were nothing more than things to keep cops and old
cks like him employed.

The kids loved him because he was fun. He'd joke
ɔund with them, make them feel at home, make them
el that whatever they had done wasn't that big of a deal.
ey were young, shit happens. The kids loved him, too,
cause any time one of them came into his courtroom with
ɔad attitude, he would throw something at the scowling
itheel. Usually a stapler, a masking tape dispenser, once
 a while, his gavel. He never hit them. He'd come close,
t all it would do is make the courtroom jump. The judge
ved the reaction. He loved the clatter, the nervous laughs.

Throwing stuff got him into the papers, got himself
 a couple of YouTube videos. The papers and the fuck-
s on YouTube loved him, too. The judge didn't care about
e fuckers on YouTube. He loved the papers, he was from
e old school and kept a scrapbook that his wife started

17.

"Hey, Booth!"

"Yeah?"

"There's some chick here to see you."

"Tell her to go home."

"You sure? A little young, but she's kind of a look

"That's my daughter, asshole."

"You sure you don't want to see her?"

"Tell her to go home."

18.

"You told her?"

"Yeah. Just like the last three times she came."

"She gone?"

"She left – gave me this picture to give you."

"Throw it out."

"Really?"

"Throw it away."

"You sure? This is a mighty cute baby."

19.

"Mama?"

"Mary Ell – it's three in the morning. What'
baby?"

"It's Shane—he, uh, he hurt somebody. I think

20.

Mary Ellis woke, Shane's breath hot on her nec

"Stop it," she said, rolling ever. But he wasn't
never was.

Not anymore.

when he was first elected and he kept it up after she died, it became his hobby. Most of the things his wife did when she was breathing was horseshit, but the scrap book was alright.

The judge loved his routines. Four days a week, up at 5:30, fifty push-ups, fifty sit-ups, some light stretching. The calisthenics was a holdover from his Army days. Even when he was in the shit of Laos, whenever he woke up, he'd do his stretching along with the rest of his company and after he was done, he would kiss his necklace of gook ears around his neck like an old Italian lady kissing a crucifix and then head out hoping to replace the ones that had rotted off the string.

Next he showered, shaved, put his teeth in, put on his shirt and tie. By this time Rosalie would have his coffee ready. He'd drink it down black while Rosalie sucked him off while he still had his pants off and finish off on her titties. He loved finishing off on her titties. They were big hangers, double D's and still brown and firm. She'd gotten real good at being gentle with him and not making his body sway too much while he was drinking his coffee. His wife never got the hang of it, and 9 times out of 10 she'd end up getting burned.

After he finished dressing, he grabbed his keys and start making his way to the courthouse.

He usually had Fridays off, which was one of the benefits of being a juvenile/family court judge. But a young colleague's wife just had her third baby, so his colleague was taking "personal time" to be with them. He didn't understand his young colleague. Having a baby, taking care of it and the other children, that was the woman's job. It was the man's job to work and keep a roof over the heads of his wife and those kids. He understood if it was the man who stayed home and cooked and cleaned and took care of the home. That he got, it was their place. His big brother did that back in the day when people looked at you funny if a man didn't have a job. Of course, his brother was a little soft in the head, but hung like a baby elephant, which kept his sister-in-law happy enough to not mind working.

His young colleague was just lazy.

Working on his days off put him in a foul mood. Fridays were for sleeping in and watching internet porn, but instead he was up doing push-ups and sit-ups 5:30. He'd forgotten to tell Rosalie he was working and had to yell for his coffee. She hustled in, but refused the blowjob, saying she had a toothache and her jaw hurt too much. The judge gave her a slap and made her wear the ball gag. He thought about screwing her in the ass, but didn't because Friday was usually her day off, too.

Lift up your skirt, he said as he was headed to the garage.

She did and he slapped her ass, leaving a handprint shading purple. She squealed around the gag.

If you take it out I'll stick you in the closet all weekend.

He knew she wouldn't, Rosalie was a good girl. Before him she was nothing but a parentless 14-year-old giving out blowjobs for bags of Taco Bell and Wendy's. She appreciated what he'd done for her.

⊙ ⊙ ⊙

What you boys got for me?

Hola, juez, Hola!

The boys are twinks. Queer as a man with a pussy. They wear makeup and clothes that don't cover their tight bellies and squish up their little cock and balls and make their ass cheeks hang out. Sometimes they dress up as girls and actually look better than most women, except if you look close; their adam's apple and hands just don't look right. But he loved them. He loved them because they were queer and Mexican, and those were tough things to be.

Qué estás haciendo también esta mañana?

The boys flutter into the towncar, all butterfly hands and rapid fire lisp lipped Spanish. Rumors about other twinks, their pimps beating them, bitch women whores beating the twinks for trying to horn in on their rough trade. The judge understood every three words of what they were saying. He thought seeing them this morning would make him feel better, lighten his mood, but all they were doing was making him boil. Seethe.

Alright, alright, shut up! Quiet now! What have you got for me?

Todo lo que tenemos es esta velocidad. No es muy bueno.

Speed was a staple. Not that he condoned drugs, but a man had to worry about retirement. He had to worry about keeping the lights on after he was too feeble to drag his body out of bed day after day. The judge looked at the crunchy 8 ball. It was the color of margarine and sunset. Like earwax. Like something dredged out of some truckers ass crack.

Fine. This is fine.

He had a criminal prosecutor who never bothered to

sleep. He would eat this up. He would pull out his wallet and put three bills in the judge's hands not caring fuck all about the quality. He needed it for work, he needed discretion about needing it for work. If he wanted discretion he would pinch it from the evidence room like a normal city employee. The prosecutor was a crusader and paranoid about his hand getting caught in the cookie jar. Crusaders were easy money.

You boys have a good day.

◉ ◉ ◉

His young colleague worked criminal court. Nothing major, small disputes. Traffic violators, small drug busts, low level assaults, the occasional confrontations with the police. Most of it was fines, dismissals. Routine. Routine. Rubberstamp. He didn't like it.

Then docket #237: Dispute of Seizure, Tammy Appleton v. AZ Department of Public Safety.

Big titty bleached out middle aged crow's feet dick sucking lips v. A couple of yahoos out of Buckeye, hoping to live a porno fantasy with Big titty bleached out middle aged crow's feet dick sucking lips.

Pulled her over for a broken tail light and New Jersey plates—bullshit—and when she got uppity they searched the car and found 1.7 million in a couple of Safeway shopping bags. Drug money, Light bulbs going off, cocks go tight against zippers. Big titty bleached out middle aged crow's feet dick sucking lips calls bullshit, throws a fit on the side of the I-10 and ends up in handcuffs and a strip search in DPS Substation #37's observation room #1.

It's mine, Your Honor. I earned it! Ten years of my life! Big titty bleached out middle aged crow's feet dick sucking lips had the documentation. Tax records, IRS affidavits. Being an Exotic Entertainer paid the pills nicely.

The dipshits were still claiming foul, insisting it's crack money. Hilly billies, nobody smokes fucking crack.

He threw the case out.

Big titty bleached out middle aged crow's feet dick sucking lips pours on the relief and thank you's. It goes on for five minutes, Big titty bleached out middle aged crow's feet dick sucking lips body dipping and swerving. Rubbing through his pants, he focuses on her lips. Glistening, pink with gloss, wet. Her bony white trash long finer nailed hands pushing against stiff silicon with her version of sincerity, orange tan plastic squeezing together, apart, together, apart, nipples making little tee-pees.

He finished with a shudder, his undershorts going so damp, you'd think he'd pissed himself.

You're welcome, Ms. Appleton, and please try to enjoy the rest of your stay here in Arizona.

⊙ ⊙ ⊙

Hola, juez, Hola!

He didn't let the boys into the car this time, just handed them a sheet of paper through the driver's side window:

Motel 6, Room #139
7116 N 59th Ave
Glendale

She has a lot of money
Mucho Dinero.

Come by the house after you're done. Dress like men before you go over to the motel and bring a camera.

Arizona law states that all seized property be returned in as close to its original state as possible, which meant Big titty bleached out middle aged crow's feet dick sucking lips would be carrying around 1.7 million in a couple of plastic shopping bags minus the hillbillies' tip money.

Even if Big titty bleached out middle aged crow's feet dick sucking lips wised up and put the money in the bank and was carrying around a cashier's check now, the boys would fuck her up enough to teach her not to drive any-where carrying around that kind of money. And at least there would be pictures of Big titty bleached out middle aged crow's feet dick sucking lips crying, mascara running, while the boys squeezed and pinched her tits and laughed at her stretch marks and brown roots.

He felt celebratory. He thought maybe he would go home and have Rosalie lube into the black plastic body suit with all the zippers to her openings. And maybe when the boys came over, they could piss on her and tell her what an ugly bitch she is.

That would be a lovely end to the day.

RUNNING LATE
Tess Makovesky

Cars scattered like lemmings before a wolf as Zak flung the squad car through the traffic, gunning through the gears and swearing under his breath. He was running late and he knew it might cost Karen dear. Trouble was the instructions had been so bloody vague—it had taken the experts at HQ nearly two hours to identify the derelict lodge in the woods on the edge of town as the location for the swap. Even after he'd taken the fastest car in the fleet he'd been held up by a constant stream of roadworks and buses and pedestrians crossing the road, until he'd been reduced to pounding the wheel in sheer frustrated rage.

Fuck... fuck... fuck. Another bus crawled past, this one filled with the grinning faces of kids on their way home from school. Time was running out. Everywhere he looked he saw Karen's accusing face—mirrored in shop windows, waiting in line at the next stop for the bus. *Hang in there love, I'm doing my best.* Only last night they'd been wrapped in each other's arms on the living room floor, television blaring unheeded, their headlong dive off the sofa scattering cushions to the corners of the room. There was a bottle of Chateau, something close enough to grab, but Karen had drunk the wine straight from Zak's mouth as they kissed. Karen had her hands on Zak's arse and Zak had his in the comforting softness of Karen's hair, knotting it as his fingers meshed. Now he felt oddly apart, removed from Karen and from the petty happenings of everyday life. A sports car roared past but he barely spared it a glance. Banner adverts for the latest movie, a new sports store on the local high street, even the late sun filtering through golden autumn leaves, spooled past the car unseen. There was only Karen, and the car, and the car's systems reacting beneath his hands.

Finally the turn appeared—a set of gates at a ferocious bend. Heart in mouth he veered across both lanes, hardly bothering to look for oncoming traffic, and bounced down the forest track under a canopy of trees. Thick mud from the unused track sucked at the car wheels, slewing the steering as he took the corners too fast. A carpet of fallen leaves covered the ground, but here and there where the mud showed through he thought he could see the impression of tires. Someone had been here, and not that long ago.

The track ended at a clearing with trees clustered round the edge as though reluctant to approach too close. There at last was the old house. It had been lodge to some long-lost estate, a quaint building with black-and-white timbers and a steeply pitched roof, but now it was in desperate need of love and repair. *Bit like me*, Zak thought with a flash of gallows humour. Then he was out of the car and running, leaving the door swinging wide. His heart beat a painful staccato in his chest and almost stopped at a sudden clatter of noise, but it was only a pigeon's wings and not the gunfire he feared. Reaching the front door in half a dozen strides he tried the handle but it was locked. That, or jammed shut after so many years of decay. He pounded on the peeling paint work with both fists.

"Karen? *Kaz*! It's me, Zak. I got what the bast—I got the

tapes they wanted. Are you in there? Kaz!" The tapes that until this morning had been in the evidence locker. The only proof of old man Heaton's confession to killing a man. The tapes that his three sons had somehow got word of, and kidnapped a serving police detective in a frantic attempt to have returned to them. You didn't mess with the Heaton boys, even the DI knew that. Which probably explained why he'd considered for all of two minutes before saying no.

Zak hadn't taken that one lying down. "What the fuck d'you mean, no? Don't you care that one of your officers could be in trouble? Don't you care that Karen's life's at stake?"

"Yes, I care," said the DI, rubbing his straggling moustache. "I'm surprised you do, though. I thought you didn't like her—you complain about working with her often enough."

Zak could understand. They'd had to pretend to a certain cool dislike. Who wouldn't be suspicious, faced with a display of blind panic over someone he grumbled about every chance he got? He stumbled out of the DI's office, waited until the man's attention was taken by something else, and ran to the evidence room to steal the tapes. It wasn't the first time he'd helped himself; over the years he'd nicked money and drugs to give to informants and the like. Not that he was bent; he always made that distinction to himself. Bent coppers did it for the money or the kudos it could bring them in the local underworld. He only ever did it to get a better result. His clear-up rate was second to none; his informants always better informed. Of course, the stealing was still the same. The tapes burned a hole in his conscience now, their flat weight knocking against his thigh.

There was no response to his shout, except for a brief mocking echo of his words. A single leaf rustled as it fell to earth; somewhere a bird chirped once; but from the lodge there was silence—the silence of utter loneliness.

"Shit!" Zak glanced at his watch. He was only three hours late—surely they'd have waited that long? The Heaton brothers might be psychopaths but they didn't lack for brains. Even they must realise that with the drop-off point abandoned and Karen dead, they'd never get those tapes.

Karen dead... The words echoed in Zak's brain, chilling his blood until his hands went numb. He beat on the door again, uselessly, ignoring shards of pain from the splinters driven deep into the flesh. Nothing. Not so much as a footstep, not so much as the squeak of a mouse. He gave up and shoved his way through the undergrowth to the back.

Straight away he saw where they'd ripped away hoardings and smashed a window to gain entry to the lodge. There was a scrap of something blue caught on a shard of glass and Zak's stomach flopped into his boots. Karen had been wearing a light blue blouse last night. Because she'd stopped at his place he'd washed and pressed it for her, and left it hanging on the chair by the bed. She was gone when he woke up—always an earlier riser than him—and the blouse had left with her. It was a fitted blouse, one of Zak's favourites since it flattered her waist and boobs, although it was a bugger to iron. Now it was torn, but the sadness gave him hope. She'd been here, for sure. All he had to do was find out when—and whether alive or dead.

He scrambled through the gap, tearing a sleeve himself and nicking his arm. It bled freely, spattering on the window frame, and he knew he was destroying potential evidence but didn't care. Finding Karen alive was what mattered now, not groping around after clues and DNA. He didn't know what he would do without her if she'd gone. She was always the stronger of the pair. She was the one who'd jumped him, at the last Christmas party. She'd laughed because her nickname was a backwards version of his name, then dragged him into the stationery cupboard and stuck her hand down his pants. She hadn't even been particularly drunk.

"Why?" Zak had said afterwards, tucking himself away. "Why now? Why me?"

"If I'd left it to you I'd still have been waiting next year," she'd said, and given his privates a pat.

She was the one who'd decided to keep the whole thing quiet, so they could go on working the same shift. The rules said you had to notify the DI if you became 'romantically involved', but that would have meant different hours, or even a move to another division. "Bugger that," Karen had said. "Don't ask, don't tell."

"That's the U.S. Army," Zak had said, but she just laughed.

He could do with the army now, or at least a few good well-trained men. You couldn't ask for backup when you'd taken the law into your own hands, though. He was on his own.

The Lodge was worse inside than out. Paint hung in streamers from the walls; the ceiling bulged downwards in worrying waves; floorboards gave, spongily, as he tiptoed across the rooms. A spider's web cast its sticky threads across his face and he wiped it away with the unripped sleeve. The smell of rot was heavy in the air but overlaying it was something sharper, fresher, more out of place—the scent of tobacco smoke. Too fresh. Possibly being smoked right now. Were they still here after all? He abandoned caution and ran toward the scent.

The stairs creaked alarmingly and the banister rail toppled as he hurtled past. It clattered to the tiled hall floor and Zak knew there was no hiding his approach. Speed was everything now.

The first room he tried was empty of everything but a broken chair and a pile of sticks in the hearth. He paused just long enough to grab a leg from the chair, then ran again. The landing held three more doors—all shut, one leaning crazily and two secure. Which to choose? Hesitating here was wasting valuable time—time Karen might not have. They'd never have got through the broken door, but one of the others had fag ash on the boards outside. He chose that, and kicked it in.

All his senses strained to pick up any trace of human presence. Was that a rustle? A whiff of aftershave and sweat? A shadow by the wall? Surely not—his mind and the dingy room were playing tricks. Then the shadow moved.

"Kaz?" Three strides took him to her side. She was bundled up with tape across her mouth and her hands behind her back, but thank God she seemed unhurt. He tackled the tape first, ignoring her yelp to yank it off. "Are you okay? I thought I'd lost..."

Too late he saw the warning in her eyes—the shock, the horror, the sudden pallor of her face. Too late he sensed a trap, and turned. Joe and Harry and George—three stocky, sandy—haired chips off the Heaton block, waited for him just inside the door. One with hands on hips, one with a crowbar, one hefting a gun. It was the gun he saw the most, looming in his vision like a cannon although it was only pocket-sized. A Walther by the look of it, probably a P99. Zak had traded one of those for a list of names only the other month, helping himself from the evidence locker when there was nobody about. He hoped this wasn't it. The irony of being at the wrong end of the barrel of his own fucking gun was too much to bear.

He dug in his pocket. "Joe? Thank God, I wasn't sure

you'd wait. I got the tapes…"

"Fuck the tapes," said the man with the gun.

"What? But I thought… I brought them all this way."

"Wasn't the fucking tapes we wanted, it was you. Giving away free drugs to old Fatface Mitchell so he can undercut us on our own fucking patch. Not on, Dad says. Got to teach you a lesson, Dad says."

Zak's skin felt chilled. Fatface was an informer—the very one who'd told him about old man Heaton's murderous ways. He'd been set up. He was hooked and sunk. "I suppose you've killed Fatface," he said.

"Let's just say he won't be making the same mistake twice."

"So what are you going to do to me?" Then, clearing his throat, "At least let Karen go. It's nothing to do with her—she didn't even know."

Joe shrugged. "Yeah, we might, if we're in a good mood. Can't say the same for you. Here, catch yourself hold of these. It'll look like a drugs meet gone wrong." He tossed a wad of notes and some packets of white dust across; Zak juggled briefly and they fell around his feet. The gun clattered, deafening in the silence of the room.

Zak heard Karen scream and thought they'd shot her after all. "You bast—" he began, but couldn't get the words to leave his throat. There was a strange metallic taste in his mouth, his chest hurt and he couldn't breathe. His legs buckled and he folded to the dusty floor. *Too late*, he thought. Too late to help Karen, too late to save himself.

He was late, all right.

LAST SUPPER
Katanie Duarte

Wes' **deep blue eyes sparkled** with excitement as he applied gel to his dark, wavy hair. Steam from the shower he'd taken minutes before slowly dissipated as he ran his hand over his freshly shaven face, admiring his flawless skin in the bathroom mirror.

As he headed to his bedroom to get dressed, he thought of her—creamy skin, vanilla scent, deep brown eyes, soft luscious lips. A memory of kissing her brought her name to his lips, "Sara." Heat rose in his body. Wes couldn't wait to be with her, to have Sara in his arms. She made him feel like he'd never felt before, made him want to be better, different somehow. And the scary part wasn't how he felt, but that he wanted to run toward it, like she was where he belonged.

Fashionably dressed in a blue v-neck sweater and black jeans, he grabbed his keys and walked out of the door. Wes could never get to Sara soon enough or never spend enough time with her. He drove his car in an anxious daze. Lights of other cars on the freeway whizzed by. It had been a long time since he was this nervous. Things usually came easy for him because of his looks. He had money, a successful career, a nice car, a luxurious downtown condo and access to more women than he could ever handle. What he'd never wanted was love, but as it turned out, love came to him without him even trying to find it, and it was anything but easy. Wes had fallen and there was no going back.

Wes' heart pounded in his chest as he arrived at Sara's picturesque little house. The house made him visualize what his life could be, and because of that, there was an image in his head of what the woman in that house could do for his life.

He composed himself and made his way to her door. Breathing deeply, he rang her doorbell. When she opened the door it took every muscle and ounce of restraint in him to hold himself from rushing to her and taking her in his arms. Sara's chestnut hair was pulled into a sleek ponytail revealing the full picture of her face. She was a vision, an apparition seen in a feverish dream; divinity just out of reach.

"I'm so glad you're here," she said.

"You look beautiful."

Lifting up on her tip toes, she wrapped her arms around his neck, tangling her hand in his hair and brought him down for a kiss. Their mouths were a tangle of lips and tongues in heat and desire. When they broke apart, Wes was left wanting. Looking in Sara's eyes, he saw that desire burned in her just as strong as it did in him, and because of this, he made no hesitation taking her hand and allowing her to lead him inside.

"Where is everyone?" Wes asked as he walked into the living room?

Sara had invited him over for a small get together. After spending several evenings and weekends together, it was time for an introduction to her circle of friends. According to Sara, her friends were curious about the guy who'd been taking so much of her time. Wes had to laugh when she'd said that because his friends had been wondering about Sara as well. So, he agreed to this dinner. Anything to make Sara happy.

"Out back," she gestured casually to toward the set of closed French doors to their left. "I didn't want to overwhelm you."

The décor in the house was just a feminine as Sara, save for a few quirks. But then again, Sara had a few quirks herself. Frilly pillows accented plush floral sofas in the light yellow colored living room. Books lined the oversized bookshelves. Candles scattered around the room, some in jars, some in glass holders and others placed in empty liquor bottles covered in wax that had been dripped from other candles. The most interesting items we're old bird cages in varying sizes hanging from the ceilings that housed porcelain dolls.

"Sara, I keep meaning to ask you, what's the deal with the bird cages?" Wes asked.

"I don't know. I just like to keep pretty things. There's something satisfying about capturing beauty and not letting it go. It's my version of a photograph."

Wes loved her vision. It made sense in a way that only could by knowing Sara.

Exhaling loudly, Wes said, "Let's get this show on the road."

"I'd like to keep you to myself just a little longer. Once we go back there's no more you and me. There's you, me, and them," she said reaching up for a quick kiss. "Sit. Let me get you a drink."

"I like that idea," he said, with a hint of relief.

"I was going to save it for later, but how 'bout a glass of wine? I picked up a really fancy Bordeaux that I've wanted to try."

"Sounds good."

"I'll be right back," she said disappearing behind a closed door.

When she walked back through that door, Wes watched her move. The black dress she wore looked like it was painted on, the short length teasing Wes by showing him her upper thigh and then covering it back again. He loved the way her body did its own dance. She was graceful and sexy, and he watched with awed attention, imagining his own body swaying with hers. Sara was like lace and lightening: soft, sexy, and radiating electricity.

Handing him a glass, she sat next to him and took a sip of wine before she placed it on the coffee table. She leaned back and focused her attention on him.

"Mmm," Wes murmured as he tasted the wine. "Come here."

Sara cuddled up with Wes, her head in the crook of his neck. She cradled herself in his arms as they sat there enjoying the wine. Moments like these, where they were together, when there were no words, Wes felt most alive, aware of his beating heart because it was Sara who set the rhythm. If he never had to move from this spot, it would be fine.

They sat silently for a while.

"Is there anything that I shouldn't bring up or say to your friends?" Wes asked.

"No, just be yourself. That's all that matters. You make me happy."

"You make me happy, too," he admitted.

Sara squeezed Wes's hand and stood. "Ready?"

Standing up, he nodded. "Let's go before I change my mind."

His feet felt a little numb. He wiggled his toes as much

as he could in his constricting shoes.

Sara walked toward the French doors and slid them apart slightly, stuck her head in and asked "Are you guys ready?"

Wes, who was right behind her, didn't hear any voices on the other side of the door. He figured that her friends were either calm or gesturing quietly. Sara slid the doors all the way open and walked in. It must have been his nerves that were making him feel so strange because as soon as he stepped into the room a surge of warmth touched his skin, but inside, his body it felt chilled, causing him to shiver a little.

The dining room had old style elegance, with walls a rich red color, like rust. Glass dining cabinets filled with china leaned against the walls. In the middle of the room five dining chairs sat around a large rectangular table with two place settings. The delicious smelling meal Sara prepared sat in the middle. At the end of the table, three severed heads in glass boxes were perched on the table where there should have been three more place settings.

"Wha…?" Confusion filled Wes' head. His breath came faster. His heart beat ferociously. The cold he'd felt moments earlier rushed to his face.

Wes didn't see Sara or where she had gone. He didn't see her when she came up behind him and pushed him down into a chair. All Wes knew was that one moment he'd been standing there looking at heads on a table and the next he was sitting at the table at the other end of them.

Sadness took over for the shock and confusion. He searched desperately for the courage to look toward her. When he did, there was intensity in her eyes that he'd never seen before, an emotion that he could not touch.

Fear should have been the first emotion Wes felt, but it was third and it came much too late.

The cold sensation he felt never went away, the numbness in his toes had worked its way up passed his knees. He broke their shared stare to look down at his legs. It was then that he truly noticed the wheelchair he sat in. Wes looked at Sara again and tried to get up. He couldn't. His body wasn't working right.

"I need to leave." The words came out slightly slurred. Panic surged through him at the sound of his own voice.

"Don't be rude," she said. "I haven't even introduced you yet."

She walked toward the end of the table where the heads sat.

"This is Ben," she said as she laid her hand on the head closest to him. "This is Ian," she said of the one in the middle. "And finally, this is Brandt."

The fire never left her eyes. It spread across her face and rested itself on her lips. The smile she wore was out of place in contrast to the painful fear that Wes felt .

"Wes, don't you want to say hello to my friends?" she asked with a threatening tone. "They've been waiting a long time to meet you. So far you haven't been very friendly."

"Hello," he said unsteadily.

Sara walked to her place at the table on Wes's right side. She carefully took her seat and began serving herself saucy cubes of meat from a tureen in the middle of the table.

"Sara, what's happening to me?" He asked.

She didn't look at him.

"Am I going to die?"

The question floated in the air unanswered.

"Ssara," he called her name again. Still, she didn't

acknowledge him.

Sara poured herself a glass of water and took a drink. When she broke her silence it wasn't in answer to Wes's question.

"Ian, do you think that you could help me hang that mirror in my bedroom tomorrow?"

Sara was talking to the heads and asking them to help her around the house. Were they talking back to her? Wes was terrified.

"Oh good," she replied to the empty air. "But, Ian, we *won't* have a repeat of what happened last time. What we had is over."

She ate delicately, and as she did, Wes thought about how he was feeling, so numb and cold. She must have put something in his wine; it was the only thing that he'd had to eat or drink since lunch. The numbness was moving up his legs and throughout his body. The cold was constant. There was no way that he would walk out of that door. Sara clearly had a plan about how the night would go. The idea that she'd been planning this was too much to comprehend.

Second, he thought about God. Wes had never really given credence to religion. It was just something that existed. He never prayed and hadn't been to church since his mother's funeral. So now, possibly being at the end of his life, he questioned whether he should have believed more, whether he should have gone to church more. More—such a simple word, but not so simple when there's no time left. There would me no more of anything. There was so much that he hadn't done. Anger fueled inside of him.

The third thought, simple really, yet he wasn't sure that he wanted to know the answer. What happened to the bodies of these men?

He eyed the tureen in the middle of the table and traced its contents to Sara's plate; to her mouth. Could it be? Would she…?

Wes was deep in thought when Sara giggled. Such an out of place sound.

"I'm not sure," she said.

Apparently, conversations were happening that he was not privy to.

"Sssa…wa." It was getting harder for him to speak.

She did not answer him. She did not look at him. Instead she looked at the clock that hung on the wall next to her. Sara was waiting. His heart thumped faster at the realization that his time was running out.

Wes began to panic. It would have been a natural reaction to hyperventilate, but he could hardly breathe, when moments before it hadn't been a problem. In fact, the way he felt had completely changed. Wherever he'd gone cold, he felt numb. And wherever he had gone numb, he could not move.

His heart stuttered

As if Sara had heard his heart struggle, her head turned toward him. Their eyes met, ocean blue to chocolate brown, and they stared at each other. Neither of them moved. With a jagged breath, an eerie calm washed over Wes.

Looking in Sara's eyes, he remembered how she made him feel before this night. He remembered feeling love, feeling like she was his home. Again he thought about God. But this time he realized that God didn't matter. He told himself that heaven was just a place to go and the only place he wanted to be was here, with Sara. This was his heaven and she was all that he needed to believe in.

Wes took a shallow breath and shed a single tear.

His heart stopped.

DANNY

Michael Bracken

Nobody tried to stop Danny when he beat the crippled kid to death with a Louisville slugger. The rest of us stood back and watched until the crippled kid's face was nothing but a pulpy mess and Danny dropped the bloody bat beside the dead kid.

Then we followed Danny to the garage behind the apartment building where Danny lived with his mother. He opened a fifth of Jack Daniels, took a long draw, and passed the bottle around. No one spoke about what we had just seen and none of us dared look Danny in the eye as we drank.

The gang drifted apart after that because Danny's family moved out of the neighborhood at the end of the school year, and the crippled kid's murder remained an unsolved crime that ultimately caused his parents to divorce and drove his mother into long-term therapy.

That none of us ever admitted to witnessing the crippled kid's death was as much a testament to our camaraderie as it was to our fear of Danny even decades after the fact.

When Danny stepped into my office one bitterly cold December morning I felt a chill roll up my spine that couldn't be attributed to the weather.

"I got a job for you," he said without preamble. "I need

you to follow a guy."

"I don't need your money, Danny," I said from behind my desk. "I'm doing just fine without it."

"I wasn't planning to pay you," he said.

"Then why would I take the job?"

His eyes narrowed as he stared at me across my desk. "Because I still play baseball."

A second chill rolled up my spine. Over the years I had faced bigger men and stronger men, but none had ever instilled in me the same level of fear that Danny had that night with the baseball bat. Despite my posturing, we both knew he had a tight grip on my balls and that I would ultimately do anything he demanded of me.

"Who do you want me to follow?"

Danny told me the name and it took me a moment before I realized he wanted me to follow the crippled kid's father.

"Why him? Why now?"

He didn't answer my questions. Instead, he gave me the man's address. "Where he goes. What he does. Who he talks to."

I found Kevin Dyson's home easily enough the next morning. He had remarried and moved to the suburbs. Dyson's wife, a lithe blonde several years his junior, left the house first that morning, and Dyson followed half an hour later. He drove to a diner in the old neighborhood and settled into the last booth, where he could watch everyone who entered. A young waitress filled his coffee cup and took his breakfast order.

A few minutes later he was joined by a pug-faced side of beef who settled into the booth opposite Dyson. They exchanged several words and then Dyson slid an envelope across the table. The envelope disappeared into the other man's jacket pocket, and he was gone before the waitress brought Dyson's breakfast.

Nothing else Dyson did that day piqued my curiosity, and when I had the opportunity late that afternoon I described Dyson's diner companion to my connections on the street, hoping someone knew him. Then I followed Dyson home and sat watching his house until late in the evening when all the lights were extinguished and I presumed he had gone to bed.

I drove to Ted Wilson's home and banged on the front door until he finally answered. He wasn't pleased to see me, but I pushed past him into his house and we sat in his darkened living room while I told him what Danny had hired me to do.

"Don't drag me into this mess," he said.

"You're already in," I said. He had been standing to my left while Danny beat the crippled kid to death, and he'd grown up to be a research librarian I occasionally tapped for help with my cases. "You've always been in."

"I try not to think about that night," Ted said, "but sometimes it's all I think about. We were cowards then and we're cowards now."

"We were kids," I said. "We were more afraid of Danny than we were of the police."

"And now?"

I understood his question, but I could not answer it. So, I asked one of my own. "After all these years, what does Danny want with Mr. Doyle?"

"How the hell would I know?" he said. "Have you asked Joe?"

Joe Zimmerman was the third witness to the crippled boy's murder. I said, "Not yet. He won't answer my calls."

"Do you blame him?"

My cell phone rang. I pulled it from my pocket, checked the caller ID, and then answered. At the other end of the call was one of my street connections letting me know that the pug-faced side of beef I'd seen taking an envelope from Doyle was some out-of-town leg breaker who usually collected debts for bookies and loan sharks.

After I ended the call, I told Ted what I had just learned.

"How does Doyle know a guy like that?"

I didn't have an answer for Ted's question. All I had were more questions, but as I stood to leave I knew I had kept the promise I had made long ago. Ted now knew that Danny was back in my life and chances were that it wouldn't be long before Danny was back in his.

Ted walked me to the door. After he opened it, he stepped to the side and said, "I'll check into Doyle's past. I'll let you know what he's been doing the past few years."

I drove home, caught a few hours of sleep, and returned to my vantage point outside Doyle's house. I was still there two hours later when I learned why Joe had not answered any of my calls the previous day. Someone had used him for batting practice and had left his body on his living room floor. The woman who lived in the apartment next to Joe's had discovered his body that morning when she was taking out the trash and noticed his door was open.

Ted seemed distraught as he explained all this to me. Then he asked, "Do you think Danny did this?"

"Not his style," I said. "Danny would have gone for the kill shot right away. From what you said, whoever killed Joe wanted to inflict the maximum amount of pain first."

"It can't be a coincidence that Danny hired you the day before Joe was killed."

Doyle stepped onto his front porch a briefcase in one hand, and looked both ways before he closed the door.

"You're right," I told Ted as Doyle walked to his car. "We'll talk about this more later. Call me when you have the dope on Doyle. I have to go."

I followed Doyle into the city, holding back a safe distance even though there was no indication that he knew he was being followed. He found an open spot on the second floor of a parking garage downtown and I had to pass him to find a spot on the third.

By the time I hustled down to the second floor, he had already left the parking garage. I caught up with him on the street when I spotted the briefcase, and I hung back half a block until he entered one of the office buildings. I quickened my step and entered the building just in time to see him enter an elevator. I couldn't catch up to him so I hung back and watched which floors the elevator stopped on before it returned to the ground floor.

The fifth floor, where the elevator made its first stop, was given over to a law firm. The ninth floor, where the elevator made its second stop, held three offices—an accounting firm, a temp agency, and an insurance broker. There was no way I could check out all four offices without either giving myself away or losing track of Doyle. So, I made myself comfortable in the lobby coffee shop and surreptitiously watched the elevator while I nursed a latte.

I picked Doyle up almost an hour later and followed him down the block to a bank, where he cashed a check for an unknown sum of money and stacked the currency inside his briefcase. I followed him back to the parking garage, but lost him when an elderly woman in a Cadillac El Dorado cut me off.

I circled the parking garage and didn't spot his car. So, I headed back to his house, where I knew he would return sooner or later. I was halfway there when my cell phone rang.

Ted was at the other end of the call. "Here's something nobody knew," he said. "Doyle had a quarter million dollar life insurance policy on his kid."

"That was a lot of money back then," I said.

"That's not chump change now, either," Ted said. "What's more, his wife didn't get a cent of it when they divorced."

"How's a guy from our old neighborhood have the scratch to buy a quarter million dollar policy?" I asked.

"He borrowed it from the Gambinis."

"Loan sharks?"

"Apparently, no one thought the kid would live as long as he did."

"What happened to the money?"

"The Gambinis got a big chunk of it," Ted said. "Doyle paid off all the kid's medical expenses and invested most of the rest. But there's $10,000 I can't account for."

"Keep digging."

"There's more," Ted said. "I've been looking into Danny's recent activities, too. He's made a mess of things since his mother died. Their house is facing foreclosure and he's had a long streak of bad luck with the ponies."

I had reached Doyle's neighborhood by then and I parked my car where I could watch the front of his house. "So what's Doyle got to do with the Danny's money problem?"

"Damned if I know," Ted told me. "I'll keep digging."

I don't know what Ted found, if anything, because he didn't live to see morning. While I was watching Doyle's house, someone with a baseball bat used Ted for a *piñata*.

I found his battered body in the second bedroom of his house, the one he used as an office. I called 911 from his landline and let myself out before the police arrived.

Instead of driving to Doyle's home to continue my surveillance, I drove to my office. Someone had trashed it but I didn't take the time to clean up. I removed the unregistered 9mm taped under my desk and slipped it into my jacket pocket.

Then I drove to Doyle's house, intending to ask him a few questions about his recent activities. I arrived in time to see his car pulling out of the driveway. I followed.

Again, he did not seem to realize he was being followed, and keeping him within sight was not a problem. Unexpectedly, he led me to Danny's house.

He parked at the curb and climbed out of his car with the briefcase I had seen him carrying the previous day. I parked half a block away and closed the distance in time to see Doyle climb the steps and push his way into the house.

I heard a loud crash from inside as I hurried up the steps, and I had my 9mm firmly gripped in my right hand before I pushed the door open. I found two men sprawled out on the floor and Danny standing with a baseball bat at the ready. When he saw me, he lowered the bat.

I didn't lower my gun. "What's this all about Danny?"

"That son-of-a-bitch—" He pointed the bat towards the pug-faced leg breaker I had seen take money from Doyle two days earlier. "—came at me with this. And that son-of-a-bitch—" He pointed the bat at Doyle. "—hired him."

"Why?"

"I was squeezing Doyle for more money," Danny explained. "I figured he could afford it after all this time. I needed it more than he did and I deserved it for what I did."

"What did you do, Danny?"

"I killed that kid of his," Danny said. "You were there. You watched the whole thing."

"Why did you do that, Danny?"

"Money. He paid me enough to buy this house and move my mother out of the neighborhood."

"And why Joe and Ted?"

"When Doyle refused to pay my initial demand, I told him there were witnesses. I told him if anything happened to me that you guys would turn him in. I told him you were in on it."

"But you knew we weren't."

"I didn't expect him to bring some out-of-town goon in on this. I never told him your names, but it couldn't have been hard to figure out. The four of us were always together back then."

I didn't know which was worse, believing for all these years that one of my best friends was a sadistic killer or learning that he had only killed for the money. Either way, he was someone I no longer wanted in my life.

I shot him once in the middle of the forehead. Then I reached down, collected the briefcase still in Doyle's hand, and carried it to my car.

After all, I deserve to be compensated for my time.

THE PLOT
Jedidiah Ayres

'm sitting cross-legged on the ground under a merciless
sun with an unruly weed-whacker in my lap, trying to
untangle the line that I let out too long in the tall grass, when
I see Austin Smith hauling his fat ass toward me across the
weedy lot behind what used to be a Famous Barr department store. I swear under my breath, not happy to see him.

I hope he gets bit by something nasty.

I put my head down, return to my work and try to clear
my expression of anything dark that he might be able to
pick up on. I hear his huffing tinged with the rattle of a
wheeze and it does brighten my countenance sufficiently
so that when he speaks at last I don't look like I want to
strangle him when I look up.

He asks what I'm doing to which I reply, "Cutting the
grass."

"Yeah, Hal, I can see that. What I'm really asking is,
'Why?'"

"Getting too long."

He claps his hand to his neck and it comes away with a
blood smear that used to be a mosquito. "Don't go getting
squirrelly on me, Hal." He waits for me to look up again
and I finally do just because I want him to leave and figure
he won't until he thinks I've heard him out and received the

message loud and clear. "It wouldn't be good for anybody."

I nod. Message received.

He starts humping back across the urban desert. *Go scald your dick in a tail pipe.*

And I'm alone again.

Two weeks later we repeat the scene, except this time, Austin stays parked in his car with the air conditioning blasting away and looks on while Dougie Rasmussen comes to fetch me.

"Hal."

"Dougie."

"Austin wants a word."

"Uh-huh."

"He's waiting."

"Just a minute."

He takes a little half step toward me, and then stops. I don't even have to look at him. He'll wait for me and just be glad that I come willingly. It takes me another minute to make the edges of my eight by eight patch of weeds neat and then I turn off the whacker and follow Dougie back to Mr. Smith's car.

When we get there, Dougie opens a door for me to get inside, but I shake my head and say, "I'm all sweaty, Austin. Don't want to make a mess of your car." Dougie looks worried. I am, after all, still holding the weed-whacker. Austin Smith insists. I shrug at Dougie and hand him the tool before climbing into the back seat where, despite the artic chill, Austin Smith has begun to sweat.

His fat hands are folded delicately across his middle and his voice is high, but I know the bite far outweighs the bark on him.

His problem is that I'm beyond caring.

"Hal, I want you to take a vacation. You're overworked and I think it'd do you good."

"I'm fine, Mr. Smith."

"No, no. You're a good worker, always do what you're told and never complain, but I can tell things are hard for you, harder than you like to let on and I'd like to give you some vacation time, maybe send you on a trip. I talked to Jill about it and—"

"I'm fine, Mr. Smith. Thanks, but I'm good."

He sighs. Settles even more. Getting down to it, finally. "Hal, I'm not going to ask you directly about what you're doing out here, but I think it's pretty clear."

"Ask me," I shrug with innocence. "I don't care."

Austin leans forward and drops his high voice an octave. "That's exactly what concerns me, Hal."

I catch Dougie's eyes in the rearview and he looks away nervously. He knows that I know what's coming. How many times had I sat where he was now and listened to Mr. Smith give some poor slob every chance to straighten up and fly right, but seen in their eyes that it just wasn't going to stick, known that I'd be coming back soon to take care of things permanently?

"You don't have to worry about me, Mr. Smith. I'll never say anything."

He smiles at me sadly. "Not with your mouth, son, I know, but hell if your actions aren't starting to betray you." I'm almost touched by his concern. He's not faking it, but I'm gone. Out of reach. "I'm just looking out for you. Haven't I always?"

I nod. Try and return some of the sincerity. "Sure. You've always been real good to me."

By now we both know that they're just words. Formalities that we feel beholden to. The course is set and we each know our parts. "Then, Hal, son, please, I'm asking you, take some time off. Think of your family." I can feel the wince that he doesn't show and he tries again. "Think about Jill and the kids. They're counting on you, and so am I."

I reach for the door and let myself out. "Thanks for your concern, Mr. Smith, but I'm just fine."

Jill's nervous. More so than usual. I can tell because she's moved beyond just being nice to me, and is now trying to anticipate my every whim. 'I made your favorite.' 'Kids, y'all leave your father be and go on to bed now.' 'C'mon, strip off them clothes and let's get to it.' 'That's right, let it all out.' But no matter. It's sweet and she's a good woman, but this situation is beyond her too.

Not that I don't strip and get to it. I'm not cruel. Not to her. When it's over, we lie in the dark and then after a while I let my arm slip off her shoulder, pretending to have fallen asleep, releasing her from her duties. Timidly, she climbs out of bed and grabs the Pall Malls from her drawer and I don't have to see her to know she's gone out and around to the south side of the house so that the wind won't carry her smoke into the children's open window. I don't have to see her to know she's crying either.

I'm at work under the hood of a Chrysler, in the third bay, and I'm trying to drown out the radio station Jamaal, has selected to torture me with, when detective Brendanowitz drops in. He puts his hand on my shoulder then offers it to shake and I straighten up and grab the rag outta my back pocket and run it over my fingers before reciprocating the gesture. "How you holding up, Hal?"

I motion with my chin toward the back office and nod to Jamaal that I'm going to step out for a minute and he needs to watch the door. Back in the office, I sit down behind the desk and Brendanowitz takes the short, vinyl couch, perching himself on the edge, avoiding the piles of fast-food containers and magazines that have collected there, a look of concern hanging off his face.

I reach into the bottom drawer and remove a bottle of bourbon and dump the melted ice into a trashcan out of two mostly clean Quick Trip cups. I hand one of them to the detective and we silently toast each other and I taste the drink before I shrug my answer.

"Jesus," he says, "Fuck."

I nod and reach to refill our cups.

"Why ain't you taken any time off, huh?"

I shrug again and down my second drink.

"Well, listen, Hal, I just wanted you to hear it from me. Least I could do, but the Circuit Attorney's being a real stiff prick on this one, and she's pressing for a 'renewed effort.' Thinks well enough ain't good enough, I guess."

I nod.

"Anyway, didn't want you to be surprised if somebody else starts poking around and asking you more questions." He looks out the office window at Jamaal, trousers hanging past the halfway mark of his ass and indicating the kid says, "Might wanna warn him too. No sense giving anybody reason to be jumpy." He turns back to me. "Also goes for Jill." I stiffen a bit, but he's not looking at me. He shakes his head. "I hate to think of her being bothered with any more questions, but I wouldn't count out the possibility. Election year and all."

My car is a nightmare of wax paper and foil wrappers, but the kids don't mind, they just brush piles off of the back seat onto the floor and search for the safety belt fasteners. They love to go to the ballpark, but it was more fun when their uncle Jesse would pick us up in his brand new F10. "Dad, when's uncle Jesse coming back?"

My voice doesn't catch. This is what I've been practicing for. "Nobody knows, sweetie. He didn't say where he was going."

"Mindy Jacobs' mom said he might've gone to Canada, but that he's probably just dead."

I whip my head over my right shoulder and make eye contact briefly before returning my attentions to the road, "Don't you believe her, sweetie. I like Mindy just fine, but her mom's had all kinds of problems even before she met your uncle Jesse, okay? And she's just saying something spiteful to help herself feel better." I tilt my head slightly for emphasis even though I'm not looking at her.

When I do glance into the rearview, Tanya looks relieved.

"But I don't want you repeating any of that, okay? Nobody knows anything for certain and everybody's gonna find different ways of dealing with it. Some of em you're not going to like, but if you go trying to make people change, you'll only make it worse."

Tanya nods. Jared scrambles to roll up his window before cutting a fart. Tanya squeals in disgust while Jared howls with mirth.

After the game I stop by Carl's like always. "Hal," the bartender greets me.

"Herman," I return. "Gimme an O'Fallon," which he

does, cracking the bottle cap under the bar. I lay down a twenty next to my hat and grab the bottle before heading over to the juke and punching a few buttons.

Back at the bar my money has changed itself and a bowl of peanuts has appeared beside my hat, just as Dusty Springfield is getting into it. I grab a handful and wash them down with the beer before making a half-assed attempt at conversation. "Whatcha know, Herm?"

"I think Lydia's getting a molar. Cries all the time."

"Next thing you know, she'll be talking. Your life is over. You gonna have more?"

"I am. Teresa's not."

I lift my beer to that. "You already got your eye on somebody else?"

Herman bends down to get at something on a low shelf beneath the bar and whispers to me, "Asshole alert," before rising again and making his way down to the far end of the bar.

I take deep breath and turn around. Brendanowitz is looking at me from the other end of the room.

Brendanowitz grabs a coffee and adds creamer and sugar without even asking me. We've done this before. I nod my appreciation and he waves his hand—no problem. We sit, silent in the gray ten by ten room, waiting for Landry, his partner, and I study my reflection in the two-way mirror. Christ, I really do look like shit. A good cop could read the signs in my face like a headline. Good thing for Austin Smith hinky feelings, hunches and body language aren't admissible. They've gotta make me say something, and we both know that's not gonna happen.

And it doesn't.

Brendanowitz puts a hand on my shoulder as we leave the station. Landry pauses, ten feet ahead of us, and glances back. I don't look at Brendanowitz, I look at Landry—who shakes his head, thrusts his hands deep into his pockets and rounds the corner out of sight.

Brendanowitz's hand is heavy on my shoulder. "Hal..."

He can't think of anything else to say.

I nod. "Thanks, Lyle."

"How 'bout a ride?"

"Sure."

Brendanowitz drives me back to the neighborhood in silence, going three blocks out of the way to avoid passing Smith's office above the deli. When he pulls up in front of my house, Jared is in the street playing football with Ryan Liberto and Aidan Cassidy. The three of them move resentfully out of our way and Brendanowitz flips his hand to the dutifully sulking trio.

When I unclick my belt he finally speaks.

"Jesse..."

I stop my exit and face forward, shoulders square against the seat.

"Jesse, he…"

My face hardens, but I keep my eyes front.

"…I miss him too."

"Fuck you," I whisper.

"No," he says matter-of-factly, "No, Hal, fuck you for letting this go." There's no malice in his voice—just quiet, resigned anger—not yet cooled to indifference.

I nearly break a tooth clenching my jaw, but I don't say shit.

"You think this is fair to Jill? The kids?"

"Why don't you mind your own business?"

He shakes his head. "Broke my heart when you two tied the knot. Pregnant or not, she coulda done a lot better." I nod. I agree. "I never liked you, Hal." There was more to that thought, but it went unsaid. I let it hang in the air, and after fifteen seconds, he keeps going. "But Jesse—he wasn't so bad, just caught crummy breaks..."

"Thanks for the ride."

I open the passenger side door and I'm halfway out when he says, "Think about it."

I do, damn him.

Jamaal is bitching about the Previa in the first bay while Steve Harvey talks about the election. I unscrew the cap from my big green thermos and tip some steaming liquid into it. It's good, strong coffee, but the sharp smell of sweat and grease from my hand lessens its impact on my headache.

When I wince down the last sip, I screw the lid back on and return to the cream colored PT Cruiser with the worn out belts. Through the open garage bay doors I spot Smith's Caddy rolling down the block and watch as it pulls languidly onto the lot. Austin heads inside and Dougie Rasmussen gestures for me to step outside for a word.

I do. "What?"

"The old man."

I blow an irritated burst of air out my nose. "When?"

"Go on by now."

"It's eleven o'clock."

"He keeps shit hours. It's either now or this evening."

Risk the wife. "Fuck. Okay."

He's arthritic and cranky, with glaucoma, and three worthless, grown kids that he hates, and who hate his guts right back. He's hard to threaten.

"Oh, kiss my dick," he says when he discovers it's me come to visit.

I push him backward into the house, and follow, closing the door behind me. With as much calmness and civility as I can, I ask, "What do you want broken?"

Dismissively, he flaps his lips and waves his hand at me, then turns around and hobbles toward the kitchen. "Take your pick, none of it works anyhow."

The room is furnished with sad-ass rundown furniture —stuffing blooming out the vinyl skin of a chair leaning on a swaybacked couch in front of a console television with a crack spidering across the dirty screen. I see what *he* means.

But he doesn't understand *me*.

I catch up to him three steps from the kitchen and, from behind, casually sweep my leg into his path, sending him sprawling onto the dingy linoleum. The sound he makes is less surprise than disgust, and stops well short of a scream, cry, or yelp, but, when I stoop and grab his right hand and snap his little finger in one fluid motion, it becomes significantly more frustrated. I'll take it.

I give him his hand back and he clutches it in his left. "What else do you want broken?" Hate is in his eyes, but he won't look at me. "Hey." I snap my fingers in front of his face. "Gramps. We can't sell any of this shit to raise your nut. You have any new ideas on getting Mr. Smith's money or should we keep going down this road?"

He still doesn't say anything, just burns a hole in the far wall with his stare.

"Fine." I grab for his feet this time and flip the slipper off the left one like a juice top, pausing with his bare foot— gnarly, yellow claws, too dull to glint—cradled in my hands, just long enough for him to spit in defiance, still not looking at me, before I twist and pop on the little toe.

He snuffs and mewls a bit now, but he's far from where I want him to be.

"Listen, old man, we both know you're never going to get it together. So, short of that, this is how you work it off." I grab the telephone from its stand on the wall just above the kitchen counter and drop it at the front door as I'm leaving, so he can call somebody if he needs to.

When I'm just about through the door, I hear him say, "This how you handled Jesse?" And I see red.

I turn around, closing the door behind me, and walk back to him.

"Fuck did you say?"

He returns to his indignant huffing and staring past my shoulder.

I grab his right wrist away from his clutching left hand and lay the whole arm flat on the linoleum. I grab the sap out of my back pocket and hold it steady over his shaking limb. I ask again, "What do you know about it?"

This is clearly more than he bargained for, and he's huffing in fear.

"Hey, old man, what do you wanna say about my brother, huh? You think I'd do this kind of shit to my own brother?" I bring the sap down on his wrist and hear the bone snap.

Now he cries. Hot, angry tears have sprung from those red, cracked eye sockets.

I haven't released the hand back to him. Instead, I hold the arm, with my left hand, above the wrist and let it dangle. With my right hand I grab the fingers and gently twist. The tears sputter, and the cries strangle. It's a victory. A big, fat, hollow victory.

I hate myself.

The grass isn't exactly cool or soft to the touch, but there is a hint of symmetrical definition to the small plot I've been grooming. I haul a lawn chair out of the trunk and set it up in the middle of the eight by eight patch and face it northwest to avoid the worst of the sun.

I don't say anything out loud. That'd be nuts.

Took the kids to a game the other day... Wasn't the same. I crack the top off my lager. It's foamy and warm. I chuckle. Jared farts a lot. Tanya hates that hotbox shit. Doesn't get it. I tell her, I don't really either anymore, but when you and me were kids we were just like that... Jill misses you awful bad, says we have to move away. But don't worry... We won't.

Reaching down for my next beer, I sense a presence behind me, and turn to see Lyle Brendanowitz on my six.

"Hal."

"Detective. You off duty?"

He nods, and I toss him a warm beer. He cracks the beverage and cops a squat on my neatly cropped patch of weeds. We share a silence and a beer, and it's almost nice, but the way he runs his hands through the fresh-cut grass bothers me. *I'm sorry.*

Finally, he speaks. "Kind of a shit view, Hal."

He's right. Weeds, abandoned strip mall, the highway in the distance passing over the old rail yard. Unused billboards with a dozen tattered, peeling, messages peeking through. It's not a postcard vista, I'll give him that. *Sorry.*

"You know, you've never been my favorite human being," I don't turn my head to him, and he continues, "but you've got your qualities. I can see that. Loyalty, for one."

I take a drink, and smother a burp in my mouth.

"Your problem, the way I see it, is you keep getting the wrong jobs. Making the wrong commitments."

"Yeah? You've got the right ones?"

He shakes his head. "No, I'm not saying that." He kills his beer and I indicate that he should help himself to another, which he does. "But I'm not burdened by your instinct for sacrifice. Pretty much always act in self-interest."

"How's that working out?"

His silence makes my point. I think.

After a moment, he continues. "You don't owe Austin Smith anything more. And he doesn't have much time left at the top of the pile. I've seen his kind when they're caught too. Think he's gonna nobly clam up when his tit's in the wringer?" He shakes his head, even though I'm not looking at him. I know him. He's shaking his head and swallowing beer. "Nuh-uh, it's gonna be a fire sale on shitheels and stand-up guys alike. Be nobody left to take care of Jill and the kids."

Bullshit. He'll be left. He'll be there for Jill. Hell, he'll be there for my kids for Jill's sake. So why's he selling me options? Due diligence? Ease that slovenly conscience of his later on when he's comforting my wife?

"You like my beer, Detective?" He doesn't answer. "How about you just enjoy what I'm offering freely, and shut the fuck up, huh?"

To his credit, he does.

He'll be good to Jill.

The next night I'm late getting home from work and the house is empty. No note, no message on the machine. I call Jill's mom in Arnold. "Hey, Betty, it's Hal. Jill around?"

"Oh hi, Hal. No, I haven't seen her. Everything alright?"

"Yeah, everything's good. Just thought maybe she'd brought the kids over."

"Want me to call anybody?"

"Nah, it's alright. Talk to you later."

I wash up and eat some cold, leftover pasta. After an hour I get a phone call from work. Somebody's there long after close. "Yeah?"

"Hal, I need you to swing by the shop." Austin Smith.

"Can it wait, I'm kind of needed at home, man."

"Hal, I sent Jill and the kids out of town."

That ball of wet rags in my guts hardens and I nearly drop the phone. "You what?"

"Why don't you come in and talk about it. I want you to go see them. Take that vacation I've been talking to you about."

"I'm coming in."

I hate doing it, but as soon as I hang up, I call Brendanowitz. He doesn't answer, but I leave him a voice message. "Hey, it's Hal… About Jesse… I think maybe… You should follow your hunches."

I'm not armed because it would hardly make a difference I were. And I suppose there's a small chance that I'm wrong about what I'm walking in to, and if I came in carrying it could give him ideas that I don't want to. Back office is the only light on and I'm meant to walk toward it. If I'm right, Dougie Rasmussen is standing in the shadows somewhere behind me, but I don't look.

I stand in the doorway and see Austin Smith sitting behind the desk, doing me the courtesy of not pretending to be busy with anything else. "Have a seat, Hal."

I don't move to sit, but I don't hover either. I try to put more patience than is reasonable into my voice. "Where are they, Austin?"

"They're on vacation, Hal, relax."

"You can't just—"

"It was Jill who came to me, Hal." That brings me up short. "At some point she has to start thinking about the kids."

Behind me, I hear Dougie Rasmussen approach. "C'mon, Hal, let's take a drive."

I turn to him slowly, "Just a minute." To Austin Smith I say, "Tell me they're going to be alright."

"Hal, what do you take me for? Hand to God, I love those kids, and Jill… She's just looking out for them. You broke her heart, Hal. And mine. Saw you out there again the other day. Talking with that cop, no less."

"He came to me, Austin."

"This isn't the time to play innocent."

"Never claimed innocence, but I've always been loyal."

"Yeah, you have, Hal, and I'm not blaming you. This thing with Jesse… It's just been more than you could handle, and I'm real sorry about that." He gives me a sad smile. "Still… I'd be a fool to wait any longer."

He would.

We take a drive and I don't complain.

WHAT ALVA WANTS
Timothy Friend

What Alva wants, Alva gets. Luster Dobbs regretted ever having made such an ignorant statement. Especially since Alva was the type to hold a hard-pecker promise over a man's head both day and night. Worse still, as soon as she got what she wanted, she wanted more. More clothes, bigger house, and now a new car. If it wasn't for all of Alva's wanting, he never would have come to the Happy Dragon during Spider's business hours.

Luster paused for a moment just inside the door, half-blinded by the sudden change from full sunlight to barroom neon. Even though he couldn't see him, Luster knew Spider was watching from his usual booth in the back corner.

He thought about leaving. Just turning around and hurrying home, telling Alva that Spider wasn't there. Maybe stall a while longer until he came up with a better idea. But he knew there wouldn't be any better ideas. He didn't do this, Alva was gone. Off to greener pastures.

Wasn't that long ago his own pastures had looked pretty green. He'd been top salesman at Roy DeFlower's Used Auto, pulling down serious cash every week. Luster's success was due to the fact that Roy's salesmen dealt primarily in cocaine. Then Roy got busted with a fifteen year old girl in his passenger seat and several bricks of coke in his trunk.

Now Luster sold shoes at the mall. His pasture was dried up, and Alva was hinting that her pussy might be affected by the drought. Whenever she wanted something that Luster couldn't afford, which was damn near every day, she threw his own words back in his face. *What Alva wants, Alva gets.*

Luster had said those words to her the first time they were together. Just pillow talk, trying to convince her she should be with him. She'd been Spider's woman then. They'd fucked in Spider's own bed while the man was tending to business right here in the Happy Dragon. Luster didn't think Spider knew about that. Hoped he didn't.

That was almost a year ago. And Alva assured him that enough water had passed under the bridge. Kept insisting that Spider wouldn't hold a grudge over it. Luster wanted to believe her, but then thought about Alva's smooth brown legs and her soft lips and wondered just how long he would hold a grudge if things were the other way around.

"Well if it ain't Luster Dee." Spider's gravelly voice heaved out of the dark. "Ain't seen you around for a while. Come on over here and sit."

Luster hesitated.

"Come on, now. I don't bite."

Luster knew this to be half true. With his gooned-up leg and scrawny frame Spider wasn't much of a direct threat to anyone, but he had a way of taking care of business indirectly. He didn't need to bite when he could have someone else do the biting for him.

The bar was empty except for Spider and the bartender. Luster weaved his way through the vacant tables until he reached the booth. Spider sat sideways with his back against the wall, his bad leg stretched out on the seat. He had a Bloody Mary on the table beside him. The light from the lamp hanging overhead didn't reach his face.

"So what brings you 'round, Luster Dee?" Spider's words were carried on a billow of white smoke. He stubbed out his cigarette in a tin ashtray as Luster took the seat across from him.

Luster felt awkward, didn't know where to start. "You heard about Roy?"

"Mm-hm. I heard about his dumb ass."

"Well, I was working for him," Luster said. "Doing okay, too. Now I'm selling shoes. Making shit for money. I was hoping you could-"

"Where at?"

"What?"

"Where you selling shoes at?"

Luster had to think for a second. "Uh...Shoe Shack. Over at Westerton Square."

"I was planning on getting some new shoes. Think you can set me up?"

"I...uh, I guess."

"I got to have'em special made 'cause of my leg. Extra wide, thicker sole. Can they do that there?"

Luster shook his head. "Naw. Just right outta the box. I don't think they do anything special."

Spider sipped at his Bloody Mary. "Yeah. Nothing special. And that's where you are now. Fuckin' Shoe Shack."

Luster wanted to box his ears. Wanted to say, "Look here, cripple, least I'm the one fucking Alva." But he knew that wasn't going to be the case much longer if he didn't make some money soon. He bit his lip and sat quietly.

"You want to work for me now," Spider said. "That it?"

"Yeah. I heard you might have something."

"Where you hear that?"

Luster didn't speak.

"Go on," Spider said. "Where you hear it from?"

"Alva." Luster's throat tightened when he said her name. "I heard it from Alva."

"Yeah," Spider said. "I knew that. Just wanted you to say her name, let you see I'm over it."

Spider leaned forward to set his drink down, and his yellowed ivory smile came into the light. "Bygones and what-not."

"Glad to hear it," Luster said. "It was just one of those things, y'know."

"I know," Spider said. "You didn't intend for it to happen."

"No, course not."

"There was no malice aforethought."

Luster stared blankly.

"You didn't plan it," Spider said.

"Yeah. No. I wouldn't do that."

"No. You ain't a planner. That's my line. You're more of a doer. That it?"

Luster nodded, not sure where this was going.

Spider leaned back, lit up another cigarette, closed his eyes. He sat quietly for a moment, then said "I might could have something for you."

"Really?"

"Yeah, maybe. I'll set up a meet with Delroy tonight. See what I can arrange."

"I thought you and Delroy were banging heads?"

Spider looked at Luster sharply, his smile gone. "Alva tell you that too?"

"No," Luster was suddenly afraid he'd fucked up. "Word just gets around. Thought you two were feuding."

"Maybe we reconciled," Spider said. "It ain't your

concern."

Delroy dealt in guns, crank and whatever prescription drugs he could get his hands on. He'd lately ventured into parts of town Spider claimed as his own. In Luster's experience these things rarely resulted in reconciliation. But like Spider said, it wasn't his concern.

"Be here tomorrow noon," Spider said. "Things go the way I want, I'll have a job for you."

Luster thanked him and got out of the booth. Halfway to the door he heard Spider call from the dark. "Give Alva my love."

Luster thought Alva would be excited to hear that things had worked out with Spider. On the way home he picked up a bottle of good bourbon he couldn't afford, hoping they could have a little celebration.

She wasn't there when Luster got home, just a note saying she had to work late. He drank the bourbon alone, just him and his hard-on. By the time Alva got home he was too drunk to do anything about it. When she kissed him goodnight—a dry peck on the cheek—he noticed she was wearing a new perfume. Probably expensive. Probably charged it to his damn credit card.

Luster fell asleep in front of the television, woke up the next morning with a headache. He took a shower, dressed and popped a handful of aspirin. He peeked in at Alva before he left. She was lying on her stomach, blankets kicked off, giving him a nice view of her firm, round ass. Luster sighed and headed off to meet Spider.

Spider was waiting for him in the parking lot, sitting behind the wheel of a brand new car. Luster didn't know shit about cars, but he could tell it was something pricey. Just the kind of thing Alva would want.

Spider rolled his window down as Luster parked and got out. His door squeaked when he shut it, and he felt a twinge of embarrassment.

"Lookin' a little rough there, Luster Dee." Spider said. "You have a late night? Alva wearing you out?"

"You know how it is," Luster said.

Spider grinned. "Yeah. I know exactly how it is."

Luster didn't like the tone of that comment, but he kept his mouth shut.

Spider motioned him closer, then handed Luster a package. It was about the size of a shoe box, wrapped in brown paper. "I need you to deliver this. Think you can do that?"

Luster nodded. "Where you need it to go?"

"You gonna take it to Delroy's place. You know where that is?"

"Sure. But why didn't you just give it to Delroy when you saw him yesterday?"

Spider pulled his sunglasses down and gave Luster a stare. "Because I didn't have it then. That all right with you? That meet with your approval, Mr. Shoe Salesman?"

Luster thought about dragging the gimp out of his car, kicking him silly right there in the parking lot. Instead he said, "Yeah, fine."

"You give that to Delroy's boys. Ask for Cole. Tell him things keep on the way they are they can expect a lot more where that came from. And you got to be sure and tell him this is from Merton."

"Merton Cullins?"

"How many fuckin' Merton's you know?"

Merton Cullins operated out of Laclede County and had made it clear that he would have no truck with outsiders. Luster had learned this when one of Roy's salesmen came back from Laclede with both arms broken. Fella's wife had to wipe his ass for two months. They were divorced now, which Luster attributed to the ass wiping. That was the sort of thing that would kill the romance in a relationship good and permanent.

"Just surprised," Luster said. "Merton's a hard man to deal with."

Spider pushed his sunglasses back up on his nose and smiled. "You know me. I'm a people person. I like to see these conflicts resolved once and for all."

Luster watched Spider drive away, then tossed the package in the passenger seat and headed out to Delroy's place. Delroy lived in a farmhouse way out in the boonies, so he settled in for a long drive.

Luster couldn't help but think about the package. It was probably money, payment for either drugs or guns. It didn't weigh much. And the comment about more where that came from suggested it wasn't a full payment.

Luster decided it was a test. If he came through for Spider this time, the man would trust him with the bigger payments in the future. And if Spider had found a way to get a piece of Merton's action then there were definitely going to be some big payments.

That was when Luster intended to fuck Spider over but good. One big score. That was all he needed. Then he and Alva could skip town, leave Spider in the shit. With a big enough stake Luster could start up his own operation. No way he was going to keep working for that crippled bastard.

A half-dozen hard looking men were outside when Luster pulled up in front of the house. Most of them were seated on the porch out of the sun, but one man paced the yard with his cell phone to his ear. A big bearded man sat at a weathered picnic table hacking at it with a knife the size of Luster's forearm.

Luster got out with the package under his arm. He could feel their eyes on him as he crossed the yard.

The guy on the phone swore and hung up. "Goddamn voicemail again," he said to the group. "I'm starting to have some serious concerns. He never goes this long without checking in."

"I'm looking for Cole," Luster called out.

The man turned and looked at him. "That's me. What the fuck do you want?"

Luster ran through Spider's message in his head, tried to get it exactly right. "This here is from Merton. He says if you keep on the way you are there'll be plenty more where that came from." Luster smiled, satisfied that he'd nailed it.

Cole took the package and tore at the paper. The other men came down from the porch eager to get a look. They stared over Cole's shoulder like kids watching someone else open a present and wishing it was theirs.

Luster noticed the man at the picnic table seemed disinterested. He just kept chipping away with his knife. The table was scarred up all the way around with little notches like maybe his whittling at it was some kind of hobby.

Cole said, "Oh, shit."

Luster looked back and saw the package hit the ground and something tumbled out. It took Luster a moment to recognize the contents.

It was a right hand cut off smoothly at the wrist, and when it landed palm down in the grass it looked like a pale, thick-legged spider. Tattooed on the backs of the first three fingers were the letters D, E, and L.

Luster couldn't manage to process what he was seeing.

He glanced back at his car in confusion. For a second he had the crazy thought that he'd grabbed the wrong package.

When he turned back the men were closing on him. Even Whittling Man had taken enough of an interest to get up from his beloved picnic table.

"Hold on, boys," Luster said. "This wasn't me. I just-"

Somebody hit him in the side of the head. Felt like a baseball bat, maybe a two-by-four. Luster couldn't tell, and the pain kept him from giving it much consideration. The second blow made stars explode behind his eyes, and he fell to the ground.

Luster heard the men cussing at him, felt them kicking him. He tried to tell them this was Spider's doing, but he couldn't move his shattered jaw. He couldn't even spit out the teeth he felt floating around in his mouth. Then he felt hands grabbing him, lifting him up, and for just a second it was like he was floating away.

"Get him on the table," Cole said. "If Merton wants to play it this way, that's just fine."

Luster wanted to tell these boys going after Merton was the wrong move. They were just giving Spider what he wanted. Then he realized that wasn't exactly true.

His head banged against the tabletop as the men dropped him. Luster saw Whittling Man looking down at him. The dead stare and half-smile on his face told Luster he was about to learn the man's real hobby.

Luster thought about Spider tooling around in the new car he'd probably been convinced to buy. Making this power play he'd been led to make, just like Luster had been led.

Luster had to laugh, choking on blood as he did. All those months ago, when he'd first said the words, he never realized how right he was. What Alva wants, Alva gets.

TIME ENOUGH TO KILL
Kent Gowran

ackie White's eyes start to blink.

Dead on the floor with a rusty hatchet buried in his head and the son of a bitch's eyes start blinking.

Cookie sees it at the same time I do and yanks a checkered tablecloth off one of the Laugh Hole's tables and covers Jackie with it. "Better?"

"Yeah."

"We should get going."

"We've got time."

"Not much."

"Plenty of it."

He turns away from me and moves to hover over Max who is doing a less than half-assed job of wiping Jackie's blood off his face.

"This is the trouble with you, Max," Cookie says. "This is why the Laugh Hole is going down the tubes."

Max stops wiping and looks at Cookie. "What're you talking about?"

"You've got no class." He holds his arms out like all of a sudden he's Jesus and is about to impart some wisdom from on high but all he comes out with is: "This place has no class."

"Give me a break." Max looks over at me for support or

some kind of input contrary to Cookie's own and I take a sudden interest counting the bottles behind the bar. Max snorts and waves his hand in the general direction of the corpse on the floor. "It's not like I go slamming guys in the head with an axe on a nightly basis."

"Hatchet," Cookie says.

"What?"

"It's a hatchet. You hit Jackie in the head with a hatchet."

"Whatever. Just the same, Cookie..." Max is wheezing. "I'm all worked up here."

"Probably not good for your heart."

"No shit." He starts to cough and it looks to me like he might pass out. "This is all your fault anyway."

Cookie smiles like it's just what he wanted to hear. "Don't forget my associate over there." He points at me just in case Max has forgotten I'm standing ten feet away. "He drove me here."

Max doesn't bother looking at me. I can see he's in bad shape, and so can Cookie. Which is the whole point of our visit to the Laugh Hole.

Cookie helps Max sit down at a table. "You want something to drink?"

"Whiskey."

"You sure about that?"

Max nods. "The good stuff."

Cookie comes over to the bar and says, "Give me a bottle of whatever's the best."

I look at the bottles and realize no matter which one I grab it isn't going to be what anyone would ever call the best. I pick one with a label I used to know a little too well and push it across the bar to Cookie.

"Give me a couple glasses, too."

I put two shot glasses on the bar. "How far are you going to let this go? He needs help."

"I've got a handle on it." He gives me a wink and takes the booze over to the table.

The last of the Friday night crowd left hours ago, and according to the digital clock set into the gaping maw of an oversize laughing mouth hanging above the bar the sun will be up shortly.

Cookie sits down. "Looks like it's the last time either of us will be drinking here." He pours the whiskey. "What're we drinking to?"

"My wife," Max says. They knock their glasses together and drink.

Cookie looks over at me. "Bring those pictures over here."

"He already saw them," I say even as I pick up the stack of photos and head toward their table.

"Give 'em here." Cookie snatches them away from he. He spreads them out across the table in front of Max. It's like watching an execution.

In each one Max sees Tiffany looking directly at the camera. Almost like she's looking at him, like she knows he'll be sitting there unable to look away. "Maybe they're old."

"Look at that one there," Cookie says and stabs at a one of the shots with his finger. "See her hand there? Pumping away on poor dead Jackie's dick? There's that big ass rock of a wedding ring you put on her finger."

The last of the color drains from Max's face. "I'm glad I killed him."

"I bet you are."

Max goes on looking at each picture over and over.

"I never made her laugh," Cookie says.

Max looks up. "What do you mean?"

"Tiffany. I never made her laugh when we were together." Cookie smiles. "But you sure did, Max." He refills their glasses. "You want to know something?"

Max stays quiet. Probably knows Cookie will go on talking no matter what he says.

"I always wanted to get you."

"Get me?"

"Make you pay."

"Jesus..."

"For taking her from me."

"That was a long time ago."

"Eleven years."

"Like I said..."

"I know how to hold a grudge."

Max's eyes open a little wider. Like now he's getting it loud and clear, if a little too late. "This was all you wasn't it?"

Cookie cocks his head in the direction of the body on the floor. "Jackie helped some."

"You took these pictures."

"Nah, my cousin Dot took them."

"The cat photographer?" He almost laughs.

"That's her." Cookie picks up a couple of the pictures and lets loose a low whistle. "After I saw these, I told Dot she should refocus her pussy snapping business."

Max shifts in his seat and starts to massage his chest. "Call me an ambulance."

"You're an ambulance."

"That's my punch line," Max says. "You don't sell it."

"You're the great comedian," Cookie says and it's not the biggest exaggeration ever. People used to know who Max was, before they knew him as just the fat guy who owns the Laugh Hole.

He leans across the table and puts a big hand on Cookie's arm. "I got a joke for you..."

Cookie looks amused. "Yeah? Let's hear it."

Max licks his lips. "Give me a minute here."

He looks around the Laugh Hole. He looks at Jackie's expensive armadillo skin cowboy boots sticking out from under the tablecloth. He looks at the bottle of whiskey and I can almost hear him wishing he'd stocked the bar with something better. He looks at the blood from Jackie's ruined head as it soaks through the tablecloth. Finally he gets around to me, and he looks at me like I should've done something to stop all of this.

"It's almost time for breakfast," Cookie says.

Max looks at him. He shuffles through the pictures of Tiffany and Jackie again.

"You going to tell the joke or not?"

Max doesn't say anything. He just smiles and then does what fat comedians do.

COPAS
Hector Acosta

The kid's first mistake was cursing at the Mexican cop. His second mistake happened midway through the stream of profanity coming out of his mouth, when the kid lost all color, hunched over, and spewed more than just curse words all over the fat cop's shoes.

"*Ese gringo lla se chingo,*" the bartender said, placing a beer in front of me.

I didn't need him to tell me the guy was fucked. Sprinkling some salt and lime on the rim of the can, I flinched when the *federal* pushed the drunken kid down to the sidewalk and started kicking him. The other people in the bar barely paid any attention to the scene outside, having long ago grown used to this type of display.

Turning my back to the action, I tried to do the same, but the sound of steel tipped shoe meeting flesh made the beer taste vile. With a sigh I pulled my stool back and threw a couple of dollars on the counter for the unfinished drink.

Not even out of the bar and already my decision to help was costing me.

"*Te voy a hacer que me limpies los zapatos con tu lengua,*" I heard the cop say, landing another kick on the American. I think if the offer was really on the table, the kid would have gladly licked the cop's shoes clean to stop the beating.

Everyone in the streets gave the two a wide berth, happy to pretend that a teenager getting kicked to death was an everyday occurrence. And while Juarez had gotten pretty bad, it wasn't at the daylight-murders stage yet. A small group stood across the street from the cop, some with their phones out and filming the whole thing.

"*Lo vas a matar,*" I said, approaching the cop with my hands up in the air to show I wasn't carrying a weapon. You only need to have a group of cops pull their guns on you once before you start to learn the best ways to approach them. Technically, the best way to approach a Mexican cop was with your wallet out and in clear view, but I wasn't feeling that much of a good Samaritan just yet.

"*No te metas,*" the cop said. At least I got him to stop kicking the kid.

"Come on Pedro, you know I'm right. A few more kicks and you're going to have a ton of paperwork to fill out." I stuck to Spanish, just so that Pedro couldn't later say that there was a miscommunication between us.

"*Pendejo* ruined my shoes. You want me to just let him go?"

"I want you not to kill him." I glanced down to the kid lying on the concrete. He looked all of sixteen, with hair so blond it might as well have been white, blue eyes, and pale skin that reminded me of the color of the milky *horchata* drink you could order in any taco stand around here. I wondered how much his looks played into Pedro's beating.

Pedro was the type of guy that joined the police force because he had a power complex that beating whores just wasn't satisfying anymore. And he'd only gotten worse ever since the Mexican army arrived in the city with their jeeps, tanks, and automatic weapons, like a child that threw a fit when a new kid showed up to the playground with a better and flashier toy than the one he had.

"You proved your point," I said.

Pedro narrowed his eyes. "What do you care what happens? What's your angle here, Thursday?"

I flinched at the name, reminded once more that I had my parents to blame for how my life turned out. Name a kid Thursday, and his chances of becoming president or finding the cure for cancer immediately went down the crapper.

"No angle. Just don't want to see a kid dead. That would probably get the bar shut down for at least a couple of days, and I like coming here."

The kid moaned, earning him another kick from Pedro.

"Stop." The firmness of my voice surprised even me.

Pedro grinned, showing two rows of pristine, clean teeth. Corruption at least paid well enough for dental checkups. "Or you'll do what, Thursday?" he asked.

Good question. If Pedro didn't want to stop the beating, he didn't have to. Despite people filming him, Pedro could kill the kid and know there would be little to no repercussions from higher ups. They had a number of ways they could spin a story like this so that Pedro came out clean. Their favorite as of late was to have the newspapers publish editorials of how the Americans that came to Juarez for the cheap beers were to blame for the drug business that had recently swept up the entire state of Chihuahua. How without the Americans and their money there wouldn't be as much of a demand for the drugs that the cartels passed through the border every day. And many Mexicans, especially the ones that served, cooked, or worked for Americans either here in Juarez or across the border Paso ate it all up.

So I briefly considered heading back inside the bar

before I made things any worse, when I caught another glimpse of the phone cameras and got an idea.

"Walk away or I make sure that people see the video," I leaned in and whispered to Pedro.

A good lie is all about presentation. The best ones work because they're served in the most direct manner possible. The gambits and elaborate con games that you see in movies and televisions rarely work in real life, because people are too lazy to follow along and keep track of all the deceit. The best way to lie is straight to the person's face, starting off with something so small and inconsequential that like a fish to bait, they can't help but be hooked from the start.

What the hell are you talking?"

"Walk away or people get to see you go into Gabriela's apartment." I crouched next to the kid and looked him over, noting that most of Pedro's work had gone into the stomach and sides, which, if there was no internal bleeding, would be a good thing for the kid-easier to hide those types of bruises. I also knew that Pedro was looking down at me, so I added, "I'm sorry, does he go by *Gabriel* when he's off duty?"

Juarez had its share of prostitutes, most of them congregating around *el centro*. They came out once the sun went down and the neon signs of the *discotecas* came on, flocks of them slowing down traffic and milling around sidewalks or venturing out to the streets, car horns drowning out the high heels pounding the pavements. And out of all the prostitutes, Gabriela was, if not the most well-known, certainly one that stood out just by sight alone. Easy to do when you were 6'2 and wore an extra four inches of heels. Then there was the fact that no amount of make up or eye catching wigs could hide her Adam's apple.

I'd once heard from a couple of giddy prostitutes ending

their night and sharing a cab with me that Gabriela had a thing for men in uniform. I filed that alongside the tidbit I'd gain from a drunk who'd ran across Pedro's wrath and told me that he had a thing for men in dresses,

In reality, I had never actually seen the two of them together, least of all have recording of them, but all I needed was for it to have happened at least once and I had Pedro.

"You're lying."

That wasn't a denial.

"I'm not," I said. "I've been holding on to it for a while, and don't mind continuing to do so. Long as you walk away from here."

"You're making a mistake, you know that right?" Pedro took a step back, which I took as a good sign.

"Probably," I acknowledged, 'But I don't like you. Never have."

Considering this was my whole plan, it was hard not to breathe a sigh of relief when Pedro turned his attention to the crowd and yelled at them to put away their cameras and disperse. Or as he so eloquently put it, 'get the fuck out of here before I send you all to jail'. He then glanced back at me and the kid and shook his head. "*Pinche gringo,*" he said.

Wondering which of the two of us he meant, I helped the kid up from the floor. "Come on, you look like you could use a drink," I said.

You couldn't find a better margarita than the one served in Club Kentucky. Deceptively simple to make, it only required a couple of ingredients—kosher salt, silver tequila, *controy*

and most importantly of all, fresh lime juice. Oh, and the experienced hands of a bartender that had shaken margaritas for Steve McQueen, Ernest Hemingway, and Marilyn Monroe, who was said to have famously bought drinks for the entire bar to celebrate her divorce from Arthur Miller.

The kid and I sat on an oak table at the back of the bar, me enjoying my margarita and him leaning his head back against the cushion of the sofa seat. He'd been pretty talky on the way to the bar, though most of it had been an incoherent mess of words that littered the sidewalk behind us. He'd stopped talking once we got inside, which suited me just fine. I sipped the drink and enjoyed the way the tartness of it made the insides of my cheek tingle, all the while keeping an eye on the front door of the bar.

I'd embarrassed Pedro. Before, he'd been annoyed at my presence but other than two run-ins with him, which had predictably resulted in a lighter wallet for me, he hadn't really gone out of the way to bother me. More than likely, he just saw me as another white guy happy to take advantage of the still strong dollar here in Juarez and then mosey his way back across the border to his home and life in El Paso. Now I'd made an enemy out of him.

Which explained why I chosen this place to hunker down in. Club Kentucky was as much of an institution in Juarez as... well, now that I thought about it, this might be Juarez's ONLY institution. Point being, Club Kentucky was famous, and famous places rarely got shot at by angry cops.

"Hey, is your name really Thursday? Like in the day of the week?"

First time the kid had spoken since getting here and it had to be a question about my name.

"Yeah."

"Huh."

I waited for the eventual follow up, but nothing came. Normally people aren't so quick to let go when it comes to the subject of my name. I've heard everything from 'What the fuck were your parents thinking', to 'Could be worse, you could have been named Friday'.

"How are you feeling?" I asked, motioning to the waiter. "You want anything to drink or eat?"

"Water," he said with a swallow, "lots and lots of water."

When the waiter, dressed in a neatly iron white shirt and tie came to our table, I ordered another margarita and two glasses of water.

What's your name anyways?" I asked

"Toby," the kid answered.

"First time in Juarez, Toby?"

He nodded.

Figured. "You here alone?"

Our waiter came back with the drinks, and Toby immediately reached out for his glass of water.

"I was with some friends," Toby said, setting the glass down on the table after drinking half of it in one gulp. "Hey, can I borrow your phone to call them? They're probably out looking for me."

"You came into Juarez without a phone?"

Toby patted his pockets and said, "I lost it."

"Knock yourself out," I said, tossing him my phone.

"Wow, I didn't think they still made those," he said, looking down at the phone I bought from the *mercado* for ten bucks.

"At least I got a phone."

"*Touché,*" he said and dialed.

I looked around the bar. Black and white pictures of

their famous clienteles hung along all the walls, keeping company to the soccer, I mean, *futbol* memorabilia that plastered the walls. The many bottles lining the back of the bar never had a chance to shine thanks to the low lighting of the room. I swear that every bar followed the guidelines that if you could see the drink in front of you, they had the lights on too bright.

There used to be a time this place would have been packed, even in the middle of the afternoon. Now though? Apart from us, the waiter, and the bartender, I counted three other people, all sitting at the bar and nursing drinks. Shit, no wonder the waiter had charged so much.

People just didn't go out as often as they used to, not with the idea of all-out war between the cartels and the Mexican army hovering in the air like a fart filled balloon. With its close proximity to the U.S, the drug cartels had always seen Juarez as a prize worth killing for, just as the Mexican government viewed the city as too important of a victory to lose. So war broke out between the Army and two main cartels; The Juarez cartel, which had control of the drug trade since the early eighties, and the Sinaloa cartel. All three factions battled it out on the streets and b put the civilians in the middle of the conflict. People moved out of the city if they could afford to, and if not, pulled their kids out of school and hunkered inside their home.

All that still hadn't stopped the death count from rising month after month. Last month alone over fifty murders were reported. This understandably put a damper on most of the tourist trade that Club Kentucky and the surrounding bars relied on.

"Cool, we're at that old bar, you know the one with the crappy looking sign that has a big beer can on it?" I heard

Toby say, "Yeah, that's the one."

Thinking about the current state of things in Juarez, I wondered what a fifteen year old white kid was doing drunk in the middle of the day. When he hung up and handed me back the phone, I asked.

"Oh," he said with some hesitation, "Well, my friends wanted to come and check out the place. Go look around the city and stuff. We agreed that it would be safer if we did it during the afternoon instead of night, when it really got dangerous."

'Didn't work out quite as you expected huh?"

"Man, what an asshole that cop was. He wanted a hundred dollars or he said that he would cart me off to jail. I hadn't even done anything wrong."

"How about underage drinking," I pointed out.

"Dude, everyone does that. It's like, totally expected."

"Cop tells you to pay, you pay. Or you go to jail. That's what's expected here."

Toby stayed quiet for a moment and then blurted out, "It's a hundred bucks!"

"Still cheaper than a hospital bill."

He opened his mouth to argue when a loud car horn cut through the bar's conversations and shoved aside the *norteña* tune playing from the jukebox. I almost jumped out of my seat and when I managed to calm my racing heart to look out the bar's window, I saw a bright yellow Volkswagen parked in the middle of the street. The driver honked again, and a blond girl in ponytails and a short top leaned out of the back side window and yelled, "Toby, you dork, come on, hurry up, we need to get going."

Toby sprung from his seat too fast and immediately doubled over in pain. Shaking my head, I got up and helped him to the door. I wanted to get a closer look at his friends anyway.

Four in all, crammed inside the small car. Their laughing and conversation stopped when they saw me walking Toby out.

The driver, a tall, black kid jumped out of the car and asked, "What the hell happened to him?"

"I'll tell you about it later, Miles," Toby said through gritted teeth.

Miles glanced at me. If he expected an explanation out of me, he wasn't getting it. Instead I looked at the other three kids in the car. All white kids wearing expensive clothes and glassy stares of drunks.

"Damn it Toby, dad and mom are going to freak," the girl that had yelled for him a moment ago said. Same blond hair as Toby.

She caught me looking at her and flashed me a smile. "Who's the old guy?"

Ouch. "I'm in my thirties. Early thirties."

"Exactly." She looked back a Toby. "Mom and dad are going to freak."

"Oh shit," Toby said, stopping to lean against the trunk of the car and turning towards me, "I didn't even fucking thank you." He explained to his friends, "It would have been worse if he hadn't been there."

"You did. Thank me I mean."

"But like, I didn't *thank you* thank you." Limping his way back to me, he reached for his wallet and took out five twenties. "What I should have paid the cop," he said.

I took the money.

Putting the wallet back in his pocket, Toby stared at me for a second and said, "You live in El Paso."

A statement, not a question.

"Yep."

"Cool. Maybe I'll see you around."

"Doubt it. Hey, you want a piece of advice?"

Toby nodded and leaned forward, maybe thinking I was about to divulge a great drinking spot or a way to avoid the cops. Instead I slapped him in the face. Hard, but not as hard as Pedro would have.

"Don't come back. At least not until you're eighteen or can hold your liquor. Whichever comes first."

Miles had gotten out of the car already, and the other kid had to hold on to screaming sister back from coming at me.

"What the fuck, asshole," Miles said, "Who the fuck you think you are?"

He would have taken a swing for me if it wasn't for Toby, who got between us. "It's cool, Miles. Let's get in the car." He kept his gaze on me.

"Let me go, no one hits my little brother. I'll fucking kill him."

I looked over Toby and pointed at his sister, "You guys better calm her down, otherwise there's no way you cross the bridge without getting some attention from the border patrol. What bridge you taking?"

"Bridge of the Americas," Toby muttered.

I checked my watch and said, "Take Ysleta. If you head over there right now, you'll get there just as they switch shifts. If you can keep her quiet and pay the five bucks, you'll pass with no problem."

Toby got back in the car without thanking me, and with the sister slinging obscenities at me, I watched them go. If they were heading towards the Ysleta bridge, they needed to take the next left. Instead, they took a right. I wondered to what bar they were now heading to before counting the money I'd taken from Toby's wallet when he wasn't looking and adding it to the hundred he gave me.

Two hundred and fifty dollars. I've done more for less.

I stuck around Club Kentucky for a couple of more hours and even though I wasn't celebrating a divorce, ended up buying the patrons a round or two. Considering it was just me and two old men over by the end of the bar, my generosity didn't even cost me much. After a while, I stuffed the remaining of Tobey's money down the inside of my left sock and decided to call it a night.

The alcohol muddled my head just enough that I didn't mind the walk over to the Santa Fe Bridge. If this had been the weekend, the bars along the Juarez strip would have been playing the latest hip hop songs or whatever *reggaeton* got the drunken girls shaking their asses the hardest. But since it was a Monday night, most of the bars stuck to playing the *corridas* their regulars wanted to hear.

I'd almost reached the bridge when I spotted the flashing red and blue lights streaking across the buildings that and washing over a crowd of onlookers. The sounds of a girl screaming pushed way all the pleasant after effects of the margaritas and brought things back into an ugly focus. My mind and body were divided in two, with all the thoughts in my head urging to turn around or slip into the nearest bar, but my body did not listening. My legs kept me walking along the sidewalk towards the lights and my arms pushed the crowd out of the way, edging me closer to the sirens, the lights, and the crowd.

And the yellow Volkswagen.

Whoever had draped the white cloth over the body had

done a lousy job it. I could see a shock of blond, almost white hair lying flatly against the gray, concrete of the streets.

"He shot him! He shot him point blank and then laughed!"

Like before, someone held Toby's sister, who screamed, kicked, and pointed to the office standing in the middle of the scene.

"*Esta loca,*" I heard Pedro tell the officer next to him. "Stupid *gringo* came at me for no reason. *Tubo muchas copas.*" Then he scanned the crowd until he found me. Pedro would have kept the body lying on the street for hours, I think, waiting for me to show up. "You know how they all are," he added, "think they can take us all on."

He kept the eyes on me, smiled as my hands shook and my vision blurred. All the alcohol I'd paid for became lodged in my throat. I pushed my way out from the crowd I released the drinks into the street, hearing people laughing and making disgusted sounds. Breathing through my nose I stayed hunched over until I was sure I wouldn't throw up again.

The Santa Fe Bridge loomed large ahead of me, a hunch-backed creation that chained El Paso and Juarez together. From this distance I could make out the tiny strobes of lights that flickered as the line of cars inched up the bridge and towards the El Paso border

My eyes stayed fixed on those lights, dancing orbs that flickered in and out of existence. I focused on them and only them, knowing that if my eyes strayed, so would my mind.

Reaching the foot of the bridge, where Mexican soldiers stood with Ak-47s slung on their shoulders, where drivers patiently waited to declare 'American, sir', and where count-less of staggering teenagers made the walk back to their homes, I found the lights no longer helped.

So I hailed and cab and asked it to take me back to Club Kentucky. Where I would drink sit at the bar and drink their Margaritas like countless better men and women before me had and try not to think of Toby. Of Pedro. Of the city I found myself in.

YELLOW CAR PUNCH
Nigel Bird

Y'ever play **Yellow Car Punch**, Colin?" The rolled-up cuffs of Giles Yokobo's white shirt flapped as he casually shuffled a deck of cards and asked the question. "When you were little I mean?"

Colin couldn't speak to give his answer, the old snot-rag filling his mouth and the circles of duct tape that were keeping it there making sure no words were going to pass his lips. Instead he nodded hard, figuring that the more enthusiastically he joined in with the conversation the kinder they'd be.

"I used to love it," Giles went on, placing the deck on a bar stool that stood between them. In the dim light of the basement, his dark skin seemed to shine more than it did in the daylight. The muscles in his forearms bulged inside his skin like an obese woman's arse inside a pair of size twelve jeans. "Probably because I could hit the hardest. And I was taller than my brothers so I got to see the cars first. You like cars, don't you Colin?"

He did. It's what had led him to this pit in the first place.

He nodded again, harder this time. Felt warm beads of sweat falling from his face like he was out in the monsoon rain.

"So I thought we'd have a little game ourselves. Just you

and me." Giles rolled up his sleeves until they wouldn't go any further, picked up the cards and passed them over to the other man in the room. "Course we can't see the cars going by from down here, us not having any windows and all, so I'm going to do it a different way. My friend Danny here is going to turn the cards over. See a yellow car and you know what to do. Ready Danny?"

Colin found himself wondering about the pair of men who had dragged him out of the pub. Who was harder? If you were given a choice between taking a beating from Danny or Giles, it wouldn't be an easy decision to make.

Giles was enormous. Could crush a skull with his grip and knock a hole through a wall with just the one punch according to his rep. And, if the stories were to be believed, he was also a mean son-of-a-bitch. Thing about him was, he wasn't a natural. It was all gym work that had his body in shape. He was muscle bound and his arms were short, so Colin thought he might not have quite the zing that he might need in a fight. Sure, he was great if you needed someone to put on a show, but might not be so hot if it came down to fast action or tight spaces.

Danny was from another mould altogether. He was a giant, but everything about him seemed natural. His body swung loose and free when he moved, like a basketball pro mid-court. He had the ease of a real fighter and the experience of life on the street on his side.

In the end, Colin decided that he was about to take the beating from the lesser man.

"Ready?" Giles asked.

There was a nod in response and Danny turned over the card nice and slowly.

When Colin saw it was a pack of Top Trumps they were

playing with, he felt a strange glow of comfort. It took him back to when he was a boy and knew all the answers in every category of the packs he owned. Even better, it was a blue car. Or a maybe it was black. Whichever it was, there was nothing doing.

The next was red. The third green. Surely it was going to be amber next.

It wasn't.

There was a yellow Ford Mondeo in the picture. It made Giles happy and his smile revealed a set of the whitest teeth Colin had ever seen.

Colin tried to shout, but his tongue was too dry and his mouth too cramped to produce anything other than a muddled grunt.

Which meant Giles got in first. Took his time about it too, pausing between the words as if he was auditioning for the villain's part in a production at the Traverse. "Yellow... car... punch." He fiddled with his rings for a moment. Centred the gold sovs on his fingers and formed a fist.

He let fly.

Colin saw it as if it were in slow motion. The arm swung low and then came back in an upper-cut. Giles lowered his shoulder to get some weight behind it and Colin tensed as many muscles as he could still control.

The fist connected with Colin's jaw. Smacked his teeth together and they crunched like line-backers on third down. His head snapped backwards and there was a crick in his neck just before his skull collided with something hard. Tingles shot through his spine and sprinted down into his fingers and toes. His head seemed to fill with spots of light as if he were a cartoon character taking a fall.

That's when the pain kicked in. His jaw screamed out

to his brain, his gums were on fire and his skull felt broken.

"Maybe I just got lucky," Giles said. "You might do better next time."

The next time was worse. The punch came from the side and loosened a few of Colin's teeth.

"See," Giles said. "This is what you get when you borrow money you can't afford to pay back. So here's what we're going to do." The voice didn't sound quite right. It was as if Colin was hearing it through ears filled with cotton wool. "We're going to keep that Saab of yours, the one you've been cruising around town in. The one you've been impressing your friends with. And before you leave here, you're going to sign the papers to transfer the ownership."

When the words and their meaning filtered in, Colin did his best to process the information. He wanted to explain. To give them the story and make them understand. Times were tough for entrepreneurs just now. He'd had a few people let him down and a few horses finish out of the frame. Sure, he'd missed making a couple of payments to Uncle, but he'd be good for the money. He'd get it back to them. He just needed more time.

"But before we get you to sign, we're going to carry on with our game. You see Colin, you need to learn a little lesson and I'm going to make sure that I teach you very well indeed."

Danny turned over another card. A yellow Ferrari. Colin nodded his head. He wanted to sign the car over right there and then. He wanted to feel that quill in his hand and the scratch of the point on the paper, but all he got to feel was another hammer blow that connected with the tip of his nose and ended up somewhere in the middle of his dreams.

When he came to, he kept his eyes shut. Let his mind do an audit of his body. Everything was still there, it just wasn't all in the places and shapes he was used to.

The pain came from everywhere. His bones throbbed with the beating of his heart, but he could handle it.

Whatever he was lying on, it wasn't a mattress. There were hard corners poking his ribs. Sharp edges cutting into his skin. Solid objects pushing him into new shapes. He needed to shift to try and get comfortable.

His eyes opened to darkness. He let his hands wander like they were his drones checking out the terrain. When they got to his head, they pushed gently at his skull. It was soft. Cold. Was oozing some kind of slop. If it was his brains, he was a gonner.

He scooped some of the matter with his fingers. Brought them to his nose and sniffed.

It wasn't the scent he'd expected. There was none of the aroma of the butcher's shop on Leith Walk. Instead it was something he recognised. Made his mouth water. Took him a while to work it out. Egg Mayonnaise. Maybe a touch of onion in the mix.

Saliva pooled underneath his tongue. Collected until it overflowed. Something about the mess he was in made him want to chuck up and his throat closed tight. He needed to spit. To get rid of the liquid. Pushed himself up until his head hit something hard. He raised his arms and pressed against the ceiling of his cell.

As it lifted a fraction, a crack of light appeared. It hurt his retinas to look at it. He pushed harder until the darkness was defeated and he was free, standing in the middle of a skip at the back of Tesco. He rubbed his eyes, covered them in the Mayonnaise and swore quietly to himself.

Giles Yokobo was on a break. A fag break. Stood on the corner of the Mile and North Bridge taking in the passers-by. Eying up the girls and calling after the ones who took his fancy. Some of them looked back. A few wandered over to chat.

The guy had some kind of magic. Was able to give out his personal cards like it was everybody's birthday and someone had put him in charge.

Colin watched on from the other side of the road, hidden inside his hood and taking everything in with the patience of dispossessed.

Losing the car had been the last straw. Set his life tumbling with the force of an avalanche. Left him at the mercy of the wind and the rain. Had him hungry for revenge.

It was when the tall blond in the mini-skirt turned around to Yokobo's wolf-whistle that Colin decided to move. He wandered down the hill until the traffic cleared, then ran across to the other side, narrowly avoiding some white van that must have been late for an appointment. It sped by with the driver shouting something Polish out of the window and using the international language of the middle finger to make sure he'd been fully understood.

Another day, Colin might have chased the bastard. Waited until he got snagged at the lights. Dragged him out and taught him a lesson about Scottish manners. Sent him home to Warsaw with his tail between his legs and a shaggy-dog story about the day he was set upon by a gang of wild men with bare buttocks and blue paint on their faces.

But not today.

When he arrived at the other side of the street, he turned again and headed up the slope, hands deep in his pockets while he stared at the pavement. He pulled level with

Yokobo, stopped and leant into the wall.

The girl Yokobo was talking to was stunning. Thick lips and clear skin. A pair of perfectly formed tits hanging loose underneath the summer print of her dress. Clear blue eyes that shone and spoke of promise. If she wasn't Swedish, Gordon would never fill out a betting slip again as long as he lived. She babbled on about the castle and the Edinburgh Dungeon in an exotic accent that could have been anything while she puffed on her cigarette and blew smoke into the afternoon.

Yokobo seemed to sense he was onto a good thing. He stood straighter and puffed out his chest so that his muscles strained against his white shirt. Listened to the girl talk, smiled in the right places and even had the balls to pick off a piece of something from the front of her dress. Practically tweaked her nipple when he did it, too. Dirty bastard.

Things like this, people like Yokobo getting to sleep with hot women, were proof to Gordon that there was no God. Which was a shame, because if there was no god there was no devil. Without a devil, there could be no real justice.

Gordon shook himself back into the moment. Pulled his gaze from the woman's proud nipples and checked out the traffic.

Someone really should do something about the way the cars hurtled down towards the New Town. People would end up getting hurt if nothing changed.

There was a taxi—a blur of black. Three green cars followed, then a red. Another black and a couple of silver BMWs. Gordon bided his time.

Another taxi, then another. Two red cars. A white van. Red Volvo. Blue Beetle. Nothing doing.

Yokobo pulled out one of his cards from his back pocket.

Was handing it over when the moment came.

A car took off to beat the lights, its exhaust emitting a low rumble as it went.

Gordon shifted on his feet. Extended his arms. Felt Yokobo's ribs against his palms. Used the weight from his rooted leg to push and before he knew it the man had gone. Headfirst into the car and tumbling over the bonnet.

There was a screech of brakes, the crunch of glass splintering and a loud scream from the Scandinavian princess, but Gordon didn't turn to look. Instead, he tightened his hood, pushed his hands into his pockets and set off to escape the gathering crowd.

An old woman blocked his way. Put her hand up into his chest and stopped him in his tracks. She was tiny and frail. Had less hair than a doll that had been given a trim by a 5 year-old. Wore a heavy woollen jumper in spite of the heat. If it had been anyone younger, he'd have pushed her out of the way, but Gordon McCrae had been brought up better than that.

"What happened? Did you see it?" she asked.

He took his hands from his pockets. Re-enacted the smash. Made a fist with his right and slammed it into the stiff palm of his left. "Yellow car punch," he told her. "Yellow car punch."

The lady looked bemused. Stood on her tiptoes to try and get a better view.

Gordon nipped off down a side-street. Decided he'd nab a car to celebrate. Maybe drive over to Glasgow to see if the grass was any greener out west. Wondered about the make and model he might go for. Didn't care, as long as there was petrol in the tank and the colour fitted the occasion.

LOVE AT FIRST FIGHT

Angel Luis Colón

You fighting tonight?" Leroy's words come between bites of a sloppy spaghetti dinner. He lifts his shirt up to wipe his chin clean and the peep show's not worth the price of admission.

"Yeah, Aleksei said I had a match at 7:30." I look at the old spook house decorations around us. There's an old neon sign that's seen better days right above Leroy that says 'The Ghost Hole'. Behind 'Ghost' it says "Hell'—an old remnant from the 70's.

He doesn't look up from his dinner and jabs a sausage link thumb behind him. "Go wait with the other assholes. They got a movie on."

"Any idea what it is?"

"I look like the fucking TV guide?"

I ain't got it in me to argue, so I give him a shrug and walk to the back. There's a closet sized room with one of those old tube televisions with the wood paneling playing the second Die Hard in Spanish. Six ashen-faced, fallen out losers do their best to share an old, leather couch without touching legs.

I lean against the doorframe. "They get up to the part where William Sadler's doing the naked karate? That shit's ridiculous."

"Nah, they cut that shit out on regular teevee." The voice comes from the very end of couch farthest from me. I don't know the guy, but he looks about as broken as any one of us. Welcome to the club.

"Who's got the 7:30 fight?" I rub my eyes. There's a headache creeping up on me.

"That'll be me." Reggie, an overweight mess of a man whose only claim to fame was getting his jaw dislocated at a bar by Mike Tyson back in the eighties, raises a hand. We've fought before. He hits like an oatmeal stuffed doll.

"Sounds good."

The movie gets to the part where John McClane is betrayed by Major Grant, then the signal shits out and all we get is snow. I decide to talk a walk to the back of the place—get a look at tonight's crowd.

It's the usual Russian and Serbian riff raff, not too sure if they have a word for white trash in Eastern Europe, but this is pretty much it. Their fists have wads of twenties and fifties in their grip. They all group up beneath the skeleton of the old gravitron ride that was housed in this space. There's a weird maze of metal piping and rotted wood above us that's in a permanent state of 'about to fall'. I still can't help but jerk my head up every time I hear a noise that seems out of place. The smell this kind of environment produces—the sweat and the dirt and the old cash—the embodiment of desperation. Nobody here stinks worse of it than the boxers.

None of us fight for money—only drugs. I fight for my weekly dose of horse. The shame's worn off by now. All I know is that there's harder ways to score than taking a few hits to the face—especially from doughy never-beens like Reggie.

◉ ◉ ◉

It's near eleven when Aleksei shows up to "pay out". I'm nursing a mouse under my right eye—more my fault than Reggie's doing—I let him get a few clean jabs there. Didn't repeat that mistake for the rest of the match. We don't fight in rounds, the state of us dictates that we go at it until someone cries uncle or gets knocked the fuck out.

I had Reggie on the floor in seven minutes—a new personal best.

"Kevin." Aleksei is your typical, boisterous, overweight Russian stereotype. He doesn't smile much, and when he does, most folks find themselves preferring he stuck with a frown. What always stands out about the guy is the long braided ponytail running from his head down near his knees. Could never get my head around the hairstyle choice, but hey, strange Russian racketeers need to have their quirks.

"Kenneth," I correct him.

"Yeah, sure. Good fight, good fight." He lifts an old doctor's bag to his chin and almost crosses his eyes into the back of his head to see. "What do you get?"

"Uh, horse…" I look around the room rather than watch him. My knuckles still burn from the fight. Those of us lucky to find gloves that fit use them. "You ever think about seeing an eye doctor, Aleksei?"

"No, why?" He keeps burrowing into the bag. "Ah, yes… here we go." Aleksei fishes a small baggie from the doctor's bag and tosses it over. "That should be enough for the next week. Unless you're one of *those* kinds of junkies."

"Yeah, thanks. See you next week." I pocket the heroin. It's shit quality, but beggars can't be choosers. I turn to get the hell out of this place and nearly walk into someone behind me.

He places a firm hand on my chest. "Easy." His brogue is thick Irish cream.

I look up expecting another gray-faced loser and instead I get the weirdest looking son of a bitch I've ever seen. He's about my height, but he's rocking one of those greaser hair-cuts that goes up about seven inches—must be enough gel in there to clog up the Hudson. His clothes—leather head to toe, a faded Bauhaus tee under his jacket and a belt buckle the size of a dinner plate—make him look like a low rent Happy Days extra. On the buckle, a young Elvis flashes the grin that made millions of panties drop.

"My mistake, sorry." I walk by and keep eyes on him. On the back of his jacket is one of those old illustrations of a black panther—the kind you'd see on a Vietnam vet's arm. Above the cat reads 'Blacky Jaguar' in gold stitching.

He turns and meets my gaze. "We good?"

"Uh, yeah, sorry. Just thought you looked familiar is all."

"Sure." He makes a motion with his hand, waving me away. "Got business with the man in charge, have a goodnight."

I don't wish it back, just beat feet the fuck out of there and wonder to myself, just what the hell is a Blacky Jaguar?

"It's his name." Leroy's sucking down on an ungodly amount of hot wings tonight.

"Bullshit. Who the fuck has a name like that?"

"Blacky Jaguar does." He leans in. "Listen, I'd keep a

clean nose about that dude. One of my buddies from the Bronx says he cleared out a chop shop in Hunts Point with a sawed-off full of rock salt and his boots. Off the boat mick maniac is what he is."

"For real? What is he doing here?"

Leroy shrugs. "No clue, all I know is he wants to fight."

"A bunch of junkies? For what?"

"No clue. He and Aleksei got some kind of weird deal going. The guy says he needs practice bashing in heads."

"That's fucking bizarre." I scratch my forearm and wince.

"Yeah, well, try not to find yourself on the business end of his fists. He broke Reggie's jaw the other night with one punch."

"Fuck. Is he here tonight?"

"Who? Reggie? That guy's done for the next few weeks."

"Fuck Reggie, I meant Blacky."

Leroy's brows rise up. "You actually want him to be here?" He scans a dirty piece of notebook paper next to him. "He ain't on the list, but I don't think he's scheduled talent like the rest of you assholes."

⊙ ⊙ ⊙

It's another month before I see Blacky again. He strolls into the waiting room and plants himself on the couch next to me with a Cheshire grin. You'd think he fucking owned the place.

"How we doing, then? Kenneth, right?" He lights a joint and looks right into me.

"Yeah. I'm doing okay. Better than that poor bastard you dismantled tonight, for sure." Something tells me Blacky's not interested in Jim's shattered left orbital. "How are you?"

"I'm doing okay, thanks. More than okay. Seen you fight. Won your last, what, six matches?" He talks in a strange mile-a-minute staccato. Doesn't work with the brogue—easy to miss words. Very unsettling.

I nod. "Not much competition."

"Suppose so…still…" He smirks and exhales a thick, strong cloud right at me. "…six less arseholes who can claim one on you." He leans in closer to me. "You fought professional level?"

"Years ago."

"Oh yeah? Where at?"

I scratch the back of my head and wonder where the hell Aleksei is with my payment. "I did the MMA thing for a while."

"Why'd yah stop? What happened?"

"Broke my leg during a fight."

"So? You can walk—can clearly still fight."

"Yeah, I'm good now, just a piece of metal and few screws in there. Kinda got hooked on the meds, though."

"Ah, there's the rub. That's why you're locked in this fucking death trap with the rest of the junkies." Blacky pulls the joint from his lips and offers it to me. "I stick with weed or Bushmills. Either do the job, together is cake and eating it. How long you've been using?"

"Less than a year—easier than convincing my doctor to let me get the pills again." I take the offered spliff. "I hear you're fighting just to fight?"

That grin comes back. "Yep. Gotta keep the blood boiling. Figure a more…coordinated event keeps me from having to stir the pot out on the streets."

"Or you could join a boxing gym." I hand the joint back.

My head's already spinning.

He laughs and nods. "That's a good point." Another hit of the joint. Dry cough. "Got another question for you while we're gabbing."

"What's that?"

"You seem uncomfortable. Why?"

"You mean right now?"

"In general. Seem to have a head on your shoulders, but sure, you're ready to jump straight from your skin."

I avert my eyes from gaze. "Well, this isn't the ideal Saturday night. To be honest, you're throwing me off a little too."

"How so?"

"Can't size you up. Doesn't make much sense that you come wandering into this bullshit for shits and giggles."

"Is it supposed to be fucking serious?" He comes off more amused than mad.

"I guess not."

"It's a good time is all. *You* need to lighten up. See, your problem…" Blacky launches into a crouch like a nightmare Peter Pan, the joint bobbing in rhythm to his words. "… your problem is the fucking junk." He fishes into his front pocket and pulls a wad of bills out. "This here? The shit you put into your veins? The fucking feeling I get when bone cracks under knuckle? It's fucking fleeting." The money's tossed onto my lap. A few hundred dollar bills—crisp and clean.

"So I should kick the habit? Go back to what, exactly?"

He's back on his ass as fast as he was up. Gives me a shrug. "Whatever the fuck yah want. Ain't got time to piddle about killing yourself if you're already fucking dying." Blacky cracks the knuckles of his left hand. "You know what you need? A proper ass-kicking." He jabs a thin, tattooed finger my way. "You and me, me and you—next week."

I laugh. He doesn't. "That a serious suggestion?"

"Very."

"I'm not sure what kind of match that would be. You're faster than me by fucking leaps and bounds. Stronger too."

"Bullshit. You're a wrestler; I can see that clear as day. Striking is good too. You have a shot."

"I'm not sure. Can't afford any new lasting injuries."

"Get off it, yah pansy bollocks. We meet next week. Bring your best god damn dress if you're gonna cry about it." He stands. "One condition." Blacky reaches down and fetches the money I'd ignored on my lap. He leaves two hundred dollar bills behind. "Buy a few ounces a'weed. No horse. You fight me at less than a hundred percent, I'll fuckin' kill yah. Understood?" He flicks the roach of his joint towards the corner of the room. Then he's up and out. No goodbye, no chance for my rebuttal.

I wait a little while for Aleksei to show up, but all I get is Leroy shoving my ass out into the night.

"Bring it up next week," he says and gives me one last push out the back door of the Ghost Hole.

I light a cigarette and have a long, hard think about what kind of shit I'm in.

I show up the next week feeling like I've been sleeping under the tire of an SUV. Three hours—it took me three fucking hours just to get out of bed. It's amazing how man can ignore his withdrawal symptoms when a psychotic greaser mick's holding the proverbial gun to his head. The money Blacky gave me is still in my wallet—untouched. Didn't bother to smoke up or drink. Too worried I'd backslide.

Aleksei's fronting the Ghost Hole. "Where's Leroy?" I ask, trying to ignore the daggers in my eyes and guts.

He shrugs. "Your fight starts in half an hour. Get ready."

I head to the common area and gear up. The crowd's thick tonight, but I'm the only fighter here. My head may not be clear, but I ain't dumb enough to ignore something's not quite right. I find a pair of decent gloves and I get a cold chill straight down my spine that's got nothing to do with the lack of dope.

Blacky walks into the room on cue. "Look at the state of you." He slaps my back—hard. "Ready?"

He's wearing a pair of black trunks with a shamrock on the ass. Without a shirt, I catch an eyeful of varied tattoos—some professional, others that faded prison grey. There's an angel and a devil perched on opposite ends of his collarbone. Between them is a sacred heart of Jesus in the death grip of a brunette bombshell spread across his torso.

Blacky reaches a hand out and knocks on my forehead. "You on the fucking planet?"

I back up. "Oh, yeah, sorry…rough week."

"You'll be fine." He goes to his jacket hung on the wall and fishes out a hand rolled smoke. It's lit in no time and he's flashing that Cheshire grin. "We're the only fight tonight, so make it special."

"Why's that?"

"Cuz I said so."

"Didn't realize you were in with Aleksei like that."

He laughs and smoke sputters out of him. "That pinko piece of shit? No communist ever tell me what to do."

"Yet I'm about to throw punches with you."

"Well, Kenny, my lad—at least you admit to your faults." Back into his jacket pocket. "Want a smoke?"

"Sure." I take a cigarette and a light. My first all week. My head goes for a long swim on the first pull. "So, if let's say this all gets weird—no hard feelings, right?"

"What do you mean?"

"If I actually win—it's not going to be a problem, is it?"

Blacky walks in close and leans his head forward. "You go in there and you fight me like an enemy, like yah just saw me with your own mum bent over a barrel—that understood?"

I nod.

He slaps my chest with a smile. "After all's said and done—Bushmills and a few lagers—on me."

"If I'm conscious, absolutely."

"Atta boy." He saunters out of the room. Blows smoke straight up. "You're gonna do fantastic." I can hear him whistle a tune down the hall.

That cigarette gets smoked down to a pinprick cherry nub that burns the fingertips of my thumb and index finger. The pain doesn't register, I'm so worried. Out in the "ring", Aleksei is saying something about Blacky. I hear my name; swallow the rock that was sitting on my tongue and head on out for my beating.

None of my other fights were like this. My head can't seem to collect any information around me. The smells, the lights, the screams from the crowd—nothing comes through.

Blacky's egging everyone on, lifting his arms up and down with a cigarette still clenched between his lips. For the first time I notice how god damned smug he is. I bob there like a kid's tub toy—my hands up, but unwilling to do anything.

Blacky walks over and stretches both arms out. "First shot's free."

I take the offer, a hard right hook to the sweet spot on his jaw. His head snaps to my left and the cigarette goes flying into the crowd. I spot it hitting one of the old timers and smile. For the first time all week, my thinking gets clear.

The punch only gets Blacky's attention. He smiles and lifts his hands up. "Fucking knew you were a good match."

Then he starts playing for real. He's fast—fucking crazy fast. Dances around me like a ferret and peppers jabs to my head. He mixes it up with a few shots to the body—taking the wind out of me. I'm able to take a few of the hits on my forearms, but blocking punches still hurts like hell. Before long my arms feel like they're on fire and filled with concrete. My hand speed gets sluggish and a few of those shots really start chipping away at me. I decide to pull back a little—try to get space—but it's a wasted effort. There's a mad gleam in Blacky's eyes. He loves this shit.

"Come on." He closes the gap between us and starts alternating punches to my ribs.

I'm in agony by the time I push him away and there's a part of me wishes that I stayed in bed—dealt with the stomach cramps and the inevitable bullet to the head. My lungs burn, sounds are garbled as if my head's in a fish tank. Still, I keep on my feet and when I see a small pause—that little window—I start punching back. Blacky's response is an increase in enthusiasm—like playing with a pit bull.

He side steps right and steps forward on his left

foot—looking to throw a haymaker. I spot it at the last moment and crouch, lean in, catch the punch with the top of my left arm as I lift it up, and put my all into a hard, right hook.

I strike gold.

Blacky's eyes lose their spark and wobble in a way that reminds me of one of those puppets you saw on children's TV. He drops like a wet sack of rocks. I go cold, but the room's probably a thousand degrees between the rush of bodies that press in. There's no way to make out what's being said, but plenty of people sound upset. Guess I wasn't the odds on favorite. A big, black hand grabs me by the arm—it's Leroy—and I'm dragged to the back. I see Aleksei collect Blacky and follow us.

We get to the cramped back room and Leroy sits me on a folding chair while Blacky gets the comfort of the couch. That last punch got the side of his swelling like a balloon.

"Time to collect." Aleksei's voice is monotone. His eyes are dark.

"You good, champ?" Leroy smirks in my direction. "Hell of a punch."

I nod. "Got a smoke?"

"Yeah." He hands me a Newport.

I hate menthol, but whatever. Leroy lights the cigarette and I puff away. "He okay?"

"He'll live." Leroy gets three beers from a tiny fridge in the corner of the room. He tosses one my way. "Just chill out, drink up—we got this."

"I don't understand."

I can hear Aleksei arguing back in the fighting pit. There are a few barks back and forth and it goes quiet. I hear the door open and shut—a sequence of locks being latched—then Aleksei walks back into the common room with his doctor's bag.

He throws the bag at Leroy's feet and follows up with a thick, yellow wad of phlegm. "There you go—*zhri govno i zdohni!*"

Leroy smiles like a god damn jack-o-lantern. "That all of it?"

"Yes."

"Fantastic." He shoves one of his bear paw hands into his jacket and out comes a Beretta. He pegs Aleksei twice in the chest and once in the head. His ponytail whips in the air and hits the ground after his body.

I nearly dive for cover. Stupid call—nowhere to go.

Leroy turns to me and slips the gun back where it came. "Easy, ain't got no beef with you."

"Beef?" Blacky interrupts. The click of a beer can tab follows. "Fuck's sake. We owe the man our everlasting gratitude, yah daft black bear. He just won us a very, very nice pot." The swelling makes it looks like he's winking. He tries to flash that grin, but only half of it shows up.

◉ ◉ ◉

"So this was all a scam?" I can't decide if I should be pissed or grateful. We're standing outside, chain smoking more of Leroy's smokes and finishing off a six pack of Molsen. Leroy's busy dousing the outside walls of the Ghost Hole with gasoline.

"That's the sum of it." Blacky exhales and teeters back and forth on the ball of his feet. "You did a right job scrambling my fucking head—though." He cackles.

"That's only because you let me."

He shrugs. "Po-tay-toe, po-tah-toe."

"That's not how that works…listen, what kind of shit are we in? What happens if Aleksei's people find out?"

"Fuck his people." Blacky tosses a butt towards the building. Frowns when a fire doesn't start. "Leroy—*all* of the fucking building." He mimes a movement that supposed to be interpreted as 'dousing the whole place' but it's more of a dance. "Kenny, listen. I got me places to duck out in the Bronx and Yonkers."

"What about me?"

"You'll be in Hartsdale."

"What the fuck is up there?"

Blacky places a hand on my shoulder and pulls a white card out of his jeans pocket. "Drug rehab center. Decent place—have a few friends that swear by it." He slips the card into my hand. On the back are three phone numbers scrawled in green ink. "Those are the places to reach me."

"What the fuck makes you think I'd call you after this shit?"

"Three reasons." Black lights another smoke. "One: I got yer money—twenty five large. Two: I got work opportunities for a man can fight and keep his fucking mouth shut. Three…" He grabs me by the back of the head and kisses me hard and angry. The way a teenager that's seen too many movies would. He pulls back with a snarl. "Seen the way you look at me."

I back up. "I don't climb that tree, Blacky." I notice the air around us has started to glow orange.

"Whatever helps you sleep at night." He exhales a stream of smoke. "Leroy will get you to your apartment and over to the center."

"Tonight?"

"Tonight."

"What about you?"

He shrugs and turns. "Man's business is never done." I watch him walk away, my eyes locked on the ridiculous black cat on his jacket. It fades into the ink ahead of me.

Leroy bumps into me with a smile. "Ready to go?" I can smell the gasoline on his hands. Stings my nose.

I look down at the card. "Yeah...I'm ready."

TRAPS
Owen Laukkanen

You find a lot of funny things in your traps when you're trying to catch prawns. Slippery cod and slime eels, ratfish with their oilslick eyes and barbed tails, spiky rockfish with their swim bladders hanging out of their mouths, ruined by the two-hundred foot rise from the ocean floor.

Octopus, too—big, angry thirty pounders, grappling with their tentacles for any way to escape. They eat the prawns in the traps and leave nothing but skeletons, twist the caps off the bait jars and eat the bait, too. They're smart buggers; they'll run through a whole string of traps, clean you out. The deckhands have a running contest, who can kill and clean the biggest octo with his bare hands the fastest.

You get starfish, too, orange and yellow and purple, big floppy sun stars and spindly, wiry things, attracted by the scent of the bait in the water. You find them wrapped around the bait jar, sucking out the fish oil, ten or fifteen sometimes to a trap.

They're mostly after the bait, those starfish. They move too slow to catch any live prey. But once in a while, the odd prawn will get caught in the mesh of the trap, halfway in and halfway out, wedged in there tight and unable to escape. And once in a while, a starfish will take notice.

The way Grady Welsh figures, it must be a hell of a slow

death for the prawn, watching that starfish inching across the ocean floor, climbing the wall of the trap, unable to do anything but sit and wait and pray for a miracle. Maybe pray for that starfish to hurry up, for death to come quick, for the waiting to end.

You find a lot of funny things in your traps, Grady's come to learn. Sometimes, you'll even find a body, but not often.

Mostly it's just starfish and stupid, doomed prawns.

⊙ ⊙ ⊙

Grady Welsh has been plotting his revenge on Kevin Autran since the day Shawna left him, five years ago, jumped off the *Tarnation*, Grady's forty-two footer, and crossed the dock to Kevin on the *Jackson 5*. Packed up her sea bag, said she'd finally had enough losing, said she was throwing her lot in with a winner. As if Kevin Autran was any kind of a prize.

It's hard enough losing a woman without having to see her on the water every day of the fishing season. Without running into her on the docks, packing Kevin's brand-new Dodge dually with groceries and gear, bumping into her and Kevin coming out of *Spinnaker's*, the fisherman's bar in Tofino, when you're trying to kick off a decent drunk. It's hard enough to lose a woman without having to see her every day, arms wrapped around some asshole, without having to ignore his big, stupid grin every time you come into harbor, without running into the *Jackson 5* on the grounds and knowing Shawna's aboard, cooking her trademark chili, humming to herself as she works in the galley. Knowing she's warming Kevin's bunk when they anchor up for the night.

Grady likes to think Shawna's leaving was the tipping point in the long losing streak that his life's become, but in truth, he and the *Tarnation* were on the slide well before the separation. The salmon stopped running, that was the first thing, back twenty or thirty years ago, ended the gold rush and turned the fishermen from lottery winners to *personas non grata* up and down the coast. Grady sold his license, got into prawns, made it stick for a while. Figured as long as he had Shawna, he was doing all right.

But things kept going wrong. Shawna wanted a baby; Grady figured, why not? Try as they might, though—and they tried—no kid appeared. The doctors blamed it on Grady, said he wasn't packing enough heat. Shawna got distant a little bit, withdrawn, and Grady couldn't fix it. Knew Shawna had her heart set on a family someday, a little girl. Knew she had to blame him a little for dashing her dreams.

The prawns stopped running, too, about the same time. Not a fleet-wide problem, mind you, just Grady. Just the *Tarnation*. Grady figured he was just distracted by the problems with Shawna, figured he needed to readjust his focus, maybe swap out to a new type of bait. But the bait wouldn't cut it, and the prawns just wouldn't show. The *Tarnation* couldn't make pay.

It was around that time that Shawna stopped coming out for the fishing season. Started staying home over the spring and summer months, taking classes at the local community college. Painting. Grady would come home at the end of the season, find the baby's bedroom entirely redecorated, elaborate murals painted on the walls—oceanscapes, whales and dolphins and mermaids and octopus. Starfish.

Try as he might, there was no bringing her back. "It's

so stressful," she'd tell Grady. "The pace and the pressure, trying to cram a year's paycheck into a few months of work. It's exhausting, Grady. I can't do it."

So Grady hired a couple deckhands, called home every night. Ate canned ravioli and slept alone in his bunk. And still couldn't catch any prawns.

◉ ◉ ◉

The Jackson 5 is tied up at the little government wharf in Hot Springs Cove when Grady makes the turn around the point in the *Tarnation*. No other boats in the bay, no floatplanes, nobody on the beach, not this late in the day. The tourists all motor back to Tofino in their speedboats by five or six; only the fishermen and the natives come around after that. Today, it looks like Kevin and Shawna have the springs to themselves.

No life on the *Jackson 5*, not that Grady can see through the binoculars. Nobody puttering around on the back deck, no shadows moving in the wheelhouse. Kevin and Shawna must be already at the springs. Just like Grady planned it.

Grady brings the *Tarnation* into shore, maneuvers up to the dock with the midships controls, steps out over the gunwale and ties the spring line to the wharf. Walks up the dock and grabs the bowline, does the same. The season's over and the deckhands are gone, paid off and put on a bus already, so Grady's working solo. Not that he needs any help today, anyway.

When the *Tarnation* is secured, Grady climbs back aboard and ducks into the wheelhouse, down into the fo'c'sle and shuts off the main engine. The silence is sudden; his ears ring. He's been living with the main's constant drone for three months now.

Grady climbs back out of the fo'c'sle. Stands at the wheel for a moment, staring out through the wheelhouse windows at the dock, the beach, the trail through the rainforest that starts the two-mile boardwalk to the hot springs. The evening is calm and very still, very peaceful.

Grady turns from the wheel. Goes into the galley, finds the 12-gauge he keeps in a locker behind the galley settee, a box of shells beside it. Loads the shotgun and stuffs the rest of the shells in his pockets. Then he ducks out of the wheelhouse again and onto the dock. Starts up toward shore and onto the trail.

◎ ◎ ◎

Shawna started coming back during the season again, after a few years staying home. Came out for a weekend or two at first, drove up in Grady's beat-up old F-150 and parked it at the end of the nearest logging road to the fishing grounds, spent a couple days cooking hot meals for the crew and working on her tan. The deckhands were taking up most of the bunk space, so there wasn't much opportunity for conjugal relations, but Grady figured this renewed interest was a good sign, anyway.

"I don't know," she'd tell Grady, when he asked her. "I just realized I kind of missed it out here, is all."

It wasn't until later, much later, that Grady realized she was timing her visits to when the *Jackson 5* was in the area, too. That she'd run into Kevin Autran in the grocery store in the offseason, a little meet-cute in the produce aisle. That they'd gone for coffee afterward—

"Traffic," she told Grady, when she showed up an hour late, "was a nightmare."

—and kept going for coffee, innocent little meetings now and then, just friends. It wasn't until later that Grady realized she was falling for the rival skipper. And by then, it was too late, much too late.

◉ ◉ ◉

Grady's footsteps resonate through the rainforest as he walks the boardwalk. The boards are engraved with the names of the boats who've stopped here, yachts and sailboats mostly. The *Tarnation*'s on here somewhere; carved with Grady's penknife and Shawna's steady hand. It's years old by now, though; so long that Grady's forgotten where to find it.

In one part of the trail, some lovelost sucker has started writing out a love poem:

And so I break my anchor chain
Spent thirty years, tho not in vain
Two hearts were one, but now undone
'Twere mine to do, I would again

She asks if

Whoever the poet is, he's lost interest or resolve three words into the second stanza. Or maybe he just found a better way of dealing with his unhappiness.

◉ ◉ ◉

This visit to the hot springs, this end of season bath, it's been a tradition for Kevin and Shawna ever since Shawna moved across the dock to the *Jackson 5*. Grady knows this, because he's been watching Kevin, watching Shawna, tracking their moves since Shawna crossed the dock. He knows they come here, every year, as soon as the season closes.

He knows because he did the same with Shawna, too, when she was aboard the *Tarnation*.

You don't get much chance for relaxation over the course of a season on the water. The hours are long and the work is steady. There's not much fresh water for showers onboard the boat. These hot springs, natural bathing pools many miles from civilization, make for a kind of finality. Step inside this steaming water and wash the work right off you, the stress, the exhaustion. Come in dirty and fatigued, come out refreshed.

In the good old days, Grady and Shawna would leave their clothes at the top of the rocks, bring their towels down to the edge of the tide pools. They'd take turns soaping up in the scalding waterfall that dropped down from the forest, gasping in the heat and laughing at each others' lobster-red bodies. Then they'd cool off in the pools themselves, nestled into the rocks and fed by tidewater and spring water in measure, working their way up from the tide line to the hottest pools again.

Invariably, they would make love, either amid the hot pools or back at the boat. It was a different kind of lovemaking than during the season, more relaxed and gentle than the exhausted perfunctory urgency of the season, when the alarm clock ticked down in the wheelhouse above, and the pillows and bedding in the bunks held as much appeal as the lover beside you.

Grady wonders if Shawna and Kevin will be making love in the hot baths when he finds them. He wonders if they share all of the same rituals. He listens to his footsteps as they pound along the boardwalk, a steady, ominous percussion, and he wonders if Shawna and Kevin can hear them.

He wonders if they're scared. If they can sense his approach, like the prawn feels the starfish coming.

◉ ◉ ◉

The sun is almost set when Grady nears the hot springs. The trail turns back toward the shore again, opens up to the beach, and the air becomes infused with the sulfury smell of the springs. Grady can hear the water through the trees, seeping up from underground and flowing down toward the shore, dropping over the waterfall and into the pools below.

The government has improved the springs since Grady first came here with Shawna; there's a changing area now, and railings to guard against lawsuits. There are signs asking bathers to please keep their swimsuits on.

Grady slows as he reaches the end of the trail. Quiets his footsteps, cradles the shotgun. It's large and unwieldy in his hands, unfamiliar, a holdover from the days he fished salmon, when seals and big, greedy sea lions would raid the ends of his lines. He's kept the shotgun on the boat since Shawna left him, waiting for his opportunity.

Grady can hear voices as he steps out of the forest. Blissful, sleepy voices. Muted laughter. He crosses the footbridge over the waterfall and reaches the changing station. Peers down through the rocks at the bathing pools below.

He can see them, Shawna and Kevin both. They've disregarded the posted signs; they're both naked, Shawna's long, black hair a striking contrast to her pale skin, Kevin a bulbous, hairy slug of a man, his ample pelt of hair a silvery grey, his belly thick and well-fed. They're lying side by side in a pool below the tide line, a cooler pool fed mostly by ocean water. They're holding hands. Shawna's eyes are closed. They don't see Grady.

Grady's heart pounds at the sight of them. His palms sweat. He's been planning this forever, for so long. In his mind, they hear him coming through the forest, hear his footsteps. They huddle close together and await their fate, helpless. In Grady's mind, they're terrified.

They'll still be terrified, Grady thinks. *Just give them time.*

He picks his way down the rocks, as stealthily as he can. Kicks up a patch of loose gravel just as he reaches the bottom, about ten or so feet from where Shawna and Kevin are bathing. Shawna opens her eyes. Sees Grady and the shotgun, and those eyes go wide.

"Grady," she says. "What in the hell?"

Grady swings the shotgun around to cover Shawna. To cover Kevin. They're close enough together, he can handle them both. "Hello, Shawna," he says. "Hello, Kevin."

Kevin's halfway out of the pool by now, water streaming down from his chest, his stomach. His eyes are dark and furious. He doesn't look scared. He looks angry.

"You followed us here," he says. "That's what you did, is it, Grady? You have something to say to us, pal?"

Grady doesn't reply. He swings the shotgun back and forth between Kevin and Shawna. Making sure they know they're both covered. Making sure they know it's just a matter of time.

Shawna doesn't seem scared, either. She seemed startled, sure, but now the surprise is fading. Now, she seems mostly sad.

"What are you doing here, Grady?" she says again. "What is this all about?"

Grady keeps the gun on Kevin. Keeps him in the pool. Keeps him from doing anything heroic.

"This was our place," he tells them. "This was our ritual, hot springs at the end of the season. This was something we did together, the two of us. This was a sacred place."

Kevin laughs. "Oh, come on," he says. "You're not still nursing the same old wounds, are you, Grady? It's been five years, man. Grow up. Move on."

"Move on," Grady says. He can feel his pulse racing. His voice is nervous, shaky. This is actually happening. "It sounds easy, doesn't it, Kevin. Just grow up and move on. To what, exactly? What do you suggest?"

He gestures around the hot pools, the rocky shoreline. Shawna.

"This is all I have in the world," he tells Kevin. "*She's* all I have. And you stole her from me."

Shawna shakes her head. "He didn't steal me," she says. "You pushed me away. Whatever problems we had together, they were ours, Grady. Kevin had nothing to do with us."

"He stole you," Grady says. "And now he's going to pay for it. Now you're both going to pay. Get out of the water."

"And what?" Kevin says. "What are you going to do? Are you going to kill us, Grady? Just shoot us right here?"

Grady shrugs. Gestures out over the shoreline, the water. "Funny thing about that stretch of water," he says. "That swell coming in from Japan's pretty hairy sometimes, you want to come out around the point and make the turn down the coast. Be pretty easy to get caught in the trough, fall overboard. Maybe your girlfriend falls overboard too, trying to save you."

"You'll never get away with it," Kevin says. "You can't just fake an accident like that. Someone will figure it out."

"You're still rigged for salmon, aren't you, Kevin?" Grady says. "I saw a handful of lead cannonballs on the stern of your boat. Tie a couple to your legs, they'll never find the bodies. I row your dinghy back to shore and the boat just drifts away, let the Coast Guard try and figure out what exactly went wrong. Way I see it, it'll work."

Kevin opens his mouth to argue. Closes it again without coming up with anything. Beside him, Shawna's just staring at Grady. Just looking at him like the first grade teacher whose star student just pissed his pants.

Grady levels the shotgun at them again. "Or maybe I just shoot you both right here," he says. "Get on out of that pool."

He's already running through the whole scheme in his head. Figuring out how he's going to corral Shawna and Kevin back to the *Jackson 5*, keep them on the boardwalk without anyone doing anything crazy. How he's going to keep them secured while he's sailing out to the point, how he'll tie a couple lead cannonballs around Kevin's legs first, push him overboard. Make him jump. Make Shawna watch, and then deal with her next. He's wishing he'd remembered to bring rope.

He's thinking about all of these things as Kevin steps out of the pool, hairy and flabby and well fed, the body of a highliner grown used to steak dinners in the offseason. Kevin reaches for his towel. Grady waves him off.

"Just stand there," he tells him. "Drip dry."

Then Shawna steps out of the pool, and Grady forgets about Kevin.

At first, he thinks she's simply gained a little weight. Thinks it's kind of fitting, her tying up with Kevin, falling into his lifestyle, getting fat in her old age. Thinks maybe bunking with a shitty fisherman did her good, kept her lean.

But it's not overeating and laziness that's creating that bulge around her belly, Grady realizes. She's pregnant.

She's pregnant.

Without conscious effort, Grady flashes back to the endless doctor's appointments, the scheduling, the fertility tests. The murals in the baby's bedroom when he'd come home from another season, all those intricate oceanscapes with no baby to enjoy them. With no baby on the way, ever.

And now this. With Kevin.

"You," he says, his voice faltering. "With him…"

Shawna colors a little. "Yeah," she says, and her hands slip down reflexively to her stomach. "We haven't told anyone yet. We were waiting until after the season."

Grady stares at her. Doesn't say anything, his mind still racing. Trying to parse this big reveal. Of all the information to overlook, this.

He doesn't realize he's lowered the shotgun until Kevin makes his move. Catches it in his peripheral vision, a big naked blur. Grady spins, raises the shotgun and fires in one motion. Nails Kevin somewhere, hard enough to send the bastard toppling backward, but he can't see where, because as soon as he pulls the trigger, Shawna's on him.

She jumps across the pool at him, takes advantage of his distraction, knocks the shotgun sideways and tackles him to the ground. Grady hits the rocks hard, bashes his head on an edge or something, sees stars. Doesn't have time to focus on them, though, because Shawna's on top of him, beating at him, clawing and punching, and it's all Grady can do to keep her from gouging his eyes out.

He gets his bearings. Shoves Shawna off of him, sends her sprawling back. Struggles to his feet, feels something warm and wet oozing from the back of his head. Ignores it and grapples around for the shotgun.

It's lying a four or five feet away. Too far. Grady picks up a rock instead, turns back to where Shawna is still on the ground, bent over a ledge, gasping for breath. Grady staggers toward her, raises the rock, about to put a braining to her, her and that baby, too, Kevin's baby, and that's when Kevin reappears out of nowhere, stumbling, bleeding from his shoulder and chest, his skin a ragged patchwork. He's clutching the shotgun with his uninjured arm, leveling it at Grady, but Grady doesn't notice it—doesn't notice Kevin at all—until Kevin pulls the trigger and the shotgun kicks and fires, sending a lot of buckshot into Grady and knocking him reeling downward on a collision course with more rock, more jagged outcroppings, and he hits those and goes ricocheting off again, loses his footing and falls, tumbling, into the hot pool.

And that's about the time Grady loses consciousness.

It's near dark when Grady wakes up again. He can hear an engine running somewhere, somewhere far in the distance. He's half submerged in water, and as he opens his eyes, groggy, he remembers he's in the little pool, the same pool as Kevin and Shawna, close to the shoreline. Shawna and

Kevin are nowhere around.

Grady blinks a couple of times. Tries to shake his head clear, can't do it. Tries to lift himself from the pool and can't do that, either. Can't get his limbs to work, his muscles. His head, even.

He remembers the shotgun blast, Kevin's Hail Mary, the sudden fire in his back. Remembers bouncing off more rocks on the way into the pool. Remembers hitting the pool, more pain—his upper back, his head, his neck. Remembers passing out.

Now he's awake. Now he can't move.

The engine noise in the distance is getting louder. The way Grady has fallen, he's facing out to the shoreline, the ocean beyond. So he can see when the source of the noise comes into sight.

It's the *Jackson 5*, sailing away from the cove. Shawna and Kevin aboard. As Grady watches, the boat motors past the hot springs, doesn't slow down. Reaches the point and executes the turn perfectly, doesn't even roll in the swell. Then it's gone, and the noise of its engine starts to diminish again, and Grady's alone in the forest.

The tide's coming in. That's what Grady notices next. The pools at the hot springs are fed by spring water and tidewater in measure, the pools closest to the shoreline the coolest. Grady's pool is close to the shoreline. He can already feel the cold ocean water seeping in as the tide rises, mixing with the hot spring water and cooling the pool. Soon, the tide will overwhelm the spring water. Soon the pool itself will be submerged.

Grady struggles to move as the chilly water seeps into the pool. Pleads with his muscles to obey his mind. Strains with every ounce of willpower he can dredge up to get up, get out of that pool, get above the tide line to safety.

He can't do it. That shotgun blast must have paralyzed him, the blast or the fall on the rocks, doesn't really matter which; all he can do is lie there, watch the tide inch toward him. Listen to the *Jackson 5*'s engine disappear in the distance.

All he can do is wait and watch the water come for him, wait and struggle to move and fail and struggle some more as the icy water overtakes him, fills the hot pool until there's no more warmth left in the water and no fight left in his exhausted body.

And still the tide rises, slow and inexorable, and Grady watches it come, feels the cold inch its way to his throat, his chin, his pursed-tight lips. Grady watches, and as the last light of day slips away, he's praying not for salvation, but for the tide to rise faster, for that final moment to come along quick.

DOWN THE RICKETY STAIRS

Alan Orloff

I **flipped a light switch** at the top of the staircase and peered down into the basement. I'd been putting it off for months, but Sylvia's nagging had finally worn me down, her pleas all variations on a theme. "Frankie, you've got to clean it out before we move on. Wouldn't be right to leave all that junk for some stranger to deal with. Them's our memories, after all, not nobody else's."

I didn't care much about some stranger, but I hated when Sylvia got mad at me.

I lumbered down the rickety wooden stairs, favoring my balky right knee, not as spry at seventy as I was at seventeen, although I was pretty sure I could still knock some heads, if it came to that. Some skills stayed with you forever: chugging beer, blowing smoke rings, knocking heads.

Lately, the past five years or so, I'd only ventured into the basement to store more crap, my claustrophobia becoming more pronounced. I hadn't taken any time to nose around, go through my keepsakes. Didn't have the energy. Didn't have the desire, either.

No one would peg me a sentimental sort, but as I got ready to *move on*, as Sylvia would say, I figured it was time. Might be something in the shadowy corners worth a few bucks, to someone—one man's treasures, yada yada.

As I reached the bottom step, the odor of moldering things, dark and dank, wafted up from the dirty floor. The house was old—older than me, which I guess made it ancient—and when we first moved in, I'd told Sylvia I'd spruce it up. Finish the basement, maybe put in a bar or sewing center, but on some level, I knew I'd never really follow through. Too busy with the guys. Too involved in my career. She'd given up asking after the first ten years, content to live above ground, enjoying all the niceties my income provided, not having to worry about what I stowed away down there, out of sight.

A single bare bulb burned overhead, and it seemed to be getting dimmer with age, barely able to cast wan shadows into the dark recesses. The basement was a decent size, but with all the boxes and bags and discarded furniture, there wasn't much room left. Not that I planned on doing jumping jacks, or anything. I just needed enough space to maneuver. My plan was to go through the junk, toss ninety-percent away and pack up the rest, nice and neat, ready to be opened when we got to our new digs.

In Scottsdale, A-Ree-Zona.

The boss was setting me up with a new identity and a soft gig, a consultant on corporate security for one of his *operations*, just something to help pass time during retirement and provide some spending money. No heavy lifting. And no more killing. I'd put my foot down. Time for the younger generation to take over. Hell, I'd earned my retirement.

And how.

I cleared off an old glass-and-wood coffee table, something Sylvia thought looked modern back in the Seventies. Then I retrieved a box from a tower of boxes, set it down on the tabletop, and opened the interlocking cardboard flaps to reveal a jumble of desk knickknacks—a paperweight, a letter opener, a few packages of paper clips.

A smile formed on my lips as I picked up the letter opener and turned it in my hands. Similar to the one I'd driven through that bastard Jimmy Bang-Bang's neck, right before I shot him in the face. It wasn't the same one, of course. You couldn't very well keep the actual murder weapon around as a memento, but it *reminded* me of the one I'd used.

Just as sharp.

I tossed it back and set the box in an open spot near the staircase. The trash pile.

I sifted through a few more boxes, then pawed through a couple green garbage bags bursting with old clothes. Nothing from the last fifteen years. Nothing worth keeping. All trash.

I moved aside an old lamp, uncovering a trophy with a gold golfer figurine atop a squat block of marble. My heart did the two-step as I recalled that incident. I never played much golf, but Tony the Elbow was a fixture at Blue Creek Country Club. One night, as Tony took a break from recounting his round in the bar to a bunch of drunks, I'd ambushed him in the men's room, jamming an extra-long golf tee into his eyeball before strangling him to death and leaving his body on the cold tile floor.

Maybe I'd take up golf, now that I'd have some time on my hands. Wasn't Scottsdale famous for that?

I tossed the trophy onto the burgeoning trash heap.

A voice caught my attention and I whirled around. I swore it sounded like someone calling my name, softly, from deep in the murky shadows. "Who's there?" I said, instinctively patting my pockets, finding them empty. Why would

I need to arm myself in my own basement? "Somebody there?"

I froze, listening. After about forty seconds, my muscles relaxed. Probably just a rodent, unhappy I'd invaded his cozy den.

A lifetime of caution—bordering on the paranoid—was tough to let go. I was a survivor. But I'd retired, didn't need to worry. My days of sleeping with one eye open and my piece under my pillow were receding fast in the rear view mirror.

Next up: a shoebox full of photos, real pictures from back when you dropped off your roll of film at the drugstore and they came back printed on glossy paper, double sets. I grabbed a handful and flipped through them. Snapshots of old friends taken during various trips, both business and pleasure. In one, Five-Dollar Phil, whose nickname sprang from his habit of tipping strippers a fin, wore a sombrero and posed with a mariachi band. That had been one wild trip down to Baja.

The next year, I'd had to whack Phil when the boss found out he'd been skimming a little too much off the top. Pity. I'd liked Phil. Liked his young wife, too.

I wondered, not for the first time, if most guys thought it was better to know you were about to die, or if they'd prefer to get whacked without any warning.

Me? I think I'd rather know what was coming. Give me time to say a prayer or something.

I came across another pack of photos, this one held together by a crumbling red rubber band. Pictures from a long-ago family picnic, every third shot featuring Sylvia cavorting in a yellow sundress. She'd been a stunner all right, and though she never really approved of my line of work, she knew it was something I was born for, something I took to, something I excelled at. She saved her harping for stuff around the house, not about my career choice, no matter how much it ate at her. Of course, the jewelry and vacations and spa treatments helped ease her pain.

Now, it was only right I should dote on her as we grew old—*older*—together.

In one picture, Sylvia's brother Angelo smiled at the camera. He was in the business, too. Or had been, until I took care of him. That had been the hardest job of my life. For Chrissakes, offing your brother-in-law! But it had to be done, and I was proud it'd been the only time I'd shed any real tears. After all, Angelo had a son to think about, Little Bennie.

I pictured the scene at Angelo's funeral, where his wife, Carlotta, dressed in black, sat next to Bennie at the grave-side, hugging him while sobbing uncontrollably.

The mental image was so clear, but something about it was off, out of focus, not *exactly* like things had been fifteen years ago. Bennie seemed older somehow, like in his twenties. And sitting next to Carlotta was Sylvia, wearing a black dress and a veil, as if *she* were the grieving widow.

I could almost hear her softly calling out my name. *Oh, Frankie, Frankie...*

Fucking mind playing tricks on me was all.

Five years after Angelo's death, Little Bennie, who'd turned seventeen by that time, came up to me at cousin Maria's wedding. Pulled me aside, him a skinny twerp with scraggly hair and big dreams, and tells me he knows I did it. Killed his father. Says he's going to get me, get revenge, cold and deadly, someday when I'm not expecting it.

I guess that day never came, did it? I still feel bad about

the hit, but bottom line, his old man shouldn't have been ripping us off.

People had to pay for their deeds. Consequences was consequences.

I stuffed the photos back in the box and hurled the entire thing onto the pile destined for the dump.

The cramped basement was closing in on me. Time for a break. I hobbled back up the stairs and tried to turn the doorknob, but it wouldn't budge. I put some force behind it, really gave it a twist, still stuck. Despite the subterranean chill, sweat dripped down the back of my neck and soaked into my collar as I wrestled with it. I gave the door a few rams with my shoulder. Nothing budged.

My claustrophobia kicked up a notch.

I swallowed, but my mouth felt full of cotton. I banged on the door, first with my palms, then with fists. "Sylvia. Hey, honey. Open the door. I'm down in the basement."

Waited.

Nothing.

I listened for her footsteps, but heard a soft voice instead. Sylvia's. *"Oh, Frankie. Oh, dear. Too early."*

My heart raced. I pounded on the door until my hands ached. "Sylvia! Open up! Please!"

I clawed at the sturdy oak door until blood ran from beneath my fingernails.

More voices now, stronger, clearer. Sylvia sobbing, her words getting louder. *"How could you leave me? How could this happen? I thought you were out of it. You promised. Oh, Frankie…"*

A piercing realization: My house didn't have a basement. My fate enshrouded me like dirt entombing a casket, pressing in on me, suffocating me.

I said a prayer, but I knew it was too late.

I wasn't a survivor.

I saw Bennie at the funeral, *my* funeral, smirking. He pointed a thumb-and-forefinger gun at the casket and dropped the hammer as his wicked smile grew.

"Ashes to ashes. Dust to dust."

BLACKMAILER'S PEP TALK
Chris Rhatigan

considered calling the cops. But I'm not a masochist, so I didn't.

I crouched on the stoop in front of John Ballard's half of a duplex, slowed my breath. Looked up and down the mediocre street where he had spent his brief, dissatisfying life, houses like gaping mouths, sky, grass, trees all a shade of industrial gray.

Nothing I could do. I'd stolen Ballard's wallet. Came to give it back but he'd blown his head off. End of story. No use asking questions. Going there in the first place was weak, made no sense.

That night I went to this bar. Ballard's wallet had forty-seven dollars in it. I used this to buy well drinks. His sullen driver's license photo kept staring at me so I took out the money, dropped the wallet in the bathroom trash.

I still had thirty-three of his dollars left. I was half-watching the Yankees kick the shit out of the Orioles when this girl walked in. We'd met at this bar two nights ago and ended up sleeping together. Morning after, I swiped several of her things—laptop, cash, some electronic tablet. I didn't recall her name, Sarah? Melissa? Joan?

This time she was with some dude who looked like he'd dropped out of an Abercrombie and Fitch catalog, except he had a shirt on. She had a grotesque rock glittering on her left ring finger. They were meeting up with some friends. The group of them laughed like they were in a commercial.

One point I caught her eye. She held my gaze for a second before looking away.

I ordered a pint and drank it too fast. Decided Sarah-Melissa-Joan would pay for her indiscretion.

◎ ◎ ◎

I sat in my car across the street from the building her penthouse was in, checking the rearview now and again, ripping butts, stuffing them in the little tin ashtray. Wiped gunk out of the corners of my eyes. This was earlier than I'd been up in a while. Being unemployed doesn't pay well but the hours are good.

Abercrombie guy left before eight in a crisp, three-piece suit. He got in a Benz in the parking lot next to the building.

I thought maybe I'd missed her. But then Sarah-Melissa-Joan came out walking fast, looking good—skirt she kept pushing down, chasm of milky cleavage busting out of a sea-green sweater.

I slid out the passenger side. Tracked her down.

"Melissa."

She turned. "My name's not Melissa."

Fuck. "Who's that guy you're with last night?"

"What do you care?"

She walked away like she was in a real hurry, didn't even know me. I scrambled in front of her.

"You're not exactly a modern couple, are you? He makes the bread and you, what, secretary?"

Her long eyelashes fluttered like I was a speck caught in her eye. "What are you doing here?"

"I assume you don't want him to find out that you went slumming." I kept repeating to myself, *This is a game of confidence. You have it. She doesn't. This is not another John Ballard.* Like a little blackmailer's pep talk. "I don't want to drag this out. No need. Let's say five thousand and we're done."

She laughed, bright and musical. "You must be kidding. I can't take five thousand dollars out of a joint bank account."

"A thousand. Meet me at China Palace. Five-thirty."

"I'm not paying you, Milo."

She still thought my name was Milo. Good. "Then hubby will know every little detail."

She headed for her car, heels click-clacking on the asphalt.

I said, "I'll let him know where your piercings are and that spot on the back of your neck and—"

"Fuck off."

She peeled out of the parking spot. Left me swimming in the scent of burned rubber.

⊙ ⊙ ⊙

I went to a café down the street. Clean wood tables and a black and white tile floor, smelled like baking bread and roasting beans. Little expensive for my taste, but so was everything in this neighborhood.

I had a cup of coffee. The saucer rattled each time I put the cup down. An old woman glared at me from behind reading glasses. I apologized for some reason, gave a little nervous laugh, said too much caffeine gave me tremors. Wondered if lying came to me naturally or if it sounded forced.

After I left, I hung around the swanky apartment building's entrance until someone walked out. I grabbed the door before it closed. Found the mailbox for her apartment number, scribbled "Kyle/Sarah Frisson" on the back of a receipt.

When I got back to my building, my unemployment check was waiting for me. Five weeks til it ran out. I was supposed to have an interview at the Nordstrom's in the mall that afternoon for a shoe salesman position, but I blew it off. Figured it would be like all my other interviews—fifteen, maybe twenty other people, half of them with a decade of experience in retail. Not that I wanted a job at stupid Nordstrom's anyway.

I googled Kyle Frisson. An attorney at Greenstein and Varachi. Photo of him in that three-piece suit, ridiculous grin, law books that looked like they were made of cardboard on a shelf behind him. I wrote down the office phone number on the back of a receipt.

Next hit was a wedding announcement on the local newspaper's web site. Married two months ago at a country club. Her maiden name was Sarah Annabelle Ralston. She worked as an assistant to the PR director at DataLink Corp. The smiling, all-American couple had hooked up in college while studying abroad in Spain.

I should've stuck with the five g's.

The more I thought about it, the more the whole thing baffled me. She was so clearly in the wrong, had so much at stake. But she seemed set in her defiance, not willing to even negotiate. Like she thought that if she ignored me, I would disappear.

She needed to understand that wasn't going to happen.

I dialed Kyle's office number on my cell. Receptionist picked up and connected me to him.

"Kyle Frisson."

I lit a cigarette. Waited.

"Hello?"

"How's Sarah?"

"Who is this?"

"Answer my question."

"What?"

He was stiff, defensive. More nasal than I'd expected. Offended that I'd even considered invading his tiny world.

"I said, answer my question. How's Sarah? I'm interested in her well-being."

"Why should I tell you?"

"You're a newly married man. Sex must be explosive. Two, three times a day, am I right?"

"Listen, buddy." He paused, hiss of breath into the receiver. "I don't know what this is about but I'll call the cops. I have your number right here."

I chuckled, smoke dribbling from my nostrils. Felt good. Loose. "And tell them what, exactly? That I asked how Sarah was doing?"

"Well, that you're, that you're harassing me."

"Am I harassing you?"

"Yes!"

"My sincerest apologies, then. We don't need to talk anymore. Just tell her Milo says 'hi.'"

I hung up. The message would find her. But on second thought, the whole thing felt grimy. Too eager, too soon. I overplayed my hand.

Should have planned it better. Maybe called from a pay phone and pretended to be an old high school buddy of Sarah's, said I was looking for her and then said something a bit off that he would pass onto her. Didn't like him knowing I was in the picture, even with the false name.

The sugary high of moments before deflated into numbness. I put on coffee, smoked a cigarette. All I had was this information. Soon as I used the information, its value vanished. It only had value when it was trapped in my head. Bizarre.

I sprawled out on the mattress on my floor. What the fuck did Sarah Annabelle Frisson think she was doing? Not even ten weeks into her marriage and she's picking up losers like me.

I almost wanted to tell her to keep her money. Her marriage was fucked anyway.

◉ ◉ ◉

The Chinese food place was set in a series of skywalks that connected one end of the city to the other. I got twitchy hanging around my apartment so I paced the skywalks for most of the afternoon.

The skywalks used to have shoe repair shops, bookstores, Italian delis, newsstands, and the like. Now the storefronts were all dark, lease signs in the windows. Carpets hadn't been cleaned in years—a network of stains stretched across each hallway, beads of moisture dripping from the ceiling and rust bleeding from the steel structure. This was one of the last places you could smoke inside with no problem— no one around to tell you otherwise.

I took a pen and a notebook out of back pocket. Sat with my back against the plexiglass. Wrote an account of my one-night stand with Sarah. A chronology that included every possible detail. I filled in a few moments that were fuzzy cause of how much I drank. Made sure I had a lot of material that only someone who'd fucked her would know.

It ended up being five pages. I liked having an object I could use. Maybe I could show it to her, make her understand the reality of her non-compliance.

Writing the letter made me aroused, so I went to one of the filthy stalls in the bathroom and rubbed one out. I kept thinking someone was going to walk in—ridiculous considering how empty the place was.

Zipped up, sat on the cold tile. Smoked a cigarette in quick drags, let a tube of ash hang there until it fell on its own.

I went to the Chinese food restaurant. Soon as I got a whiff of the grease, I realized I hadn't eaten all day. The sleepy old woman working the counter blinked at me like customers were the last thing she expected.

I ordered sweet and sour chicken. She said nothing, rang it up.

I said, "When's this place closing down? You know, like everything else up here."

She scowled, went back to the kitchen. Few minutes later, she handed me a styrofoam plate, pointed at the plastic utensils and napkins on a counter.

"Are you a fucking mute or something?"

I kept taking my phone out of my pocket, flipping it open. Five-thirty passed. Cleaned my plate. Felt half alive at best, a mass of food in my stomach.

It occurred to me that I'd approached this all wrong.

Maybe I was selling Sarah a product—this letter—and the product had a set value. Didn't matter how much money she did or didn't have, like anyone else, she didn't want to get ripped off. Maybe her flat rejection of my proposal was the beginning of negotiations. Of course, she knew I would press her for more if I got the thousand right away, so she couldn't just cave in.

I was walking back when I noticed someone—big guy, maybe six-two, black t-shirt stretched by bulky chest and arms—following me at a distance. Kept catching his reflection in the glass. I didn't turn around, accelerated my pace. My footsteps, his footsteps, echoing through the halls.

At one point I doubled back, went in a square past China Palace again. He was closer now. No question he was following me. Food sloshed around in my stomach, nerves gnawed at my skin.

Instead of going back to the parking garage, I hung a left toward an escalator that went to a hotel lobby. Walked down the steps and stopped in the middle of the lobby. Soft leather chairs, oriental rugs, people with convention tags hovering around the front desk. Figured he wouldn't try anything in a place like this.

He came right up to me, sported a cocky smile. "Milo, right?"

"Sure."

"Got a message for you."

"Did you need to follow me to tell me the message? Couldn't have just come up and said it to me?"

"Back off, man. Leave Sarah alone."

"Or what? She'll have—who are you?"

"None of your concern," he said.

"You her brother?"

Shook his head. Pursed his lips and sniffed. Some act like he was losing patience. "She didn't send me. Just back off. If you know what's good for you."

"Then what, a friend, cousin? Did she want you to rough me up or something, you couldn't do it? Afraid it'll taint your squeaky clean record?"

Guy poked my chest with a finger. "You don't want to see me again."

"Whatever."

He left through the revolving doors. I sat down in one of those cushy leather chairs, laughed, hand covering my mouth, for almost a whole minute.

Outside, I smoked in the fog. Could barely see ten feet in front of me. People emerged from the hotel's revolving doors, fading the other way seconds later. Seemed comic or tragic or something.

Sarah had shown how much was on the line. That she'd tell a friend or whoever to follow me, maybe push me around. Seemed almost absurd. She was afraid of Kyle finding out about the money. Thought she could scare me off with no real effort.

I went back to my apartment, worked through my next step. This was different than John Ballard. With him, I'd been trying to create something out of nothing. Guy I saw on the street who I arbitrarily decided to rob. Sarah was an opportunity that I had to capitalize on. Question was how.

I didn't sleep much that night. Kept waking at weird hours—young couple upstairs screaming at each other, drunk people next door laughing and stomping around.

Fell back to sleep as the first rays of sun bled through the blinds. Woke up a couple of hours later, showered, combed my hair and put on a shirt with a collar. As close to respectable as I could get.

Stopped by a gas station for coffee and fresh cigarettes. I sat on the curb and smoked a few. Coffee was scalding and had been sitting out for a few hours, but I drank it anyway. A headache crept in from lack of sleep and the roar of nearby traffic.

I went to a stationery store and made copies of the letter. Put the original in an envelope with Kyle's work address and sealed it.

Found her office out in the suburbs without too much trouble and parked across the street. Hers was the only white BMW in the parking lot. I slipped a note under the windshield wiper. *Your big friend is cute. Meet me at 5:00. Orange Ave Tavern.*

I had considered sneaking into her building, passing by her desk and leaving the copies. But that was too risky. Thought about sending her flowers. Kind of liked that one. I could picture her rolling her emerald eyes, dumping the flowers in the trash. But that would set me back at least fifty bucks and accomplish little.

Settled on putting the copies in a manila envelope and leaving them at the front desk, saying they were her wedding photos (ha ha). The girl at reception didn't question the bullshit story at all and was taking the envelope back to Mrs. Frisson as I left.

I went to the Orange Avenue Tavern early. I killed one

pitcher of beer quickly and nursed a second. I didn't like the place. Bright and noisy with twenty TVs all blasting ESPN News from every possible angle. Bunch of shit on the walls—old-time bicycles, photos of high school softball teams. The more I drank the more everything annoyed me. I got an order of mozzarella sticks and devoured them.

Sarah walked in at about four forty-five. With her husband and those same friends. They got a booth and she made a point not to look at me.

My first instinct was to go over to her table and make trouble, but I thought better of that. Maybe it's even what she wanted me to do—make a fool of myself with a public display, damage my credibility.

I didn't finish my beer. Smoked the whole drive back, lighting one cigarette with the previous one, swerving between lanes as I did so.

I sat on the stoop of my apartment building. Few doors down, two guys made a quick drug deal. I wondered what it was for and how much.

She had almost asked for it. Maybe she liked the drama. Maybe she wanted to drag it out, or maybe she wanted a divorce.

But none of those options fit—if that was the case, why did she wait for me to make the first move? And why did she send her friend after me?

I walked down the empty street, long shadows of sunset swallowing the parked cars. I reached a mailbox, opened the lid. I hesitated, then dropped in the envelope—the one with the originals inside and Kyle Frisson's office address on the front.

First thing I did when I got back to my apartment was find out how to look up divorce records on the county court's web site.

I've gone to that web site every day since then, looking for the name Frisson.

Nothing yet.

WITH A LITTLE BIT OF LUCK

Bill Baber

'd just had my favorite kind of sex: hard, fast, and just a bit on the rough side. It was with a burgundy-haired bitch with hard pointy tits that I'd picked up at a local dive.

My dump of a motel in Florence, Arizona, was named the Mountain View. This was ironic, since the only view was of the state penitentiary just across the highway. When I pulled into town, I got chills after I saw the razor wire on top of the fence shine eerily in the light of a nearly full moon. I should have known that the sight of the guards in the towers cradling their rifles was nothing but a bad omen.

Just about every town of any size in Arizona has a state pen. I'd never been inside Florence but it had a reputation as a mean old shithole. My best friend growing up got shanked in a yard fight just inside that wire fence. I'd done time in Picacho, fifty miles to the southwest, as well as a county hole or two—all country clubs in comparison to Florence. As an added bonus, Florence was home to Arizona's death row. It was no place I wanted to end up.

I hadn't planned on sticking around. I had valuable, ill-gotten cargo hidden in my ride and I needed to keep moving. But, shit, you can't blame a man for having a thirst for a beer or two, especially when a hot and willing chick is added to the mix. Right? But I guess I should have just grabbed a six-pack like I originally planned and kept on going.

She was sitting on a stool near the door at The River Bottom, a bar located in the last building along the highway on the north side of town. It was frequented by an ugly and volatile mix of prison guards, bikers, cowboys, and a few ex-cons thrown in for good measure. The juke box alternated between George Jones, Skynyrd and the Stones. It wouldn't take much to light a fuse there and at any moment a spark could cause the place to explode.

I bought her a beer. In the dim light and thick smoke I couldn't see the fine lines around her eyes and mouth and the striking color of her hair. But, I *could* see the cute little nipples that pressed against her thin shirt. A small diamond glittered on the side of her right nostril.

"This isn't a good place to hang out." I told her, ignoring the hard stares from the rednecks nearby.

"Been in lots worse," she said.

She told me she was from L.A. Recently, she'd migrated to Tucson and got herself involved with a speed freak that had gotten her hooked and wanted her to do things she had just enough pride left not to. She said she had been clean for three months.

"I'm looking for open roads. She said. "There aren't any streets I want to walk back there."

I didn't give a shit what her story was. I just wanted to fuck.

Afterwards, I was resting on top of sheets soaked with sweat and sex. The mattress was as old and lumpy as a retired Tijuana whore. Hard tits was in the bathroom, "freshening up." There were a couple of beers resting in a bucket of mostly melted ice on the beat up dresser, and I was considering reaching for one when that dumbass Braxton kicked in the door.

Braxton Reams had always been a stupid little shit. He'd grown up with me and my crew in midtown Tucson. He always wanted to fit in; was always trying to be a tough guy. Mostly, what that got him was his ass kicked. I hadn't seen him in a few years; he was even skinnier than usual, and he had the sunken checks and fucked up teeth of a meth head. He looked pathetic. But, with a stainless .45 pointed at me, he managed to look pretty damn tough. Good thing he was still dumb. If he had been tailing me, I thought, he would've known I wasn't alone.

"Get dressed," he said. "You're taking me to the money."

"What money?" I said.

"Don't bullshit Me." he said. "The word is that you're the guy who took down that jewelry store at Encantada."

He was right; I had gotten a boatload of jewels and a good chunk of cash. It had been an easy score: Encantada was an upscale mall up in the foothills, and Harry Noble's was an independent jeweler that skimped on security. It had been a week before Christmas; all I had to do was dress up a bit and walk in carrying a couple of shopping bags. One of the two clerks that were working was at lunch and the old guy that was minding the store looked like he was going to shit when I put a gun in his face. After scooping up jewels—including a display full of Rolex's and another of diamond tennis bracelets—I cleaned out the register and got lost in the crowd of holiday shoppers.

I'd laid low for a month, and now I was headed to Vegas to piece the loot out to a standup guy I knew. Marvin would wash the cash and take the jewelry off my hands, leaving me with nearly three quarters of the take. Before that prick

Braxton came along and complicated things, next on the agenda was supposed to be a Mexican beach and a life of sun, senoritas, siestas and cervezas until the money ran out.

Walking up to the edge of the bed, he prodded me with the pistol. Just then, the girl with the burgundy hair silently eased open the bathroom door. There was something small and dark in her hand. With an amazing lack of hesitation, she shot Braxton in the head and his blood and brain matter oozed all over the already filthy sheets.

In the end, all wanting to be a tough guy had gotten Braxton was killed.

"Jesus Christ," I mouthed to no one in particular. Then, "Let's get the hell out of here."

I pried Braxton's piece from his dead fingers on the way out the door.

There was already a crowd gathering outside the motel and more than one of them was on a cell phone, alerting the police to the sound of a gunshot from upstairs. Since the next day was visiting day at the prison, the place was nearly full. I was driving an '89 Ford pickup stolen from a construction site at the north end of Tucson earlier in the day. No one was going to miss it until Monday, but now, the cops would have a description. I didn't have time to look for another ride.

Luckily, I remembered that an old cell mate, a Pima Indian by the name of Johnny Cueto, lived nearby on the Gila River Reservation. If I could remember how to find his double wide, which was located somewhere between Bapchule and Sakaton, I was sure he'd help.

We headed west on a county road that crossed over I-10. It was a blustery January night. Dust and desert debris scurried across the road in front of us. It was chilly and I cranked up the heater. In the glow of oncoming headlights, I could read the excitement in my passenger's dancing eyes.

After coming to a crossroads where there was a convenience store and gas station, I thought we were close to Johnny's. A mile or so further down the road, I saw his old Camaro in front of a place that still had lights on. I pulled the truck around the back where it wouldn't be seen from the road. My knock was answered by a slender Indian girl in her early twenties. She was trying to cover acne scars with too much make up. She was at least fifteen years younger than Johnny. Across her neck were the scrolled letters of a tattoo with a heart at either end proclaiming that she was his property. Not for long I thought. Not unless my old pal had really changed.

She glared at us for a moment without speaking. When I told her I was a friend of Johnny's she looked at me like she didn't believe it. Finally, she opened the door without taking her eyes off of me. She called to Johnny.

He was a little drunk, and the smell of weed was thick in the trailer. When he saw me, he broke into a grin. Johnny was a big dude: six foot three or four and nearly three hundred pounds—none of it soft. He grabbed me off the ground and hugged me hard. The bones of my spine popped like small arms fire.

He tossed me a beer from the fridge, not offering one to either of the women.

"What the fuck man? It's been a while, the hell are you doin' here?"

"I need wheels." I said. "I'm in a bind."

Johnny knew what I meant. He'd done two different stretches for armed robbery. We used to talk all the time about how we never wanted to be locked up again.

"Kalisha, give him your keys."

She hesitated and Johnny shot her a look.

"Give him the fucking keys. Now."

She did, and scowled at me. She was one mean looking girl.

"Don't fuck it up," she spat.

After setting down my half-finished beer, Johnny and I hugged again. Before letting go, he slipped something hard and cold against my back.

"Good luck man." was all he said.

Kalisha's car was a newer silver Honda, perfectly non-descript, making it seem perfect for my needs. I drove the pick-up a mile or so further down the gravel road. The girl with the burgundy hair followed. There was a line of mesquite trees leading down into a wash. The jewels and cash were stashed behind the seat. I retrieved the bundle and stuffed it into my duffle, hoping she didn't see. Then I pushed the truck down the incline into the trees.

It wasn't much past eleven and there was still quite a bit of traffic on the freeway, especially as we neared Phoenix. I wasn't sure what I was going to do with her. I figured I'd leave her in Flagstaff—the sooner the better.

Staying in the center lane, I was cruising just over the speed limit. I noticed a car closing fast behind me. The rear view filled with red and blue. I signaled and pulled to the shoulder. When the trooper walked up to the window, I could smell dust and after shave.

"Good evening," he said. "You have a tail light out. May I see your license and registration please?"

The tags were current so I figured we might be okay. How the hell was I supposed to know Johnny's little squeeze had a felony assault warrant?

"Step out of the car sir, with your hands on top of your head."

Suddenly, that Mexican beach was mighty far away. I didn't want to do another stretch but this looked bad. I didn't know if there was any way out.

He led me to the passenger side of the car. Suddenly, the freeway was devoid of traffic in both directions. It was very still. The trooper frisked me and found the gun I had taken from Braxton.He pulled his own, putting mine behind his back.

"Don't fucking move," he said.

I did as he said, watching, not knowing what the hell that unpredictable bitch might do.

"You," he said to her, "out of the car with your hands up where I can see them."

She opened the door and—just like that—blew away the side of his face. I guess I wasn't surprised. This chick liked shooting people, especially in the head.

Taking advantage of the lull in the traffic, I got out of there. The next exit was for Maricopa. I could take back roads all the way out to the west end of Phoenix. I didn't know what would happen after that.

I didn't wonder for long. We hadn't gone far when I heard a click that turned my blood cold. She had the gun pointed at me and in the dash lights I saw an evil smile on her face.

"Let's talk about that money and the jewels," she said. "There was no way I was going to let Braxton share in the spoils of our little plan. Too bad things have to be this way; you seem like my kinda guy."

Figuring she would shoot me as soon as she got a chance, I swerved hard to the right, throwing her against the door.

At the same time, I pulled the piece Johnny had slipped me from where I had stuck it between the seats on my left.

It was just like that scene in Scarface. She was dead and splattered all over the passenger side of the car. I felt bad for a moment but shit, she would have done me in a heart-beat. I never even knew her name. But, there was one thing I *did* know: that since I saw those damn walls of Florence State Penitentiary and first encountered the girl with the burgundy hair, everything had gone to shit. Then I thought, you stupid bitch—look at you now.

I saw a dirt road that led off into the desert. After a quarter mile, I grabbed my duffle, left the car and started walking through the cold night thinking about those guard towers and razor wire. But with a little bit of luck, I'd make it to that Mexican beach. And, once there, the only thing I'd want to see shinning in the moonlight was the long black hair of a beautiful senorita.

CUTE AS A SPECKLED PUP UNDER A RED WAGON

Tony Conaway

Please, sir," she said. "I can see you're in pain. Let me help."

I had just left a Starbucks and sat down in my truck when she came up to me. I'd gotten a taste for their coffee when I was in the Sandbox—yes, big military bases actually have Starbucks. I drink it hot, even on a 95 degree East Texas day. And I was trying to stay sober. Hence the coffee, when what I really wanted was some 120 proof paint thinner.

If it had been some ass-clown who wanted to sell me an Herbalife joint-pain reliever, I would've snarled something like, *Well, my dick ain't gonna suck itself—you want to help with that?* But this was a young girl, and a looker.

I wasn't going to curse her out until I'd eliminated the possibility of fucking her.

She almost ruined it when she opened her mouth again. "Please, I'm... I'm just so filled with the power of Jesus. He wants me to help you, I know he does. Please, can I lay hands on your knee and pray for Him to heal you?"

Now, I don't believe in God, Buddha or Allah. But hey, I'm a guy. If a pretty girl wants to put her hands on my thigh, who am I to say no?

I figure she'll want to go inside the Starbucks to perform this party trick. But no, she surprises me again. I'm still sitting in the driver's seat of my pickup, my feet outside on the parking lot. (My knee is bad enough that I have to grab that leg and swing it up into my truck.)

And damned if she doesn't kneel down right there, on the dirty tarmac of a hot parking lot! She's wearing jeans, but still—kneeling in a parking lot?

She goes right into her routine, laying her hands on my leg and praying up a storm, asking Jesus to heal me in a loud voice.

It takes a lot to embarrass me, but a girl kneeling in front of me in public comes close. I look around to see if anyone is watching.

And it turns out that everyone in the Starbucks is pressed up against the windows, watching…what? What do they think they're watching?

Then I realize that, from their angle, it looks like some girl is blowing me, right in the parking lot! Most of her body is hidden by the open door of my truck, so all they can see are her legs…and the top of her head. Which bobs up and down while she's praying.

I decide that, even if she doesn't care about her reputation, I ought to. I pull her up, then stand myself.

"Look, it's too hot to do this out here. Let's go inside where it's cool."

"What, into Starbucks?" She notices the people staring, and waves at them, as if she's about to sail off on a cruise. "I'm OK out here."

"Yeah, well, in my experience, Jesus only comes to places where it's under 95 degrees." I lock the door to my truck and start to guide her down the block.

She smiles as if she's talking to a none-too-bright child. "Silly. Jesus is everywhere."

"Trust me, I did two tours of Iraq. Jesus doesn't live there anymore."

I guided her up a few blocks and around the corner, to a place that called itself

Ivan's Icehouse. Of course, it was no more a genuine, old time Texas Icehouse than it was a church. It had electricity and indoor bathrooms, both of which disqualified it from being an actual icehouse. But it was open at this hour, and we'd walked just far enough in the summer heat to work up a thirst.

She demurred when I tried to guide her inside. "I—I can't. I'm 20 years old—I'm not old enough to go into a bar."

"Don't worry about it. Anyone asks, tell them you're married to me." That's one of our quaint Texas customs— an underage person could drink if she was married to and accompanied by someone aged 21 or over. They've probably changed that law, but I also knew that they didn't care that much about proof of age in this place. Not for pretty girls.

I'd been sober for almost two months, so it irritated me that Bob the Bartender showed no surprise to see me back. He just nodded and went back to watching candlestick bowling on the bar TV. Even with satellite TV, there are hours when your choice of sports is limited to an obscure pastime out of Boston.

I sat her at a table then got us some drinks. I figured she wasn't an experienced drinker, so I ordered her a Long Island Iced Tea. That's a potent drink with several types of alcohol, yet doesn't really taste like it. Myself, I downed a shot of Jack Daniels at the bar. If I were a religious man, I would've shouted "Hallelujah" when that shot of Jack hit my gullet after two long dry months. I got a bottle of Shiner bock to chase it with.

She wanted to get started on her faith healing of my knee, but I convinced her to take a few swallows first, while I enjoyed my cold beer.

As soon as I finished, I left her to sip her Long Island Ice Tea, and I headed back to the pool room. I figured Denny the Weasel would be back there. I was right.

I caught his eye, then nodded towards the men's room. He smiled and joined me in the none-too-large bathroom.

"I need the best painkiller you've got."

"Oxy?" he asked.

"Oxycontin or oxycodone?

He held up a baggie with six oxycodone caplets. Solid pills, so you couldn't open them to snort the drug. Three day's dose for normal person. Probably only last me two.

"How much?"

I'd just cashed my disability check, so I had enough. I realized that was being wildly optimistic, that I would be able to spend two days in bed with this chick. Or maybe I was thinking that, if I was going to fall off the sobriety wagon, I might as well do it in a big way.

I paid the Weasel, put one pill in my mouth and chewed it. Oxycodone is a time release drug, made to be swallowed whole, but it works faster if chewed. I washed it down with a handful of water from the bathroom sink. I'd learned how to dry-swallow pills in the Army, but I never liked it.

Sometimes I had nightmares where I was still in-country, lying under camo, waiting to ambush some ragheads. In the dream, it's time to take my anti-malaria meds. I'm trying not to move or make noise, so I dry-swallow the pill. But it gets stuck in my craw, and I can't keep myself from coughing, which alerts the enemy—you get the picture.

So I don't like dry-swallowing.

Before limping back to the girl, I went to the bar and got two more beers. There weren't many guys in the bar at that hour, but one wannabe cowboy was already talking to her, trying to pick her up. I returned to our table and chased him away. Everyone in town knew I was a crazed vet who had killed more than my share of axis-of-evildoers overseas, so not many people were willing to stand up to me.

I sat. "There. It's good to be out of that heat, ain't it?"

"Yes." She looked around. "I've never been in a place like this before."

What I wanted to say was, *You've never been in a place where every man there wanted to fuck you? Sure you have. You just didn't realize it.*

Instead I said, "Inside a bar? You must have seen one on television. Or in movies."

"No. My parents were awful strict. No TV, no movies. Until they sent me to the Bible College at the edge of town, I'd never even been away from home."

Well, that explained a lot. I felt the oxy kicking in, so I figured it was time to get down to business. "You want to do that laying hands on my knee now?"

"Here? I suppose."

And she kneeled in front of me and started praying again. Everyone in the bar was staring, but they were staring at her before anyway.

When she finished, she said, "How does that feel?"

I stood, slowly. Thanks to the oxy, I could move my knee as if there was nothing wrong with it. I walked around the circular table without limping. She was thrilled. I figured she would be.

When I made a complete circuit of the table, I took her in my arms and kissed her.

Yes, she'd just downed a strong drink. But it was her excitement at healing my knee that made her kiss me back. And follow me out of the bar, back to my truck, over to my place, and into my bed.

Praise Jesus, indeed.

◉ ◉ ◉

The next morning I stumbled out of bed around 8:30 am. It was already over 90 degrees, Fahrenheit. I'd brought two six-packs of beer last night, but they were gone already. So I made do with coffee, and toasted to the fact that I was back in a country where they used Fahrenheit instead of Celsius to tell you how uncomfortable it was.

Sarabeth—that was her name—bounded out of the shower naked. That was just one of the revelations she'd discovered last night: that it was fun to walk around bare-assed. She had the body for it. Apparently her parents had considered nudity to be one of the seven-hundred-and-nine deadly sins.

I continued to stare out the kitchen window at the tangle of weeds that used to be my late mother's garden. But I couldn't ignore the 20-year-old girl who wrapped her still-damp arms around me and rubbed her tits into my back.

"Good morning! Good morning! Good morning! Isn't it a beautiful day! Did you make me coffee?" "I reckon it is. And no, this is one of them one-cup coffee-makers. You can pick what you want to drink—coffee, tea, even hot chocolate." I took a box of K cups out of the cabinet. The teas and the chocolate had come with the coffee, and I hadn't touched them since I bought the damn thing two years ago. But I don't think those things go bad. I'd used up all the coffee that came with it, but I had a bowl with an assortment of Starbucks and Dunkin Donut coffee K cups. Folks in AA take their coffee even more seriously than soldiers.

She rummaged excitedly through the containers. "Oooh, hot chocolate! My Grammy used to make me hot chocolate."

Grammy, I thought. *I'm fucking a hardbodied girl barely out of her teens, who used to have a Grammy. Is this a great country or what?*

We spent most of that day fucking. Sarabeth wasn't a virgin, exactly. But apparently, yesterday was the first time she *liked* having sex. I figured she'd been molested by some assistant pastor or had a quick tumble with a clueless prom date in the back of a Buick. I didn't ask. It's hard enough to get women to shut up, even without asking them questions.

Thankfully, I was unemployed, so I didn't have to call out sick. We did go out for some food and—of course—more alcohol. I spent what was left of my disability check on six cases of beer and a dozen different bottles of liquor, so she could try them and see which ones she liked.

I shouldn't have been surprised that she liked the sweet stuff: rock and rye, amaretto, and Bailey's Irish Cream. None of which is cheap.

I got her good and drunk that evening, just so I could get some rest. I'm not a teenager, and I was having more sex than I'd had in ages.

When she was drunk and snoring on the bed, I staggered out and went to where I usually sleep. Call them nightmares, call them PTSD, call them night terrors—I have these episodes where I wake up and I'm back in the Sandbox.

My wife left me because she was afraid to sleep next to me. She said that she was afraid I'd hurt her.

Or at least that's what she said at the divorce hearing. Who knows with women?

But, when I have these bad dreams, I sleep in the closet. I'm more comfortable there, waking up in the dark. It's small enough so I can reach out and touch a wall on all four sides.

I don't have a dog any more, but now I understand why dogs like to sleep in a doghouse that's just big enough for them to lie down in.

But I still had to drink most of a bottle of Canadian to get to sleep.

◉ ◉ ◉

There's no justice in this world. The next morning I was hung over, while Sarabeth was as chipper as ever.

"Good morning! Good morning! Good morning!" She wrapped herself around me from behind. "Why are there so many books? There's a full bookcase on almost every wall."

I may talk like a redneck, but that doesn't mean I'm ignorant. But I wasn't about to explain that to Sarabeth when

I was hung over. Right then even my nostrils hurt when I inhaled.

"Book club," I whispered.

"Book club? There must be two, three thousand books!"

"Once you join, they're hard to get out of."

"Okey-dokey," she said. "Well, if you can find room for me somewhere in your library, I think it's time I moved my stuff here."

The truth was, that was the last thing I wanted right now. Why can't they ever just fuck you, then go home? But it was easier to give in then argue.

◉ ◉ ◉

Three hours later I was back in the bathroom of Ivan's Icehouse. I had just come from the bank, where I'd cashed in my lone CD. I needed money for more oxy.

"Need anything else?" asked Denny the Weasel.

"Yeah." I hated to admit it, but I was thirteen years older than Sarabeth. I needed some help to keep up with her in bed. "Got any Viagra?"

"Shit," said Denny. "The average population of this town is, like, ninety. Everyone young gets out of town. 'Course I got Viagra, and Cialis, too. You bonin' that pretty young blonde I heard about?"

"Yeah. She's got my truck now, loading it up with her belongings from Bible College."

"You ain't helpin' her move?"

"She said her roommate would be happy to help, just to get rid of her. I figure if I step foot on sanctified ground, I'd burst into flame."

"Huh! Like a vampire going into church? You that bad a man, Able?"

"No," I said as I paid him. "I'm worse."

Afterwards I nursed a few beers until Sarabeth got back. She sauntered into the bar, looking happier than ever.

She greeted me with a kiss fit to suck the fillings out of my teeth.

"Hey, you got any money on you?" she asked. "I need a few things while we're here in town."

I though about my rapidly-diminishing savings. "As long as it includes a few cases of beer."

◉ ◉ ◉

Next morning I was hung over again. I sat on my front porch in my robe, pretending there was a breeze. I watched a robin search for worms on the stony, sun-dried plain that passed for my lawn. When I joined the military, East Texas got thunderstorms every day in the summer, and this lawn was like a jungle. When I was discharged, we were in a drought. Now it looked too much like Iraq for comfort.

The robin scratched at the hardpack soil with one foot. The *scritch* was audible. It hurt my hung-over ears.

"G'won, get outa here!" I croaked. The robin ignored me. Cocky motherfucker. Robins think they own your property. I looked around for something to throw at him.

When I'm sober, I kept my little house squared away, like a good soldier. Now, after just a few days of drinking, there was crap everywhere. I found a scuffed workshoe on the porch railing, and threw it at the robin.

At that very moment, a man stepped around the corner.

He showed no surprise that there was a shoe flying at him. He caught it effortlessly.

"And good morning to you, too, Able."

Shit. It was my AA sponsor, Cornthwaite. He probably parked on the street so he could sneak up on me.

"Didn't see you there, Cee. I was tossing that at a snake, over yonder."

He nodded as if what I said made sense, then came up on the porch. He sat down across from me, without asking. The shoe hr placed just outside the front door, like this was a fancy hotel that shined your shoes if you left them out.

"Haven't seen you at the last few meetings, Able. You haven't returned my calls, either. Thought I'd look you up."

"Yeah. Been busy. Got a new girlfriend."

"She named Margarita? Because I can smell the tequila on you from here."

"She's real enough. She decided she wants to take up jogging. I bought her a new set of workout duds yesterday."

"Well, Able, you know that we don't recommend that you start any new relationships for your first year of sobriety."

"I know."

"You've got to get *yourself* right first, before you can handle getting involved with someone else."

"Yup."

At that's when Sarabeth came jogging back, her new tee-shirt clinging to her. Sarabeth—and the look on Cornthwaite's face when he realized she was with me—was probably one of the top ten finest things I've ever seen in my life.

"God damn!" said Cornthwaite. "She is cute as—"

And he uttered some stupid expression they say in rural Florida. I don't remember what it was. But then, some things I try to forget.

⊙ ⊙ ⊙

After introducing Sarabeth to Cornthwaite, they went inside. I stayed out for awhile. As much as the sight of Sarabeth took my breath away, her constant chatter wearied me. Let Cee talk to her for awhile.

For no good reason I looked for the other workshoe, the mate to the one I threw at Cornthwaite. I finally found it in the mailbox. Then I took both shoes inside.

I was not surprised to find that Sarabeth was doing most of the talking.

"The sex is what changed my mind. I was always taught that sex is something awful, to be ashamed of, that you have to apologize to God for even thinking about. Your dead relatives in heaven watch you when you masturbate, right? But sex is wonderful! And I thought, if they were lying to me about sex, what else were they lying about?"

"Well, that's a natural reaction," said Cee. "Lots of us lose our faith over one thing or another. But many of us find life easier when we come back to it."

Sarabeth suddenly peeled off her sweat-soaked tee shirt and stood there in her new sports bra.

"They wouldn't even let me jog! I used to love running when I was a girl. Then I grew breasts, and they convinced me that I shouldn't run any more. They said that men would be driven to sin just from watching my breasts bounce when I ran! But they wouldn't let me wear a sports bra to hold down my breasts—noooo! A sports bra was somehow sinful. Show me where it says *that* in the bible!"

Cee smiled, and she smiled back. I knew he did well with women. They loved his dark eyes.

Me, I thought his eyes looked like two little piss holes in the snow.

"You're absolutely right," he said. "You have wisdom beyond your years."

Sarabeth looked at me for confirmation of her wisdom. Instead, she saw my disapproval of Cee's flirting and took it for disapproval of her.

"Oh, relax, Able! Plenty of girls wear just a sports bra. It's practically the same as a halter top."

"Yes," said Cee. "You should be proud of Sarabeth, Able."

"Say, how did you get a name like Cornthwaite, anyway?"

Oh, God, don't ask him that! I prayed silently.

But God reminded me that He didn't exist—He let Cee go into his speech.

"I'm named after a famous ancestor, Cornthwaite Hector. He was one of the founders of a town called Melbourne, Florida. Curiously, although he came to Florida by way of Australia and New Zealand, the Melbourne in Florida - "

"Florida? You're from there? I always wanted to go to Disney World!"

I sighed, rose, and went back outside. The robin was still there. I threw both shoes at him, one at a time. They didn't hit him, he just hopped out of the way. Couldn't even be bothered to fly—he just hopped.

"If I still had my guns, you'd be nothing but feathers!" I said. But they took my guns away. They do that when you've been convicted of a felony.

I walked out to retrieve the shoes. The robin hopped a few feet away and looked at me. I threw the shoes at him again, and missed again. I was not doing the Marines proud.

On the other hand, the Marines never trained me on throwing work shoes. The robin and I played this sad game until Cee exited and told me that I had to come back to the AA meetings. He'd escort me to one now if he had time, but he had to get to work.

He left, but I knew he'd be back. Not for me, but to get another glimpse of Sarabeth.

◉ ◉ ◉

It was that afternoon that Sarabeth got to the inevitable question.

"I don't know," I said. That was the truth, too.

"How can you not know if you killed someone in Iraq?"

"Because you're never alone—you're squad is with you, and they're probably shooting what you're shooting at. So you don't know which one of you actually shot the *Muj.* And because you don't usually get to go and examine the corpses. Most of my work was protecting convoys. Someone shoots at us, I shot back with a big, turret-mounted 50 caliber machine gun. The convoy doesn't stop, and whoever shot at you is soon behind you. And it's worse at night—the muzzle flash from a 50 cal ruins your night vision."

I cracked open a fresh bottle of tequila and poured myself a shot. "Now I've got some serious drinking to do. Go watch your cartoons."

Sarabeth's parents hadn't let her watch TV. She loved SpongeBob.

Me, I loved drinking.

◉ ◉ ◉

To my surprise, I slept OK that night. Sarabeth insisted that we both sleep naked, which was no hardship in the Texas heat. She spooned me from behind, one hand reaching around to hold my dick. She stayed like that all night, as if she was afraid that I was trying to run away. The one good thing about it was that I was sure I wouldn't have a nightmare and hurt her. No *hajji* ever held my dick.

In my cynical moments, I decided that she figured that, if I did get away, at least she'd still have my dick. If she had that plus my wallet, that was all she needed of me.

Things seemed to go downhill after Cee visited.

"Hey, maybe we should go easier on the drinking, you think?" She had just downed a mixed drink called a Nutty Irishman, which is made with Bailey's and Frangelica. Not one expensive type of alcohol. Two!

"Got to celebrate tomorrow. It's a holiday: Juneteenth."

"You celebrate the day Lincoln freed the slaves?"

"Of course. I'm a proud black man."

"Really?"

"Really–truly. My great-grandmother Enid was a Negro. That makes me one-eighth black. If they still had laws in this state against miscegenation, young lady, you'd be breaking the law."

This seemed to amuse her. "One-eighth? That makes you an octoroon, then?"

I nodded. "Stick around 'til the Fourth of July, and I'll take you to the big Spackman family picnic. You'll see I got kin both black and white."

She grabbed me by one hand and pulled me towards the bedroom. "Well, Mr. Octoroon, let's find out if it's true what they say about black men."

But, try as I might, I couldn't get it up that night. Not even the Cialis helped. I slept in the closet that night, but it didn't keep the nightmares away.

I had a new dream that night. I dreamt of something we only did a few times, when Fallujiah was going crazy. My squad was sent on foot patrol.

This is how you do a foot patrol in an urban environment: The point man looks ahead and scans the roofs of buildings for snipers. The man behind him looks for snipers on the top floor, in the windows or on the balconies. The man behind him looks for snipers on the level below. And so on, down to ground level. (Of course, the Marine in back has to cover what's behind you.)

I dreamt that I had the middle. Most buildings in Fallujah were only three stories tall. There were a few tall apartment buildings, but the majority were pretty short. I walked near the middle of the squad, looking for trouble on what we'd call the second floor. I kept glancing from side to side, because I was watching the buildings on both sides of the street.

Then, in my dream, the buildings became four stores tall. We didn't stop and assign someone to watch the new floor. I did it.

Then the buildings were five stores tall, then six. I was watching an impossibly broad area. Any one of those windows might have snipers.

Now I was watching a dozen stories. I never saw an entire street of skyscrapers in Fallujah, but they did in my dream.

There was no way I could effectively cover so much terrain. We were keeping silence, but I gestured to my Sergeant. He ignored me.

Then a dozen *Muj* popped out of the windows that I was supposed to be covering and cut down my whole squad. I found cover under the wreck of a car, where I watched my guys getting cut down.

I woke up screaming in my closet. If Sarabeth heard me, she didn't bother to get up.

◉ ◉ ◉

Cee kept stopping by, and eventually he said that he couldn't protect me from the law. I may have been an atheist, but a judge had sentenced me to go to AA meetings for three years. If I didn't go back, my parole would be revoked. I still drank, but I went back to the meetings.

Barely a week after I started going back to AA, I got home one day to find Sarabeth's stuff was gone.

It turned out that she had gone off with Cee. He took her back to Florida to see Disney World. And they stayed there.

I didn't stop drinking and using drugs right away. The last drink I had was at that Fourth of July family picnic. That's when I was disinvited to future family picnics.

◉ ◉ ◉

So now I'm sober again. Will it last? I have no idea. I hope so, but what are hopes worth? I do know that, each time I have to get sober, it gets harder, not easier.

I never saw Sarabeth again. (Or Cee, for that matter, but

him I don't miss. I got a less-annoying sponsor after that.) But here's the strange part: when I finally quit the drugs, my knee didn't go back to hurting. It was as if her faith healing actually worked after all.

Did Sarabeth really cure me? Damn if I know.

Was it worth losing my sobriety, taking painkillers for my knee to trick Sarabeth into fucking me? That I do know. Oh yes, that one I know the answer to.

CHIPPING OFF THE OLD BLOCK

Nick Kolakowski

I.

Jake Thompson, sixteen years old going on a hardboiled forty, celebrated the Fourth of July by lighting a rag stuffed in the gas tank of his school principal's Buick. He expected some merry flames, but what happened next took his life to a whole new level.

Jake's friend Bucky stood ten feet behind the Buick, hopping from foot to foot like a cheap windup toy. Bucky had spent his formative years huffing glue out of paper bags and swallowing anything on his mother's dresser that looked like a pill, frying his brain to the point where he couldn't spell 'dog' unless you spotted him the 'd' and the 'g.' But he was loyal to Jake, which meant he was okay in Jake's book, where the definition of a good guy was one who did as told.

"Get back a little bit," Jake told him.

Bucky didn't hear, or else the danger of turning a piece-of-crap car into a Molotov cocktail hadn't yet registered in his substandard noggin. It registered with Jake—he stepped backwards another twenty feet, figuring the bulk of the flames would shoot upward and spare him an unexpected barbecuing. The empty parking lot gave them plenty of room to spread out. Hopefully principal Taylor wouldn't come outside in the next five minutes, although who knows what he was doing alone at school in the first place—probably thinking of new and exciting ways to suspend Jake and any other kid who dared speak his or her mind.

When Jake moved back, Bucky did the same, staying behind the car as he pulled his phone from his back pocket.

"I better not be in the shot," Jake said.

"You're not."

"Seriously, dude, I want to see the video before you put it online or whatever," Jake thought about pulling out his own phone, to capture the burn from a side angle, and thought better of it. If you do something bad, his eldest brother Kevin always told him, make sure you're not carrying evidence of it on you. Kevin was a very smart dude.

"I won't. You're cool." Bucky turned his fancy phone on its side, for the widescreen effect.

They waited. The tip of the rag flared and crisped black, the flames bubbling the Buick's jaundice-yellow paintjob. Jake scanned the parking lot again, his eye drifting to the brick monstrosity of the school looming over it. So far this experience was underwhelming, and he started feeling idiotic about his earlier excitement, when they had first spied the principal's car parked all by its lonesome.

"It's just gonna burn like that?" Bucky asked, shaking his phone in frustration, as if that would make the fuel torch faster. "Or is it gonna go *off*?"

"Like a soft fart so far," Jake agreed. "Maybe we should—"

The car hood exploded with a belch of smoke and oily fire, baking Jake's skin, crisping his eyebrows. The blast kicked the Buick backward. Bucky was slow in the head but his reflexes were fine-tuned by a childhood of dodging thrown bottles, and he managed to dive ninety-five percent of his body out of the vehicle's fiery path. The remaining five percent was his right foot, which crunched like twigs as the Buick's left-rear tire rolled over it.

Bucky howled and dropped his phone. Jake ran to comfort and assist, his throat tightening like it always did when he freaked out—but he wanted to laugh, too, how messed up was that? The Buick, slowed not a bit by its collision with Bucky's foot, rolled across the parking lot like a funeral pyre on wheels. Who says the universe doesn't have a sense of humor? Who says the cosmic forces out there—or whatever Deity of your upbringing—hadn't arranged for a construction crew to build that parking lot at a slight gradient sloping toward the front of the school, creating a natural path for two tons of steel and burning plastic to follow? Who says those cosmic forces, gifted with a finely tuned sense of aesthetics, didn't want to demonstrate their displeasure at the architectural travesty of John Jay Public School?

Jake could only stand there, flabbergasted, as the Buick crashed through the glass doors of the school and proceeded to flambé the front hallway, the ceiling tiles popping in bursts of Halloween orange, the fire alarms shrieking in panic. His best option at that moment was to run, and he even turned on his heel to do so—but Bucky on the ground, mewling in pain, made him stop. As they say in the war movies, you never leave a man behind.

Bucky's body seemed heavy and soft as a burlap sack stuffed with doughnuts. Jake grunted as he hoisted that weight onto his shoulder, ready to begin the long journey for the woods at the edge of the parking lot, when the school's side door crashed open and a shirtless Principal Taylor stumbled out, pale and wet as a manatee hoisted from a Florida swamp. Behind him came Rebecca Smith, Jake's science teacher, also missing her shirt. Jake stopped in his tracks, stunned by this sight of naked adulthood: webbed with veins, saggy with fat, notched with scars and moles and red marks from too-tight clothing: two pieces of animated beef jerky primed for heart attacks and cancer and death and other indignities. Jake suddenly wondered if dying young and leaving a beautiful corpse wasn't nearly as bad as it sounded.

Taylor caught sight of them, and his mouth opened. His fists balled. He seemed on the verge of unleashing one of his patented tirades, but stopped before a single word came out, because Jake's grin said he was more than happy to share this story with anyone who'd listen. Taylor returned a tight-lipped glare that suggested he was ready to overlook Bucky and Jake—not to mention the loss of his motor vehicle and considerable damage to his institution—if Jake was willing to disappear and never mention this situation to anyone.

Jake agreed to the deal by turning around, re-hefting the almost-comatose Bucky, and taking off for the woods again. He was ten yards from freedom when the local fire department, breaking its all-time response record by two minutes, came screaming down the school driveway, followed by a police cruiser with its lights flashing. It was only then, as he gently lowered Bucky to the grass and stood tall to take his medicine, that Jake started laughing his head off.

II.

He was still laughing when the cops dragged him into Captain Keegan's office and shoved him into the world's most uncomfortable metal chair. Keegan sat behind his monolith of a battered-steel desk and stared at Jake as if the kid were a particularly interesting booger. Keegan was the kind of cop who ordered his officers to blast the "Star Wars"

Imperial March from their squad cars patrolling the neighborhoods—nothing intimidating about that, no sir, just your friendly local fascists interfacing with the community.

"You," he told Jake, "are in such deep crap, it boggles my mind."

Jake shrugged. "You gonna charge me?"

"Am I going to charge you?" Keegan chuckled without an ember of warmth. "Kid, if it was up to me, I'd drag you out back and shoot you in the back of the head. Try and put an end to that twisted bloodline of yours. But unfortunately, we have things like due process in this country, so yes—alas—we will have to merely charge you for your crimes."

"Lawyer," Jake said.

"Why would you need a lawyer?" Keegan squinted as if this were the oddest request he'd ever fielded in his twenty-one years of policing. "Tell me everything now, and I'll persuade the state to give you a break, as much as I'd hate to do so."

No way the state would give Jake a break. No, the state would ship Jake down to Cremaster Academy, a remedial institution of higher learning known not-so-affectionately by every unlucky student forced to grace its halls as 'The Ballsack.' Cremaster's sadistically avuncular staff forced students to line up in the hallway each morning, pull up their cuffs, and submit to a weapons search. The basketball team's record stood at 2-59, with those two wins coming from tragicomic matches against a special-needs school downstate. The whole thing was just sad.

"You have no power. District attorney can hear your recommendation and recommend you shove it." Jake kept his tone perky. "You know it, I know it. Lawyer."

"You little sociopath." Keegan grunted. "Your brothers

taught you well."

Jake took issue with the term 'sociopath.' If I hadn't stopped to haul Bucky to safety, he thought, I wouldn't be sitting here right now. Besides, it's not like anybody's ever convicted me of squat, and the last time I checked, here in America, you're innocent until proven guilty. Anything else is *le bullcrap*. "Lawyer," Jake said again, and offered the cop his widest grin, one that reminded Keegan so much of the kid's father.

III.

Jake's brother Ernest ("As in Hemingway," is how he liked to introduce himself. "I'm a serious guy") swept in like a force of nature an hour later, accompanied by a local lawyer who advertised on bus benches and wore a suit so shiny you could adjust your hair in the reflection. The lawyer spent the next thirty minutes comparing the county government to Judaea under Pilate, and sprinkling his full-throated roars with lots of Latin, before exiting the building with a happy Jake on one side and a dour Ernest on the other.

Ernest waited until the parking lot, and the lawyer's departure in a battleship of a Cadillac, before he slapped Jake on the back of the head. "You still smell like smoke," he said.

"Thanks for getting me out," Jake growled.

Ernest unlocked the doors of his fine muscle car and gestured for Jake to climb inside. They boomed onto the highway at whiplash speeds. "You bored with video games or something?" Ernest asked. "Figured you'd liven things up burning down the school?"

"They won't charge me," Jake said.

"You sound awful sure of yourself."

"No witnesses." Jake began ticking points on his fingers. "Bucky won't say squat. We caught the principal screwing one of my teachers, so he won't say squat. County don't have the money for forensics on something that didn't kill anyone. So why don't you cut me a little frigging slack?"

Ernest drew one of those prissy yellow cigarettes he kept loose in the breast pocket of his tailored button-down shirt, lit it with his silver Zippo infantry lighter, and took a few soft puffs while he thought the situation over. "You know we can't have anyone looking at us, with all Kevin is working on, right?"

"Right."

"Can't have any police sniffing around, no school people…"

"Right, right. I get it."

"So you're grounded. If you're going to set stuff on fire, stick to the property." Ernest leaned over and hit the radio button, twisted the knob until heavy metal shook the car's frame, his message clear: end of discussion.

"Poop," Jake yelled over the noise, leaned back in his seat, and pulled out his phone to text Bucky. With any luck, the video of the burning car was salvageable enough to put online. If they could rack up sufficient eyeballs on the destruction, it might translate into enough ad money to secure Jake a bit of beer and weed. A kid could always hope. Otherwise, the rest of this summer was going to be sadder than a Stephen Hawking exercise video.

IV.

Bucky fought through his morphine haze long enough to email the video over. As Jake uploaded it to YouTube he thought about doing something nice for his injured pal—a subscription to a prime porno site, maybe, so Bucky wouldn't go completely insane recuperating under the roof of his fundamentalist parents.

The video was pure Hollywood: the Buick centrally framed onscreen, the crisp pop of flames eating away the rag, the white flash as those flames hit the gas tank, the trunk rocketing toward the viewer at what seemed like a million miles an hour. He heard Bucky scream in high fidelity, and the view smeared as the phone went flying, bounced off the pavement once, and landed with its lens pointed at the perfect blue sky. That was worth a half-million viewers, easy. Before uploading, Jake spent fifteen minutes going through the video frame by frame, seeking any incriminating glimpses of his face. None. Perfect. At least something today was looking up.

He heard footsteps downstairs, the click of the refrigerator opening, and the faint rattle of a beer bottle pulled from the machine's frozen guts. That meant Kevin was home from whatever sketchiness he was building in the shack at the far end of the property. Jake closed his laptop and headed downstairs for a powwow.

Kevin sat at the kitchen table, the overhead light burning down like an interrogation lamp. When Kevin returned from Iraq after four years of vaporizing insurgents, he had a catlike ability to predict where people would appear, and when, and would wait for them in his most frightening pose: massive arms crossed over his chest, eyes locked in his best Badass Stare. Kevin shaved his head every morning but allowed his beard to grow into a bear pelt dangling from his chin.

"Heard you blew up the school, little bro," Kevin said.

"Just burned it a little," Jake said. "Can I have a beer?"

Kevin tilted his head toward the fridge, and Jake retrieved a cold one. Say what you will about Kevin, he always chose the best microbrew, even if it required driving forty-five minutes to buy some from the fancy store in Growler. If I'm going to soak my liver in alcohol, Kevin always said, I might as well soak it in the best.

"Which cop talked to you?" Kevin said, gesturing for Jake to sit in the chair across from him.

"Keegan."

"Huh."

"Told me he'd shoot me in the head, except the state wouldn't look kindly on that," Jake said, anxious to earn a little respect in his brother's eyes. "Threatened me in all sorts of ways, and you know what I said? I looked him dead in the eye, said I wanted a lawyer."

"You didn't tell him anything."

"No, sir."

"You're sure?"

"I got nothing to tell him. It's not like anyone around here's sharing with me what's going on. I know it's big, whatever it is."

"We don't share, and it's for your own good." Kevin's voice rose a half-decibel but to Jake it was the same as if he'd started screaming his head off. "We share, you know a little something, you're a tempting target for those who might get in our way. You understand?"

Jake stared at the scarred tabletop. "Yes."

"Good. Because I love you, buddy. We all do. So what happens now?"

"In terms of what?"

"In terms of the court, you dumb monkey. You facing charges?"

Jake laughed. "Nope."

Kevin's stony face cracked, his eyebrows colliding in curiosity. "Why's that? I thought you didn't tell them nothing?" His hand tightened on the beer bottle, squeaking the wet glass.

"I caught the principal with a teacher," Jake said, chuckling as if it were the most hilarious thing in the history of comedy. "They must have been boning in the office or something, they came running outside with their clothes undone. They can't say they witnessed anything without it wrecking their marriages, yeah?"

But Kevin's face stayed stony. "You know where they live?"

"I wouldn't worry about it, bro. Seriously." The fear hit him, that electric jolt that rocketed up his spine so often when talking to Kevin.

"We'll see," Kevin said. "You got any evidence? Shooting a video with your phone, anything like that?"

"We shot a video," Jake said. "Why else set the car on fire to begin with?"

"Okay, delete it."

"Aw, man..."

"I am serious as a heart attack. Get rid of it."

"It's got nothing incriminating, no faces or anything," Jake snorted. "You're taking away my ad revenue, man."

"How much you'd earn off that?" Kevin asked.

"Maybe five hundred," Jake said, inflating future revenues by a generous margin.

"I'm not one to separate a businessman from his money." Kevin tugged his cash-roll from his jeans and peeled off several large bills. "This look like enough to you?"

Jake nodded, his mind crackling with images of fragrant

weed.

"I'm buying something with this," Kevin said, as he laid the bills on the table with slow ceremony. "Stay out of sight. Cops come around, call the lawyer, don't engage, you get it?"

Jake pocketed the bills.

"I'll take that as a yes." Kevin stood and headed for the kitchen doorway, revealing the skull tattooed on the back of his neck. "I got to head out for a little bit, but you stay out of trouble, you hear?"

V.

Kevin's pickup chased its headlights onto the empty highway, Kevin making a phone call before hanging up and letting his mind drift into the night. He thought about his younger brother acting hard beyond his years, in that way of teenage boys. The kid hadn't known pain yet—true pain, the kind that comes with watching your platoon buddies scream and die—and Kevin wanted to keep it that way for as long as possible. The scars appear soon enough.

Twenty minutes later Kevin pulled into the Smokehouse's parking lot, taking care to choose a spot where he could slam the gas and rocket onto the main road, yee-hah and gone in five seconds.

When Kevin walked in, he made a point of dumping fifteen quarters into the vintage jukebox and cueing up the entirety of Bruce Springsteen's catalog, setting "Radio Nowhere" first, because anyone who didn't like the late-era Boss was either dead inside or un-American. The music for the next three hours having been set, Kevin took a seat at a rearmost table and waggled his eyebrows at Lola, who worked Tuesday and Thursday nights and managed to sling heavy trays despite a left hand missing two fingers. Kevin saw Lola as a fellow survivor, another member of the Missing Body Parts club, although in Kevin's case it wasn't so much lost limbs or digits but roughly a pound and a half of flesh cored from his torso, calves, forearms, and back.

"You want that fancy stuff, right?" Lola asked, swooping near.

Kevin nodded. "Yeah, and some nachos, extra everything, please and thank you."

She offered a little smile and disappeared into the crowd, returning a few minutes later with the beer and food. Kevin had scooped out the first bit of salty nacho goodness when Jeremy appeared at the far end of the room, in his pearls and bright purple shirt, blending in among the late-shift autoworkers and roughnecks about as well as a rose in a rusty scrap heap. He offered Kevin a finger-wiggle and sauntered over.

Kevin wiped his hands on a paper napkin and leaned back in his seat. "Hello again."

"Hello, handsome." Jeremy took a seat, crossed his legs, and made a show of adjusting the alligator-leather strap of his very expensive wristwatch. "I hope you haven't been waiting too long."

"You're actually on time, for once." Kevin knuckled the nacho platter an inch in Jeremy's direction, and the man winced as if Kevin had shoved a corkscrew through his palm—probably concerned about consuming a plateful of cholesterol. Kevin didn't expect to live much past thirty-five, which meant he could gleefully consume any greasy, spicy food his tongue desired: yet another benefit to being an outlaw.

"I do my best," Jeremy said, trying to wave down Lola.

Kevin ticked his peripheral vision a few degrees to the left, to better scope the four cowboys hanging out by the dingy pinball machine, all of them glancing over with unfriendly eyes. "How are you?"

"Friggin' great," Kevin sighed. "My little brother just tried to set a school on fire."

"Why would he ever do that?"

"Because it's school. What, you were never a teenager?"

"Did they arrest him?"

"Yeah, but it's okay. He's getting off." Kevin helped himself to another handful of nachos, scanning the pinball cowboys again. He didn't like the way they kept looking at Jeremy. "We're grounding him for the rest of the summer. You got my USB stick?"

"Darling, I would have just emailed you the files."

"No good. Don't you know the NSA watches everything?" Kevin laughed. "Last thing I need is more government up in my business."

Jeremy rolled his eyes. "Yes, I brought it. What are you planning to do with it?"

"What do you care?"

"I like knowing what I'm an accessory to."

"We're starting a cute little flower store. Reach under, you want your cash." Kevin slipped the fat envelope from the inner pocket of his jacket and passed it under the table with a hustler's slight of hand. Jeremy tugged it away, and Kevin kept his arm under the table until he felt a bit of cold plastic in his palm.

"You think grounding your brother is the best idea?" Jeremy asked.

"Why?" Kevin said, pocketing the USB stick.

"He sets the school on fire, gets away with it, that's not

someone you ground—that's someone you give a job." Jeremy toyed with his pearls. "Sounds like he's a chip off the old block."

Kevin's eyes flickered with emotion. "I don't want him getting hurt."

"It's life, dear: he's getting hurt one way or another. He might as well make some cash doing it." Jeremy tilted his head toward the pinball machines. "Speaking of hurt, see those crackers over there? I don't think they like my *style*. Walk me out?"

"No. Go out the back."

Jeremy sighed. "Why are you always so cruel?"

"We walk out together, maybe get into a fight with those guys, people will remember. Last thing we want is people remembering us here."

"Thanks for nothing." Jeremy mimed spitting into the nachos. "But seriously, consider taking the kid on. You had to learn somewhere, too, right?" He stood, with another anxious look around. "Actually, never mind my advice. You're a bastard. Goodnight."

Kevin almost responded with something witty, or at least profane. Instead he kept his gaze fixed straight ahead as Jeremy disappeared down the hallway that led to the bathrooms and the rear exit.

When Kevin glanced back at the pinball machines, the cowboys had split, leaving their beers and half-finished games behind. Kevin drained his glass, sighed, and stood up.

Outside he saw Jeremy first, his shirt a flash of purple at the edge of the bar's flickering neon glow. The darkness made it an ideal place for a pack of drunks to kick someone to death—and here they came, slinking between the parked cars like wolves.

Kevin took a deep breath, his heart racing like it did every waking minute in Iraq. He came up behind the last cowboy in the line, wrapped both hands around the man's neck, and slammed his skull hard into a convenient truck door. The man went down without a groan, but his boots hammered the dirt loud and that made the rest of them turn around. Kevin already had his fist rocketing into the surprised face of the next-closest cowboy, who squealed as he fell. They were soft, these punks, and too drunk for hard work. The other two ran away.

To his credit, Jeremy seemed calm as he squinted to examine the bodies. Something in their broken forms met his approval: he smirked and nodded before unlocking his garish rental vehicle. "Like I said, take your brother on," he said as he buckled in. "The world can use more people like you."

"Maybe I will," Kevin said, and stood watching as Jeremy's car raced for the road. The idea made sense. Hadn't he started out as a vandal, too? We all need to begin somewhere.

YOUNG TURKS AND OLD WIVES
Shane Simmons

The **apartment tower** sticks out of the neighbourhood like a single broken tooth. Chipped white concrete exposes the rusty checkerboard rebar just under the surface. If somebody doesn't condemn the building, it'll fall down all on its own one day. Sooner rather than later, fingers crossed. A pile of rubble would be less of an eyesore. Wipe that fuck-ugly building off the map and the money would still be left standing. The money wouldn't go away. It would find another dark corner to go hide in, like the rats and the cockroaches.

It's the first of the month which means rain or shine, shit or storm, I have to get my ass down there to cook the books. They send a car around to pick me up at my house. It's not that they don't trust me to show up on time, it's that I don't trust that hellhole to leave my car alone for a ten-minute appointment. This is one of my conditions. The other is that they send a respectable looking driver in a respectable looking vehicle. No gangstas in a muscle car, hopping around on hydraulics and jacked up on blow. What would the neighbours say?

Today it's a new guy and a new car, both acceptable. The car is luxury but non-descript, the driver sharply dressed, also non-descript. We don't bother with introductions. It's not important we know each other's name so long as we know where we fit in with the organization.

"You new?" is all I ask him.

He's too mature, too well dressed, carries himself too well, to be new talent. But I haven't seen him around before. He's either from out of town, or operates locally in circles I have no personal contact with.

"Not really," is as much explanation as I get from him. It suits me. We listen to the radio instead of making small talk.

Half an hour later, we're in another world. Urban sprawl gives way to urban blight, and finally urban apocalypse. This is the part of town the degenerates and lowlifes look down their noses at. Nobody comes here unless they're looking to score, and nobody stays longer than it takes to get well. Even the hard-core junkies, jonesing for a fix, will wait until they're clear of the area and among a better class of scumbag before they shoot up.

We pull alongside the curb and I have to look through the sunroof to see the top. Thanks to some zoning kickbacks decades earlier, it's the only tower for blocks. Once upon a time, somebody wanted to build a high-rise and paid the necessary bribes down at city hall to make it happen. Maybe they thought it would be catching, that urban renewal would spread like a virus. They didn't realize the whole neighbourhood was already terminal.

In a dodgy corner of town, the tower was gleaming and modern for the first few years. But it was cheaply built, badly maintained, and by the end of its first decade of existence, it was such a dump it looked like it had been standing there as long as all the century-old tenements it dwarfed. When it was repurposed as something known locally as The Factory many years later, all those levels were put to good use. These days there's a meth lab on seven. The coke-cutters are on nine. Stolen brand-name meds are packed and distributed throughout three and four. Homemade pills are milled out on five and six. Everything is nicely compartmentalized on a floor-by-floor basis.

Eleven through fourteen serve as a grow-op jungle of pot plants and sun lamps. The windows are painted black to keep the place from shining like a lighthouse beacon all night long. Extension cords run across telephone poles and plug into neighbouring buildings to help distribute the energy demand, but the lamps suck up so much juice the electric company has to know they're feeding a mary-jane greenhouse. And if they know, the cops know. But a raid has never materialized. Cops like a toke of quality weed just like the next guy, and who wants to fuck up a good thing? Through hassle or hustle, one way or the other they all get their piece once the goods hit the street. Nobody is willing to step up, make an arrest, and become the most hated boy scout in the troop.

Or maybe the cops just don't want a high-profile drug collar to turn into an even higher-profile bloodbath. The lobby of the building is always thick with lookouts. There's never a shortage of young men willing to keep an eye out for a small cut of the take and a taste of the wares. Paranoid and packing, they're itching for a fight that might be coming with every strange face that walks down the street, every unfamiliar car that drives past their block.

We pass one of the boys on the way inside. I know him by his ink, but I can't remember the name. He's standing at the base of the building with a long rubber hose running back to a tap inside. The way he's spritzing the landscape, he looks like a gang-banger gone straight, trying to care for his lawn in some upwardly mobile suburban bliss. The problem is there's not a hint of grass in sight and it ruins the effect.

"Trying to grow a garden of weeds between the cracks?"

"Boss is doing some spring cleaning around here."

There's a dark patch on the concrete where he's been hosing it down. The water running into the gutter still hints at a pinkish-red colour. Somebody probably got shot. Somebody probably got dead. Ambulances won't come here. Nobody will call 911. If you get shot or beaten badly enough, you'd better be able to drag yourself to a hospital. Nobody will lift a finger to get you help while you're alive, but they'll all lend a hand to make sure your body disappears if you die on the premises.

"Looks like somebody had a bad day," is my comment.

"A lot of somebodies are having a bad day today," he says.

"And here you are, mopping up the mess."

"Cleaning up is a dirty job."

"That's profound," I told him. "You should write that one down. Stuff it in a fortune cookie."

"Fuck you."

"These kids," I tell my driver as we head for the front door, "None of them know how to take a compliment."

"Maybe you don't sound sincere."

"I said it with a smile."

"Accountants don't do sincere smiles."

Over the life of the building, low-rent housing for the poor had become a no-rent factory for the 82nd street drug cartel. Not to be confused with the 83rd street drug cartel, the boys on 82 are big time, dealing a little of everything in the recreational-narcotics spectrum. Their vast empire spans all the way back to 79th street and the two blocks bordered by boulevards north and south. That comes to nearly five and a half square blocks where they own the exclusive rights to deal to every degenerate who juices, shoots or puffs on that postage stamp of concrete. As a client base goes, it's a good whack of addicts who have decided to call the neighbourhood home—or at least decided it was a good enough place to get high, piss their lives away, overdose and die. There's money to be made. Not a huge amount—there's only so much a bunch of late-stage terminal junkies can steal to support their habit—but it all belongs to the cartel.

Inside we're met by more of the hired help. The day watch, same as the night watch, fuelled by a speedball cocktail of cocaine and heroin, lubricated by half-sugar, half-caffeine energy drinks that are designed to keep you up and burn you out. Most of the boys have been awake for days. Their version of down time is a burgers-and-fries snack and a 48-hour coma on one of the bare mattresses in the building's former laundry room. Then it's back to the vigil and a fresh shot of junk to keep them wide-eyed and aware like a good guard doggie—paranoid and suspicious of everything, ready to bark at a passerby and bite an intruder.

I run my own laundry room, only mine doesn't house a bunch of stressed and stoned lookouts trying to grab a nap between hits. The work I do for the cartel—and a select few other gangs—is to turn their ill-gotten proceeds into legit numbers in a bank account. I count the money, crunch the numbers, wave my magic accounting pen, and turn it all into taxed, legal and unquestioned tender. Oh, they keep plenty of piles of cash on hand to throw around and play at being big men in a small neighbourhood. But paper piles up, and nobody wants to leave too much money stacked around the workplace. Even crooks get robbed. And the top guys are bright enough to plan for the future. What good is profit if you can't spend it on a nice car, a nice house, or a high-dividend stock to see you through your retirement if you ever live that long? You can't buy these things with cash-on-hand unless you want a visit from John Law.

So I make the money look good by running it through a series of businesses. I've brokered the sale of a number of fronts at bargain prices. Currently, the cartel is the proud owner of a restaurant nobody ever eats at and a bar nobody ever drinks at. Then there's the long-term storage facility that only stores row upon row of empty lockers. They have two dance clubs downtown. One of them never opens its doors, the other never shuts them because the place is gutted and full of pigeons and pigeon shit. There's also the landmark movie theatre that hasn't shown a movie since colour was a novelty and the debate raged on whether talkies were here to stay. On paper it's a community centre, even though no one from the community has seen the inside of the place since it was boarded up twenty years ago with placards that announced "Under renovation" and "Opening soon." Failed businesses all, but in the books they're gold mines. If you tell the tax man your dive bar is the hottest watering hole in town, he'll just cash your cheque and congratulate you. You think he gives a shit it's all drug money? Of course not. So long as you can produce enough fake numbers to convince him you're not guilty of tax evasion, he doesn't care what else you might be guilty of.

There's a fire burning in the lobby. No fireplace, just a fire. Trash is being burned in a garbage can in the middle of the floor so the watch dogs can keep warm. With so many broken windows, the place gets drafty. I'd be concerned about an open blaze setting off the fire alarm or the sprinklers, but none of that equipment has worked in years.

When my driver and I get closer, I can hear the boys talking tall tales. With nothing better to do than get high and tell each other work-related anecdotes, they can always be counted on for a good story or two when I visit. I might as well be witnessing primitive man from a hundred thousand years ago, telling ghost stories over camp fires. The ghost stories change, the fuel that's burning in the pit changes, but man's still primitive, superstitious. Savage and fearful.

I linger, so my driver stops to listen too. "Skiff" is what they call the scrawny collection of bones and needle tracks who has the floor. He recognizes me from my monthly visits and nods a greeting. Skiff is always there, always on watch, always ready with a story. Every first of the month I experience the same mild surprise that he's still alive, still bullshitting. But he'll outlive the building, that Skiff. Like the rats and the cockroaches and the money, Skiff will go on.

"Stop me if you've heard this one before," he says.

We're all heard this one before, but nobody stops him.

"This one time, Dunlan's in an elevator. Derek Dunlan, right? You've heard of him. Everyone's heard of him. He's in an elevator and it's packed. No room to breathe, no room to slouch, people are standing shoulder-to-shoulder. Everybody's in everybody else's personal space, got it? And then the elevator stops. Dead. Power failure, or it just breaks down, or something. It's not important. Just know that this motherfucker isn't going anywhere anytime soon. People bitch, people complain, but not our Dunlan. He just stands there, quiet, doesn't say shit. He closes his eyes like he's going to sleep or meditating or some damn thing and he's a statue. Meanwhile everybody else is freaking out. Slow at first. Situation like that, you want to stay calm, be polite, be considerate of your fellow man. Whatever. But after ten, twenty minutes, folks get antsy. After an hour they're going fucking nuts. The air's stale, everybody's sweating, it's hot like a sonofabitch. And this is what happens.

"One guy lights up. I don't know if he's claustrophic, or a nic addict, or just a miserable fucking asshole, but he takes out his pack of cigarettes and lights one. People complain. Obviously. Shit like, 'You're not allowed to smoke in here,' or 'We can hardly breathe as it is.' And he's all like, 'Fuck you! I need this!' And people shut up because they don't know if the guy's a freak or not. But our Dunlan has something to say. Understand now, Dunlan's been quiet as the dead. He hasn't said a word the whole time. He hasn't moved or opened his eyes in about an hour. Hell, he's not even sweating. But now he opens his eyes and says very calmly, very politely, 'Please put that out.'

"The guy puffing away, I don't know what he says. Maybe he gives Dunlan another 'Fuck you,' or maybe he doesn't have anything to say. Bottom line, though, is that he's still smoking. So Dunlan tells him, still calm, but a little less polite, 'Put it out, or I'll put it out for you.'

"This time I'm sure the smoker gives Dunlan a 'Fuck you' or worse. Whatever he said, a second later he's screaming. And I mean screaming his head off worse than you've ever heard anyone scream in your life. Because Dunlan leaps across the elevator. There's nowhere to move, but suddenly everybody just somehow finds room to get the fuck out of his way. The sardines part like the Red Sea and Dunlan's all over the guy. He lets him have a knee in the groin to give him something to think about, and before anyone knows what's happening, he's got the guy's head jammed in the corner of the car. With one hand he's forcing the guy's eye wide open, with the other he pops the cigarette out of his mouth and he stubs it out right in his eyeball. And none too fast either. He lets it simmer there for a bit. And that's when the screaming starts and it just keeps going and going, even after Dunlan lets the guy drop and flicks the dead butt at him.

"So Dunlan goes back to exactly where he was standing and assumes the position like nothing happened. Everyone's too stunned to say dick. And even if they had anything to say, no one would have heard it because smoker-boy is still screaming himself horse. Dunlan lets this go on for a little while, but it only takes him about a minute to have had his fill of that shit. So he just says all soft spoken, 'Quiet please.'

"Nothing. The guy's still screaming like he didn't hear, which is probably the case. So Dunlan repeats himself, 'I said, quiet please.' And the smoker must have heard that one because he says something back. 'You burned my fucking eye out!' which is stating the obvious, but at least it's a little more articulate than all that hollering. And Dunlan just tells him, cool as a cucumber, 'You saw what I did to make you stop smoking. You don't want to see what I'll do to you to make you stop shouting.' And that does the trick. The guy shuts the fuck up in a big hurry, but then some other people in the elevator start thinking they can talk shit to Dunlan. Maybe they figure he's just one guy and they outnumber him. Who knows, but one big guy right behind Dunlan thinks he's got balls.

"'You're a fucking psycho,' the big guy says. And Dunlan turns around to look this guy right in the face. He's stares at him, not hard or mean or anything. He just stares at him, indifferently, like he's watching paint dry. And you can practically see this other guy shrinking. He doesn't know where to put his eyes, so he tries to out-stare his shoes. And

Dunlan says, calm and quiet and composed, 'That's right. I'm a psycho. And you're all locked in here with me. So I want everyone to be on their very best behaviour, because if you piss me off I'm going to kill every last one of you.'

"And Dunlan turns back around, turns his back on all of them, and closes his eyes again and waits for the doors to open. Six hours he stands there not moving a muscle. By then, everyone else is all over the floor, lying on each other, trying not to crush each other. But they make sure Dunlan's got his space. A little halo of elbow room so no one has to touch him or disturb him in any way. And it's like that until the elevator starts moving again and the doors open on the main floor. The emergency crew's there, and paramedics and maybe a real doctor or two in case people are passed out or worse. But everyone's fine, except for the guy with only one eye, but even he's not complaining. And the owner of the building asks, 'Is everybody okay?'

"That's when Dunlan opens his eyes again and just says, 'Quite.' And he walks off that elevator like the whole trip downstairs took only two minutes. Seriously though, six hours with that many people all jammed together, the medics were expecting to find half of them dead. And except for one of them, they were all in perfect health. They figure Dunlan probably saved lives that day by keeping everybody calm, or at least too scared to panic. Yeah, that's right, Derek Dunlan saving lives. Who'd have thought? Of course the cops wanted to talk to him once they found out what had gone down in the elevator, but by then he was long gone and no one there knew who he was. The last time they ever laid eyes on him, he was heading out the door of the building. And you know what? He was lighting up."

There's a respectful, contemplative silence from the

watch dogs. Derek Dunlan stories are the local boogyman stories, and nobody ever wants to be the first to speak afterwards. So I do.

"Last time I heard that one, nobody said anything about Dunlan smoking."

"I told you to stop me if you'd heard it before," says Skiff, sounding hurt.

"Well you know me, I just love listening to your beautiful speaking voice."

I've opened the flood gates, and now the rest of the boys want to know more details, question the facts, reassure themselves that there really is no boogyman.

"Anybody ever lay eyes on this Derek Dunlan?" one wants to know.

"Sure, I seen him," is the answer. "Biggest nigger you ever saw. Built like a wall of cinderblocks."

"I heard he was little wop," comes a dissenting voice, "no more than five feet tall, but all muscle."

"Hey, Jimmy! You a wop?" one wants to know of his fellow watch dog.

"Quarter wop. My granny on my mother's side was from the old country."

"Sicily?"

"Queens."

Their brand of racism is so casual, so familiar, it's impossible to take offense.

"With a name like Derek Dunlan? Bullshit," declares another dissenting voice that nudges the conversation back on topic. "He's gotta be a mick. Fire-engine red hair and everything."

I have to laugh at these young turks and their old wives' tales. This can go on for hours and I've heard enough of the debate already. Before long, they'll be speculating that Derek Dunlan is a Martian. There's an appointment to keep so I hit the call button for the elevator. My driver steps inside with me when it arrives. He pushes the button for twenty-two, the top floor. I've never been up that high. Accounting is on seventeen, between heroin on sixteen and bath salts on eighteen.

He catches my eye on the button that lights up red.

"Boss wants to see you," he explains.

I've never had the pleasure.

"Really?" I say, flattered. "The penthouse."

He shakes his head.

"One higher."

There's nothing higher.

"The roof?"

"Boss wants to see you pass his window on the way down. Says you've been skimming."

And suddenly the new driver and all the talk of spring cleaning makes sense. I consider bolting, but I know I'll never make it past the dogs, never make it outside, never even make it as far as that stain on the pavement before I've made it a twin.

My hands shake as I reach for the pack of smokes in my pocket.

"Mind if I have a last cigarette?"

"Help yourself."

"Want one?" I offer the driver, trying to hand him one between fingers I hold as steady as I'm able. I'm hoping a bit of courtesy might buy some compassion. If I'm nice, polite, maybe he'll make it quick and let the drop do all the killing.

He doesn't take my offer.

"You said it yourself. I don't smoke."

And as the doors shut us in together, I realized that some of the tall tales are true, some of the ghosts are flesh and blood. And in a day, a week, a year, I'll be another anecdote connected to that underworld boogyman, Derek Dunlan. They'll all remember me and my last words to them over a fire and a story, but nobody will recall the face of the man who rode the elevator back down alone.

THE HANGOVER CURE
Seth Lynch

Anyone who drinks, drinks a lot, has a hangover cure. Something to push them through the long, pounding, headache hours of morning. I've witnessed sufferers knock back a vile medley of tomato juice, Tabasco sauce, and raw eggs in one sickening draft. Others have been known to flail themselves with birch twigs until their backs bleed—people so dedicated to their cure that they'll take it with or without a hangover. For most of the folk the cure is more booze, a neat whiskey or a vodka and orange for breakfast. For me, it's Greenbank Lucy.

Lucy is only available on Sunday mornings. Sunday being the one day of the week her kid, Sammy, isn't around. Neither is her husband—she calls him that 'though they never got married and now they've split. I've got a few names I call him but I'll save the expletives for later. Besides, the point is, on Sunday mornings he gets the kid and I get his wife. And yeah, I call her that.

This Sunday morning there's a steam roller working my head and two baling machines giving demonstrations in my gut. I've a feeling they just found the place where Saddam hid his weapons of mass destruction. I don't usually drink that much, that quick, but last night was a blow-out. Three beers in and there's a tap on my shoulder. Not the filth, they don't do anything so gentle as tap. I turned around, half-expecting a fist in the mouth, only to see Fat Ellis and his Siamese twin of violence, 'Normal' Norman Machin. They helped me finish my drink, by pouring it over my head, and then, in case I might be in danger of fainting, they each took an arm lifted me a few inches off the ground. In this elevated postion they carried me outside to show me their car.

You can tell how expensive a car is by the size of the boot. This car is in the mid-range price bracket. I had enough room to roll on my side but not enough to stretch out my legs. The drive was smooth, I only hit my head twice and just once had to hold back on a serious stomach lurch. For that I'm grateful, the last thing I needed was to cover my clothes in vomit. In fact I'd call an day a success if I can get through it without throwing up on myself.

Between thinking about the size of the boot and hoping the socks they shoved in my mouth were clean, I forgot to count the bends and twists in the road to work out where we were going. No big deal, I knew where we were going. If I'd been dead I'd have guessed at a discreet burial site some-where deep in Leigh Woods. But as I wasn't dead, yet I was in the boot of Ellis and Machin's car, I figured we were on the way to Frosty Farrow's place.

Frosty, despite his nickname, is a fiery bloke. He runs his rackets hard, with Ellis and Machin his front-line enforcers. The fact I was still alive was not a good sign, it probably meant Frosty wanted to watch me die. And if he was going to watch then it'd be a slow and painful death. I don't mind slow—preferably over another 60 or 70 years with no not-icible symptoms—but I'd rather skip the pain part. And the being watched, I'd like to skip that too.

Those morbid thoughts were about to overpower me

when the boot popped open and Ellis and Machin lifted me to my feet. I was feeling a little shaken by this point and needed a drink—it felt like years since I'd had a sip of beer or a sniff of whiskey. I could only hope that Frosty was either in a hospitable mood or that he'd grant me a last request before I died.

The hands which lifted me out of the car maintained their tight grip and turned me around to march me towards Frosty's lair. I freely admit I wished I was somewhere else. Anywhere else. Whatever Frosty wanted it wasn't going to be pleasant. The best result would be if he had some work on offer. You know me, I'm always ready to do a job and I'm not that fussy either. But if he's asking me it's because everybody else has already turned him down. And it takes serious balls to turn Frosty down. The work, therefore, must be a king-sized shit of a job.

So, you wonder, why couldn't I turn him down too? Because my name would be last on his list of asking, two or three below the dross at the Sally Army joint. If he accepts a no from me then he accepts the job won't get done. And there's no way Frosty would ever accept a scheme he's cooked up won't get done. I either do it, and probably get busted, or I don't do it and face the consequences. Even in my panicked state I couldn't help thinking I'd stand a better chance escaping from a prison cell than a grave.

Like I was saying, a job would be the best of it. The worst of it? I've heard a lot of tales. Flailing a man alive, emasculation, disembowelment, all manner of fun selected from Frosty's Bumper Book of Medieval Torture Volume 2. My problem is a vivid imagination. If someone tells me they're going to cut my balls off, I picture them doing it 'til I almost felt the pain. Then I'd have to feel it all over again when they actually did the cutting. I have a good memory too so I'd be reliving it all once it was over.

"Sit down, Smith, you half-arsed little scrote."

That was Frosty, who seemed to be in a good mood. He was sitting in his conservatory wearing nothing but a dressing gown and a pair of boxer-shorts. A fat cigar stuck out from between his thin lips. Skin, dark from years spent holidaying in Spain, was spread wrinkled over a body which has shrunk in some places and ballooned in others. I didn't want to stare him out in case he took it personally. I didn't want to look at his pigeon chest or his gibbous gut either. This left his crotch, no no no, his bony ankles, or the ceiling. I opted for the ceiling.

Whilst I was doing this opting Ellis found a chair and twisted me into it.

"What are you staring at my ceiling for, you fucking weird little freak? Look at me: I'm not made of shit."

I tried to focus on the bridge of his nose. He has a scar there, I wouldn't have noticed but it's highlighted by his deep Spanish tan. Frosty's gnarly face looks as if someone's had a go at embalming it. Short and sparse grey hair has been sewn into his skull. His nose, pitted with holes and covered with blackheads, must have been broken once a week every week for twenty years. It has bends which make me feel dizzy just looking at them. His yellow teeth took a personal dislike to me and kept snarling from around the cigar. My mini-contemplation of Frosty's head was brought to an abrupt end by the encroaching presence of Machin and Ellis.

The two goons stood on either side of me, each rested a grizzled hand upon my shoulder. Frosty lit a new Cuban cigar, coughed up some phlegm, which he gobbed into a bin, and said "I've got some questions for you."

"Do you worst," I said.

"Last night there was a game on, a game I was running. Some little fuckers came in and helped themselves to the winnings. And when someone takes something from me I like to take something from them."

"Like their life," Machin said. He and Ellis started laughing.

"What miserable swine would steal from you, Mr Farrow?" I said, hoping that would be enough to convince him it wasn't me. Which it wasn't by the way.

"I know you, Smith, and this job has got your mucky fingers all over it. They even used an explosive to get through the front fucking door. I also know you get mouthy when you've had a few. So," he said and produced a bottle of Jack Daniels, "you're gonna 'ave a few."

For a moment I thought I'd landed in an obscure form of heaven. Had Frosty really dragged me across the city to drink a bottle of Jack? He must have known that I'd have come willingly if he'd told me there was a drink in it. I reached towards the bottle while looking around for a glass and not caring too much if I found one.

Before I could lay my hands upon the bottle the iron grips of Machin and Ellis had me restrained in my seat. I caught a glimpse of Frosty rising from his chair as my head was jerked back. Ellis had a handful of my hair and was using it to hold my head in place. I stared at the same cracks in the ceiling I'd been looking at when I first arrived. This time I was trying to avoid the view straight up Ellis's hairy nostrils. Machin's rough fingers clamped around my jaw and forced my mouth open. Call me slow witted but I was starting to get nervous.

Frosty took glorious delight in pouring the booze down my throat. At first I tried to drink but I couldn't swallow fast enough. I choked and the whiskey spluttered back up before dribbling into my eyes. Frosty held off for a moment. Half-blinded, with snot pouring from my nose, I started to struggle. I was thrown to the floor where I began retching. Just as I was getting used to my freedom they yanked back into my seat. My head was pulled back and Frosty started pouring.

With the bottle empty, the questioning began. "Where were you last night?"

It took me a while to work out what's going on. The room had started to spin and my eyes had difficulty keeping open. I felt as if I'd been punched in the guts, which I may well have been. I could hear Frosty talking and Machin replying. A door opened somewhere. There was a short chuckle before a jug of water was tipped over my head.

"Where were you last night?" Frosty asked again.

"I was in the boozer."

"Which bloody boozer?"

"The Cherry Tree, I always drink there."

"Who saw you?"

"Machin, for fuck's sake, Machin. He was there all night too."

"Is that right, Norman?"

"Yes, Gov. He was on the pool table. Got on everyone's tits, him lying on the table when they wanted a game. Eventually he fell off, with a bit of help from Jo the barmaid."

Machin and Ellis started laughing again. Sounded like two donkeys being castrated.

"Jesus Christ, Norman," Frosty said. "Why didn't you tell me this when I told you to go fetch him? I mean Jesus fucking Christ."

Frosty was talking to me again but all my concentration was being used to stop myself from throwing up over his shoes. Then I was in the car, back seat this time. We stopped on a few occasions and I took the opportunity to vomit in the gutter. Come to think of it, that might have been why we stopped. Next thing I know it's Sunday morning and here I am drinking a jug of water and thinking about Greenbank Lucy.

◉ ◉ ◉

Lucy answers the door, she looks worse than I feel. Her bottom lip is swollen and her right eye is puffy and brown. There's a small plaster stuck over her left eyebrow.

"What happened?"

She opens the door a little wider for me to enter.

"Usual," she says.

The ash from her cigarette falls to the carpet. She hardly notices. My guts are twisting in on themselves. I can feel the hangover about to send me down on a self pity trip.

"He's got no right," I reach out and touch the side of her face.

"It's not about right or wrong, he hits me and that's all there is to it. I tried to leave him once but he waited outside my mum's house 'til I showed up. Then he beat shit out of me while his brother drove us back here. Poor Sammy was cowering in the corner of the van. He's said he'll kill me if I ever called the cops and we both know he would. So what choice do I have? I'd stab him in the guts but then he'd be dead and I'd be doing time and who'd look after Sammy?"

"The man's a Bastard."

"Forget about it, Harry, it's only pain and bruises."

She slumps down into the sofa and I flop down beside her.

"You look rough," she says.

"I feel rough."

She takes my hand and we sit in silence a while.

"You could leave again, don't go visiting your mum this time," I say. "Take little Sammy and up sticks."

"I don't have anywhere to go and I've got nearly no money. This house is in both our names. I'll need his agreement to sell and then he'll find out where I am. He won't stop at a few slaps if he catches up to me then."

I put my arm around her shoulder. If I'd only managed to hold on to some of the cash that's passed through my fingers over the years. She shrugs my arm away and stands up to go and make some tea. While she's in the kitchen I make a dash for the downstairs lav. I've got a bad feeling I'm gonna puke.

I don't puke but I do stick my head under the cold tap a while. Just as I start towling my hair dry I hear the front door burst open. The sound of voices fills the hallway. One of them I recognise, little Sammy.

"What's going on?" Lucy says.

"Take the brat, we've got to get out of here."

I recognise that voice too, her husband. There's another voice, less distinct, must be coming from out on the street. I can't be certain but I'd say it was his brother. My hand pauses at the door handle. A big part of me wants to get out there and smack her husband's face in. And, if it were just me and him, I probably would, although he'd beat the living crap out of me without breaking into a sweat. I scan the floor of the toilet hoping to find a discarded poker or heavy lead candlestick. There's nothing but a stray pube so I take a seat and wait—with one proviso—if he hits her I'll 'ave 'im. I may even land a few punches before he works out what's happening.

"What's going on?" Lucy asks.

"We need to get away for a few days, 'til things cool down."

"What have you done?"

"None of your business but we knocked over a game Friday night and it's getting hot."

Front door slams and a few moments later a car screeches away up the road.

"You can come out now," Lucy says.

I open the bog door and peer around it into the hall. Sammy's holding his mum's hand and looking dejected. I pull a funny face and wink at him. For that I get the briefest of smiles.

"I thought it best to keep out the way," I say.

"I'm glad you did, don't want to spend the rest of the day cleaning your blood off the carpet." She sends Sammy to the living room to play with his toys. We stay in the hallway.

"Where they off too?"

"Probably his cousin's place on Exmoor. He's got a farm-house a mile outside Porlock. They always go there when they've got to hide out." She heads back to the kitchen to finish making the tea.

"I need a breath of air," I say and make my way out to the back garden.

Once outside I close the back door and take out my mobile, "Hello, Mr. Farrow, how well do you know Porlock?"

HIGHWAY SIX
John L. Thompson

The glow of the New Mexico sun was high in the sky and bright enough to chase the shadows into hiding. Jack watched the desolate highway with casual interest from a rocky outcropping that was a high vantage point overlooking the highway known simply as Highway Six. The narrow asphalt road snaked its way through the desolate landscape of tumbleweed and shallow rocky canyons. He shifted an M4 carbine that was slung across his chest to a better position, cursed silently and continued waiting. Mitch, his old combat buddy, sat on a nearby boulder with an AK-47 resting on his lap while he studied the same stretch of asphalt through a pair of binoculars.

"We should use the .50 Cal." Jack sucked in the acrid smoke from his cigarette and broke the long silence between them.

Mitch paused, lowered the binoculars. "We've already had this discussion. The IED is in place and we can't turn back now."

There was a long pause before Jack spoke again to change the subject. A soft breeze kicked up a small dust devil across the road and it reminded him of what the Natives had said about this stretch of land. "They say this stretch of highway is cursed."

Mitch had resumed his watching of the road. "Whose 'they'?"

"The local Natives…Pueblo people."

"Indian locals?"

"Yeah."

"Bullshit."

"No serious." He sat up on the boulder to a more comfortable position. Sitting for the past hour had rubbed a sore spot on his ass. "I remember that some Wells Fargo armored truck guard got murdered along this stretch of road back about '94. The Natives kinda stay away from around here."

Mitch shrugged his shoulders. "I was in middle school back then."

"Yeah, I was in middle school too but I remember all the news coverage." He crushed the remaining cigarette under his boot heel. "It always stuck with me though for some reason."

"How did this guard get killed?" Mitch continued watching the highway.

"Ambushed. A couple of bad guys were waiting along the side of the road. The Wells Fargo guards come driving up in a rental van…"

Mitch interrupted him. "Wait, rental van?"

"Yeah, their normal armored truck broke down or something so the Wells Fargo guys rented this van."

"No armor?"

"No."

"That's stupid. So let me get this right. The Wells Fargo guys come bee-bopping down the road in this rental van. The bad guys were waiting at some bend in the road and hit 'em. What'd they use?"

"I heard some .223 and 7.62 casings were recovered at the scene."

"And these bad guys shot the van to shreds."

"Pretty much but the interesting thing is that the case is unsolved. Feds been looking for them ever since."

"How much did they get away with?"

"Nothing. A hit-run thing. Maybe got scared when the surviving guard shot back. They shagged ass and disappeared."

"Disappeared? How the fuck can that be? There's nothing out here and nowhere to go."

"It's easy enough to disappear around here. The Laguna Reservation is right over there." He pointed out to the vast open lands to the south. "Easy enough to haul ass through there since the local cops ain't allowed on the Natives land. It's considered a 'Sovereign Nation.'"

Mitch snorted. "Sounds like it was an inside job."

"You think so?"

Mitch lowered his binoculars. "Of course it was. Look at it this way. How the fuck do a couple of bad guys know that the van was going to be a rental that day? How did they know that the van was going to be carrying no armor? How do they know that the van is going down this stretch of road at this exact time frame?" He shook his head and held his hands out in disbelief. "I doubt these bad guys just woke up and decided to do a hit on an armored truck that morning at so and so time and know that van was going to be a fucking rental to boot. No way. It sounds like someone was giving out info to these guys. Maybe some fuck-stick guard that worked with them hoping for a nice cut of the action passed on the info." He shook his head and went back to watching the road. "Those bad guys sound like a bunch of amateur dumb-shits. Nothing like the *Muj* that we both have had personal experiences with. Even the US military never went out on missions without some armor."

Jack nodded. They had their share of blowing the insurgents into the haji-afterlife but even though the *Muj* were untrained insurgents, they were still a far better caliber of people than the two bad guys that had botched the robbery of the Wells Fargo van. "You may be right but I still think the Natives are right about this land though."

"Superstitions never made people rich. I don't believe in anything being 'cursed'. The Iraqis…remember that one hadji bastard claiming that Allah and his prophets were going to come down and turn the deserts red with American blood?"

Jack could remember the incident all too well. It had cost them several of their buddies' lives and an innumerable amount of wounded over a course of several months. Every mission had turned into a major fire fight. It was only through a five-hundred pound bomb courtesy of the Air Force that put an end to the radical cleric who had deep ties within the Al-Queda organization. "Yeah, he said something about it was 'destiny' and written in the Holy Book or some shit."

"All of it was superstitions made to incite riots and killing and all that shit. But what happened? We painted the deserts red with *their* blood."

Jack and Mitch had spent a couple of tours in Iraq doing missions, house to house searches, KBR convoy escorts and had dabbled in disarming IED's. The training in IED's was invaluable in learning the construction of a simple device that could disable just about anything the US Military had in terms of wheeled or tracked vehicles.

When they finally had come home to a hero's welcome, the newness of a civilian life had eventually worn off. The jobs were not fulfilling, women came and went and money was forever out of reach it seemed.

That was until they saw the lone armored truck cruising along Highway Six.

The idea of hitting an armored truck had come about over straight shots of Crown Royal and beer chasers. Flights of fantasy at first but then blossomed into a full-on planning. For the first time since they had returned to civilian life, they had found a 'mission'.

That IED training would hopefully pay off today. Jack had wanted to use a .50 caliber rifle. The slug would blow a hole through the motor with ease and they could easily over-power the guards but Mitch was insistent on constructing an IED. He wanted no chance of the driver or messenger guard using any radios, guns or even the will to fight back. It took a couple of weeks to construct the device and hopefully the damned thing would work. The biggest fears would be if the thing would detonate at all or if it was too much explosion. This was their first time constructing one.

They had followed the armored truck on numerous occasions. Carefully noting the number of stops in the Los Lunas and Belen areas before it moved out onto Highway Six towards the main Interstate 40. The lone stretch of road was rarely used and traffic was sparse or non-existent. The messenger guard and driver were just the usual 'Barney-Fife' security types. They were careless and never were aware of being watched. They carried their .38 caliber pistols low, like modern-day gunslingers. Jack and Mitch agreed that the two idiots would never have lasted in Iraq.

Mitch dropped his binoculars and took hold of the nearby remote switch that would detonate the IED hidden on the road. The days to construct the devise would hopefully pay big. The device was stuffed into the carcass of a dog, a blue heeler from the looks of the remains and Jack had hated scraping up the remains off the frontage road in Albuquerque the day before. "We're on."

The sound of a vehicle coming down the road sliced through the air. It was distant at first but Jack could see the distant blur pass by a rocky out cropping. After several seconds, the sound of the lone diesel engine came to within ear shot.

Jack checked the M4 and quickly slid forward onto his haunches and squatted down. Instincts took over at this point. He could see the armored truck moving down the road toward them. The truck slicing through the air reminded him of an angry stink bug that had arched its ass when agitated.

When the truck had passed a certain point, Mitch thumbed the switch and ignited hell.

The explosion ripped through the air. Jack could see the armored truck burst. The walls buckled and pushed outwards, its back doors flew open and flames shot out. The diesel engine had quit running but continued to roll toward the curve in the road. The truck tipped up and over the edge and rolled down the side of the embankment trailing thick plumes of flames and smoke.

Jack and Mitch moved down the embankment and forward just like the old days in Iraq, with their rifle pointed out and held high. Jack noted the burning currency under his feet and floating through the air. When they had reached the armored truck, the scent of cooked meat and burning paper greeted them. The truck was engulfed in flames.

Jack lowered his M4 and cursed. There was not going to be a big payoff. "Too much 'boom' boss." He lit a cigarette and looked around. "Maybe the Natives were right about this road."

Mitch held up his AK-47 and watched the smoldering money floating down from a burning heaven. "Maybe we should've used the .50 cal."

BIOGRAPHIES

PATRICIA ABBOTT is the author of the forthcoming novels CONCRETE ANGEL (June, 2015) and SHOT IN DETROIT (Polis Books). More than 135 of her stories have appeared in print, many of them with SHOTGUN HONEY. She also published two ebooks (MONKEY JUSTICE and HOME INVASION) through Snubnose Press. She lives in Detroit.

MICHAEL MCGLADE's short stories have appeared in *Spinetingler, The Big Click, Cracked Eye,* and *Plan B.* He holds a master's degree in English and Creative Writing from the Seamus Heaney Centre, Queen's University, Ireland. You can find out the latest news and views from him on McGladeWriting.com.

BRACKEN MACLEOD has worked as a martial arts teacher, a university philosophy instructor, for a children's non-profit, and as a criminal and civil trial attorney. His short fiction has appeared in various magazines and anthologies including *Shotgun Honey, Sex and Murder Magazine, LampLight, Every Day Fiction, Shroud Magazine, Reloaded: Both Barrels Vol. 2, Ominous Realities, The Big Adios, Widowmakers, Femme Fatale: Erotic Tales of Dangerous Women, Beat to a Pulp, Splatterpunk,* and *Shock Totem Magazine.*

He is the author of the novel, MOUNTAIN HOME, and a novella titled WHITE KNIGHT. His next novel, STRANDED, is coming soon from Macmillan Entertainment and TOR publishing.

TRAVIS RICHARDSON has been nominated for Anthony and Macavity awards. His novella LOST IN CLOVER was listed in Spinetingler Magazine's Best Crime Fiction of 2012. He has published stories in several publications including *Thuglit, Shotgun Honey* and *All Due Respect.* He edits the *Sisters-In-Crime* Los Angeles newsletter *Ransom Notes,* reviews Anton Chekhov short stories at www.chekhovshorts.com and sometimes shoots a short movie. His latest novella, KEEPING THE RECORD, concerns a disgraced baseball player who will do anything to keep his tainted home run record. www.tsrichardson.com

MARIE S. CROSSWELL is a novelist, short story writer, poet, and graduate of Sarah Lawrence College. Her short crime fiction has previously appeared in *Thuglit, Plots with Guns, Flash Fiction Offensive, Beat to a Pulp, Betty Fedora,* and *Dark Corners.* Her long short story "Dreamland" is available on Amazon.

She lives in Phoenix and digs black cats.

FRANK BYRNS lives and writes in Maryland, halfway between the nation's capital and the nation's heroin capital. His crime fiction has appeared or will soon appear in such markets as *Shotgun Honey, All Due Respect, Out of the Gutter, Powder Burn Flash,* and *Plan B Magazine.* Visit him online at www.frankbyrns.com.

KEITH RAWSON is the author of over 200 short stories, essays, interviews, and articles. He is a regular contributor to *LitReactor, The LA Review of Books,* and *Spinetingler magazine.* He lives in southern Arizona with his wife and daughter.

Liverpool lass **TESS MARKOVESKY** is now settled in the far north of England where she roams the fells with a brolly, dreaming up new stories and startling the occasional sheep.

Tess writes a distinctive brand of British comédie noir and her short stories have darkened the pages of various anthologies and magazines, including *Shotgun Honey, Pulp Metal Magazine, Out of the Gutter Online, Betty Fedora, 'Exiles: An Outsider Anthology' (Blackwitch Press), 'Drag Noir' (Fox Spirit),* and *'Rogue' (Near to the Knuckle).*

You can follow her ramblings (both literary and literal) at her blog: http://tessmakovesky.wordpress.com.

Katanie Duarte is a native of Los Angeles, California. By day, she's a stay at home mom, suffocating in suburbia. By night she's a blood spilling, knife-wielding writing machine. Her short stories have appeared in *Paranormal Horror-An Anthology, Paranormal Horror Anthology Two: An Anthology* and *Liquid Imagination.*

Although he is the author of several books, including the private eye novel ALL WHITE GIRLS, two-time Derringer Award-winning writer **MICHAEL BRACKEN** is better known as the author of more than 1,100 short stories. His crime fiction has appeared in *Crime Square, Ellery Queen's Mystery Magazine, Espionage Magazine, 50 Shades of Grey Fedora, Flesh & Blood: Guilty as Sin, The Mammoth Book of Best New Erotica 4, Mike Shayne Mystery Magazine,* and in many other anthologies and periodicals. He lives and writes in Texas. Learn more at www.CrimeFictionWriter.com and CrimeFictionWriter.blogspot.com.

JEDIDIAH AYRES is the author of PECKERWOOD, FIERCE BITCHES and a collection of short stories. He is the editor of the anthologies NOIR AT THE BAR volumes I & II and keeps the blog Hardboiled Wonderland.

TIMOTHY FRIEND is a writer and independent filmmaker whose fiction has been published in *Crossed-Genres, Thuglit,* and *Needle: A Magazine of Noir.* His western novella THE GUNMEN will be release from One Eye Press. He is the writer and director of the feature film, BONNIE AND CLYDE vs. DRACULA, distributed by Indican Pictures. He holds an MFA from the University of Missouri-Kansas City. For more information, visit http://www.timothyfriend.net

KENT GOWRAN lives and works in Chicago. His stories have appeared in *Needle: A Magazine of Noir, Plots With Guns, Beat To A Pulp,* and other wild venues. In 2011, he created the flash fiction webzine *Shotgun Honey.* Stories and other jive can be found at kentgowran.blogspot.com.

No one has ever bought **HECTOR ACOSTA** a drink. He's pretty upset over that, but makes do by funneling his bitterness into his writing. He's had stories published in the last two volumes of Shotgun Honey, Weird Noir, and Thuglit. He can be found on twitter @hexican.

NIGEL BIRD hails from Scotland. His work includes the collection DIRTY OLD TOWN, the novellas SMOKE and MR. SUIT and, most recently, the novel SOUTHSIDERS (published by Blasted Heath). He also has a couple of half-baked crime buns in the oven.

ANGEL LUIS COLÓN's fiction has appeared in multiple online and print journals like *Shotgun Honey, The Flash Fiction Offensive, Revolt Daily,* and *Thuglit.* His story, 'Separation Anxiety', appearing in All Due Respect earned him a 2015 Derringer Award nomination for best Long Story. When not working on his own projects, he's busy reviewing mystery/suspense for My Bookish Ways and helping out as an editor at Shotgun Honey. His debut novella, THE FURY OF BLACK JAGUAR is due out this summer from One Eye Press.

OWEN LAUKKANEN has fished commercially on both the Atlantic and Pacific Oceans. He is the author of the critically-acclaimed "Stevens and Windermere" series of FBI thrillers, and, as Owen Matthews, one obnoxious young adult novel. Laukkanen lives in Vancouver, Canada, with his girlfriend and their rescue pit bull, Lucy.

ALAN ORLOFF's debut mystery, DIAMONDS FOR THE DEAD, was an Agatha Award finalist for Best First Novel. He's also written two books in the Last Laff mystery series, KILLER ROUTINE and DEADLY CAMPAIGN (from Midnight Ink). Writing as his darker half Zak Allen, he's published THE TASTE, FIRST TIME KILLER, and RIDE-ALONG. His latest suspense novel, RUNNING FROM THE PAST (Kindle Press), was a Kindle Scout "winner." Alan lives in

Northern Virginia and teaches workshops at The Writer's Center in Bethesda, MD. For more info, visit: www.alanorloff.com

CHRIS RHATIGAN is the co-publisher of *All Due Respect Books*. His short story collection, WAKE UP, TIME TO DIE, was released last year by *BEAT to a PULP*.

BILL BABER has had over two dozen crime stories published and his work has recently appeared in *Rogue* from *Near to the Knuckle* and *Hardboiled Crime Scene* from *Dead Guns Press*. His 2014 short story "Sleepwalk" was nominated for a Derringer Prize. He has also had a number of poems published online and in the occasional literary journal. A book of his poetry, WHERE THE WIND COMES TO PLAY was published by *Berberis Press* in 2011. He lives in Tucson with his wife and a spoiled dog and his been known to cross the border for a cold beer. He is working on his first novel.

Born in Philadelphia, Pennsylvania, **TONY CONAWAY** has cowritten non-fiction books for McGraw-Hill, Macmillan and Prentice Hall. His fiction has been published in four anthologies and numerous publications, including *Blue Lake Review, Danse Macabre, qarrtsiluni, the Rind Literary Magazine* and *Typehouse Literary Magazine*.

He has also written and sold jokes to The *Tonight Show*. Sadly, David Letterman never returned his calls.

NICK KOLAKOWSKI is a writer and editor living in New York City. His work has appeared in *Shotgun Honey, McSweeney's, Playboy, The North American Review, The Evergreen Review, Carrier Pigeon,* and *The Washington Post. Someday* he'll learn to shoot well enough to take down the drone that keeps buzzing over his house.

SHANE SIMMONS is best known for his graphic novels, THE LONG AND UNLEARNED LIFE OF ROLAND GETHERS and its sequel, THE FAILED PROMISE OF BRADLEY GETHERS, which have been published in multiple countries in multiple languages to great acclaim and few dollars. To pay the bills, he writes for television, mostly animation. When he's not scripting innocuous cartoons for children, he spends his time writing grim comedy, violent crime and troubling horror stories to relax and unwind. He lives in Montreal with his wife and too many cats.

SETH LYNCH is the author of SALAZAR, a P.I. novel set in 30's Paris. His next novel is due out in Feb 2016 and features Chief Inspector Belmont of the Paris Police. He currently live in Wiltshire, England with his family where he's pretty much outnumbered 3 to 1. Find him on Twitter @SethALynch or on FB https://www.facebook.com/sethlynchauthor

JOHN L. THOMPSON currently lives in New Mexico with his wife of twenty-three years. When he is not working the daily grind or hiking the vast terrains looking for remnants of the old west, he can found writing short stories and novel scripts.

MEET THE EDITORS

JEN CONLEY'S stories have appeared in *Thuglit, Needle, Beat to a Pulp, Out of the Gutter, Grand Central Noir, Literary Orphans, Crime Factory, Trouble in the Heartland* and others. She's been nominated for a Spinetingler Award and shortlisted for *Best American Mystery Stories*. She lives in New Jersey.

CHRISTOPHER IRVIN has traded all hope of a good night's sleep for the chance to spend his mornings writing dark and noir fiction. He is the author of FEDERALES and BURN CARDS, as well as short stories featured in several publications, including *Thuglit, Beat to a Pulp, Needle,* and *Shotgun Honey*. He lives with his wife and son in Boston, Massachusetts.

ERIK ARNESON's fiction has appeared in *Needle, Thuglit, Otto Penzler's Kwik Krimes, Out of the Gutter Online, Beat to a Pulp, Shotgun Honey,* and more. He hosts the *Title 18: Word Crimes* podcast, which features stories by the likes of Merry Jones, Jon McGoran, and Duane Swierczynski. Erik's comic book FORTUNE is available as a free download via www.ErikArneson.com.

RON EARL PHILLIPS resides in the foothills of West Virginia with his wife, daughter and one too many cats. He spends his days writing code for a newspaper media company, his nights writing and editing fiction, and his weekends avoiding a never ending honey-do list. His work has appeared in anthologies such as OFF THE RECORD, LOST CHILDREN, BEAT TO A PULP: HARDBOILED, and FEEDING KATE. Visit www.RonEarlPhillips.com.

READ MORE FROM ONE EYE PRESS

SINGLES
Federales by Christopher Irvin
White Knight by Bracken MacLeod
Gospel of the Bullet by Chris Leek
Knuckleball by Tom Pitts

FUTURE SINGLES
The Gunmen by Timothy Friend
The Fury of Blacky Jaguar by Angel Luis Colón
Hurt Hawks by Mike Miner
Goldfinches by Ryan Sayles
Texas, Hold Your Queens by Marie S. Crosswell

MAGAZINES
The Big Adios Western Digest (Fall 2014)
Blight Digest (Fall 2014)
Blight Digest (Winter 2014)

ANTHOLOGIES
Shotgun Honey Presents: Both Barrels
Shotgun Honey Presents: Reloaded
Shotgun Honey Presents: Locked and Loaded

Visit us today at OneEyePress.com